Always on His Mind

by

Barbara Lohr

Purple Egret Press

Purple Egret Press
Savannah, Georgia 31411

This book is a work of fiction. The characters, events and places in the book are products of the author's imagination and are either fictitious or used fictitiously. Any similarity of real persons, living or dead, is purely coincidental and not intended by the author.

Cover Art: The Killion Group
Editing: The Editing Hall

Print ISBN: 978-0-9908642-8-8
Digital ISBN: 978-0-9908642-9-5

*For Ted, the man who's always
on my mind and in my heart.*

Chapter 1

Mercedes missed Manhattan. Missed the fast pace and crazy excitement like she missed the Prada sunglasses she'd left on the subway. Sometimes she still felt those phantom glasses pushed up on her forehead. Although she was home in Gull Harbor now, the pulse of New York City still echoed inside. Pulling into a parking spot along Whittaker Street, she strained to hear blaring car horns, smell a pork taco or rub dirt particles from her eyes after a bus wheezed past.

How pathetic. She even missed the annoying parts.

When she stepped out into the searing August sunshine, a Lake Michigan breeze ruffled her hair with the rich beachy smell. This street held a lot of memories. If she closed her eyes, she'd be homecoming queen again, waving to the cheering crowd from the white Olds convertible. Today her ears rang with the silence. Mercedes Kennedy had fallen in the crack between the past and the future.

No career. No luxurious condo. Nothing.

Well, except for Stephan but he was still in New York.

Smoothing back her rebellious blonde bob, Mercedes studied Michiana Thyme. The former gift shop now housed the town's PR department, with her sister Kate in charge. In the back of the green frame building sat an attached restaurant. A smile teased Mercedes' lips when she remembered camping out in that cafe with her girlfriends on lazy Saturday afternoons. They'd sip root beer floats, giggle and trade lipsticks until Loretta, the owner, shooed them out. After all, they were townies taking up valuable tourist space.

It felt strange to see the empty windows without mannequins or sale signs. A curious choice for the public relations office. But Kate's fiancé, Cole Campbell, was handling the renovation and repurposing of the shop.

The day was heating up, and Mercedes unbuttoned her black Donna Karan jacket. Even though this was just her sister, she'd dressed for a business call. Head down, she hitched up her Hermes shoulder bag and headed to The Full Cup across the street. In Manhattan, no one arrived for a cold call empty-handed. Kate's friend Sarah now ran her parents' coffee shop and bakery. She'd know what Kate liked.

The bell over the door jingled when Mercedes opened it and she tensed. Being unemployed had made her short-tempered, even though she'd been getting a disgusting amount of sleep since arriving in Gull Harbor last week. The past year had chewed her up and spit her out, not that she'd admit it. Mercedes smiled as a young family with two little kids brushed past. Their summer shorts and tank tops made her Donna Karan separates feel out of place. The mother couldn't have been much older than Mercedes, and they exchanged a smile.

"Mercedes Kennedy, as I live and breathe." Face flushed, Sarah smiled at her from behind the glass counter. "Kate told me you were coming home. Staying long?"

"For a while. Nothing definite." Mercedes basked in the unconditional approval Sarah always sprinkled with a giant sifter.

"Aw, that's so nice. Probably help with the wedding, right? Wasn't that great news about Kate and Cole? Your mom must be so thrilled."

"Ecstatic is more like it. About the only thing I can remember is that Cole and my little sister were in the debate club together, right? It's been ten years." The details were fuzzy in Mercedes' mind.

"Made for each other." Sarah's face got all dreamy. "A perfect couple."

"I'm glad Kate's happy. Mom is too." Her voice softened. The Kennedy family had been short on happiness in recent years. And her own business failure? She hadn't really gone into any detail with her mom and sister.

The smell of sugar hung in the air like the Goodyear blimp. Mercedes could almost feel her thighs swell. But her sister loved this stuff. She motioned toward the display. "Do you know what Kate likes?"

"Cheese crowns," Sarah said without any hesitation.

"Great. Could you give me a half dozen or so?" Did Kate have a staff in her office? Mercedes had never asked.

"Coming right up." Reaching behind her, Sarah swept up a waxed tissue. "So you're headed across the street to visit your sister?"

"Right, want to see what's happening in that PR department."

"She must be so happy to have you home." Sarah carefully

chose six enormous pastries. The overhead lighting bounced off the thick glaze.

"Truth is, Kate's so busy. She hardly knows I'm here."

"Her big sister? Kate always adored you." Sarah struggled with the flaps of the bulging box. "Gull Harbor really needed a marketer. Why, summer's almost over and then comes a sharp drop in business. Can you believe it?"

"No." Fall was advancing on Mercedes like a client deadline. Only she didn't have clients. Not anymore.

"How's your mom doing?" Finished, Sarah nudged the box across the counter.

"Still recovering from the stroke but she seems happy." The shiny box felt smooth and cool in her hands, uncomplicated like Gull Harbor. Her sister Kate had come home to recoup following that messy divorce. Maybe Mercedes was doing the same thing after her embarrassing bankruptcy.

"Well the way things worked out, your mom needed her anyway. The stroke and everything."

"Right. Kate carried the ball when I couldn't get back here last spring."

While Sarah rang up the sale, Mercedes studied the pictures of men in uniform taped on the register. A handsome guy in a Marine uniform was in several shots. "That your husband?"

Sarah glowed. "Yeah, that's Jamie. Remember him from high school?"

She squinted at the picture. "Not really."

"Jamie was in our class but didn't play varsity football until his junior year. You'd graduated by that time."

"Right." This trip home had become a Scrabble game in another language. For now, that felt fine. Mercedes wanted to keep to herself. No sense in having the whole town know their success story had failed.

Failure. The thought turned her tongue tinny and she swallowed. Dropping her head, she checked her Rolex. What if Kate left for an early lunch? "Guess I should be off. Nice seeing you, Sarah." In high school Sarah had been one of the girls who sprawled on their screen porch with Kate. Giggles would drift up to Mercedes' window while she got ready for a date.

"Say, maybe you'd want to join our book club?"

"Don't know how long I'll be here." Mercedes edged toward the door.

"You're always welcome. Kate has the schedule."

"Thanks, Sarah. I might have my hands full for a while."

"Sure...the wedding and everything." Sarah squeezed her shoulders together. "Busy, busy."

"See you later. I'll think about the book club."

Outside, the morning sun blinded her. No cars, so she could jaywalk without being mowed down by a crazed cabbie. She didn't see the strip of tar in the street until her shoe was sucked into stubborn softness. Mercedes was stuck.

"Oh, my Louboutins!" Six hundred dollars down the drain. And that wasn't the only problem. One wrong step and she could break her ankle. Cissy Grantham ended up on crutches after snagging her heel in a grate on Fifth Avenue. Mercedes couldn't afford to be laid up.

That did it. She lurched out of the shoe.

The road blistered the bottom of her foot while she struggled to keep her balance. When she threw her hands out, the box sailed through the air. The tearing sound of her kick pleat was the last straw.

She would not cry. She just would not.

Behind her, the doors of Rosie's Breakfast Club burst open. Guys laughed, promising to "hit the links together." To top it off, dogs yipped with excitement. She had to get out of here. If she could just reach that shoe.

No luck. She couldn't snag the shoe and her kick pleat tore higher. A breeze tickled the backs of her legs. Damn. She was blinking back frustrated tears when muscled arms closed around her and she fell onto a chest smelling of bacon and hash browns. Two small brown and white dogs barked at her heels. A wet tongue licked her leg.

"Looks like you need some help, pretty lady."

She was unceremoniously swept up. The smiling grey eyes reminded Mercedes of her favorite winter jacket. "Th-Thank you."

"Don't mention it. Shouldn't jaywalk, you know."

The dogs wouldn't quit.

"Quiet, Elvis. Wiggy, no." He gave them a stern look.

"Elvis?"

When he shrugged, she felt the ripple of a muscled chest. Blessed silence fell. "The crews don't tar near the crossing so you're safe there. Always cross at the light." He sounded like a boy scout but looked like Super Man.

"Why didn't they just resurface the whole street?" She spread her fingers flat on his muscled chest.

"No budget for it." That smile could sell toothpaste. "Mercedes? Finn Wheeler. Remember me?"

Heat shot up her cheeks. This was a man she should remember.

"High school." His arms cinched tighter. Like they had a right. "Chemistry class?"

Her mind bounced back through the years like a beach ball. "Sure. Right. Finn." Only the gawky teenager with that name had worn dark-rimmed glasses, framed by huge ears. He'd been skinny as a golf tee.

Finn set her down, where she wobbled on one foot. Her whole world felt lopsided. The dog gave her another lick. "How're you doing...Finn?"

"Terrific, except an old friend is in trouble."

You have no idea.

"I can take care of that."

Her heart stopped when he wrenched the shoe from the tar and handed it over. "Red soles, huh?"

"Yes. Thank you." She closed her fingers around the gooey mess.

The dogs were nuzzling the pastries scattered on the ground. Finn snapped his fingers. "Sit." They obeyed.

Mercedes watched him tuck the cheese crowns into the box. She'd always had a thing about a man's eyes and hands. They said it all. Was he kind? Callous? Finn knew how to treat a cheese crown with respect. Elvis and Wiggy panted but they stayed put.

Mercedes wanted to pant too, but she was losing her balance and reached for his back. Very slowly Finn straightened, a steadying hand on her arm. "You need more help?"

"I think I can stand on my own two feet."

"You always could, Mercedes."

"Right." She planted her bare foot on the blazing hot street.

"Where you headed?"

Gritting her teeth, she pointed to Michiana Thyme.

Handing her the box, Finn Wheeler swept her back into his arms. "Just a stone's throw. Elvis, Wiggy? Come." The dogs clicking along behind him, Finn marched down Whittaker Street. Mercedes hooked one arm around his broad shoulders, enjoying the view. At the stoplight, he pressed a button and she swallowed a chuckle while they waited. After all, not a car was in sight. When the light changed green, he took off toward Michiana Thyme. Kate would never believe this.

"So, you in town for long, Mercedes?"

"I don't really know. Could you take me to the back door?"

"No problem." His strides lengthened. The dogs picked up their pace, little tails waving briskly.

"So, you don't believe in a leash for your dogs?"

"No need. They obey me." Finn grinned. "So, you don't believe in stoplights?"

Point taken. She'd forgotten the dry humor shot from the corner of his mouth. This was the boy who coached her through chemistry. Now Finn's chest felt comforting, as if she hadn't slept in months and he was a soft bed. Her head jerked up. But her wandering right hand crept back to his chest, tucked under the box so he wouldn't see. Apparently he could feel. His eyes slid to hers with a naughty crinkle. A chill skittered down her spine.

"When did you get back?"

"Last week." Since when did she have a breathy voice?

The back door of the building stuck from layers of green paint. No problem for this boy. Finn rammed it open with a shoulder and took the four stairs in two lunges. The dogs kept pace.

Did Finn have strong thighs that matched his chest and arms? Her mind wandered, and she squeezed her eyes shut. How ridiculous.

After all, there was Stephan in New York.

Not answering her calls.

Her sister's handwriting was scrawled across a sign taped to the door. "Gull Harbor Public Relations Office."

He pushed the door open. "Hey, Kate. Look what I found." Elvis trotted in ahead of them as if he owned the place. Wiggy followed, sniffing as she went.

The scent of crisp summer linens and body creams still lingered in the empty shop. Hangers hung haphazardly from rods along the walls. The PR department didn't look ready for prime time but at least Kate had a job. That was saying something.

Reaching to pet Elvis, Kate turned from a desk set among the old wooden counters that needed dusting. "What happened?"

"Jaywalking." Finn set Mercedes on her feet.

"I got stuck in the tar." Mercedes kicked off the shoe still in decent condition. Now she could stand, but her toes curled on the carpet that needed cleaning.

Finn studied her feet. "All women should paint their toenails pink in the summer."

Kate's laugh echoed in the empty room. If Mercedes had been uncomfortable before, now she was in full-fledged blush. Finn set the bakery box on Kate's desk and the two dogs continued exploring.

"Is this what I think it is?" Her sister inhaled as if she were breathing in hallowed incense.

Mercedes plopped down in a chair that tilted under her. "Sarah says they're your favorite. Cheese crowns. Probably six hundred calories per bite."

"You can help Kate with those, right?" When Finn put a hand on Mercedes' shoulder, a crazy tickle raced down her spine. "You could use a pound or two, pretty lady."

She bristled. Staying a size two required painful vigilance.

"Funny you should run into Finn right now…" Kate began, glancing down at the wires snaking across the worn carpet.

But he raised a hand and backed toward the door. "Elvis, Wiggy? Come. See you later, Kate. You too, Mercedes. Later."

Would there be a later? The man didn't know she was a walking train wreck. "Thanks so much, Finn. You're really very h–helpful." Good grief, she'd almost said hot. Was Kate giggling?

The door closed behind him. "What the heck was that?" Kate's eyes circled between Mercedes and the door.

"My knight in shining armor, right?"

"Finn Wheeler is all of that, and he definitely seemed interested." Her baby sister was laughing at her.

"Don't be silly."

She was relieved when Kate's attention dropped to her feet. "Do you think nail polish remover will take care of that tar?"

"My feet? Probably. The shoes? Not so sure."

"We'll work on that in a minute." Kate's attention shifted to the box on her desk.

"Sure. Just a half for me, okay?" She was starving.

Grabbing a plastic spoon from her desk, Kate hacked at the pastry and handed her a chunk. "Mom will know what to do. Those shoes cost a bundle, right?"

"Louboutins? Of course." Mercedes bit in. Layers of sweetness dazzled her taste buds. She chewed slowly, managing to croak out, "I never knew these were so good."

"You bought six, huh?"

"I thought your staff might want some."

She thought Kate mumbled, "What staff?" Hard to tell when her sister had so much in her mouth. "If you don't slow down, I might have to give you the Heimlich, Kate."

"What? So we're back in grade school?" Her sister's tongue darted out to capture the last crumbs.

Mercedes eyed the empty room. "You're in this all alone?"

"Gull Harbor isn't that big."

"I know." That was becoming clear. "I thought maybe you might need some help."

Kate peered into the open box. "You looking for something to do?"

"Just willing to, you know, help out." After all, this wasn't fair. It wasn't Kate's fault that Mercedes was unemployed.

"I appreciate that, Mercedes. And I'd be glad for any ideas. But Gull Harbor can barely afford my part-time salary." Kate glanced around the shop she called an office. Mercedes saw her point. "At least this is a step up from the flower stall I ran this summer in front of Ignacio's and Chili's vegetable store."

"Mom told me about that. You sold flowers?"

"Kate's Blooms. That's what Cole called it. He helped me." Her sister got all fidgety and flushed. "We were in Debate Club together, remember?"

"Vaguely. Anyway, I'm glad it worked out for you. Barry, well..."

"Over and done. I'm past Barry Bankoff and my ruined marriage. In a weird way, selling flowers felt healing." A silly smile tilted her lips.

"And Cole helped you."

"Yep, yep he did." Kate twirled a curl around one finger.

Time to change the subject. "Actually, I wanted to offer my help in planning the wedding. Neiman Marcus is having a fabulous sale on wedding gowns right now. Designers like Vera Wang or Givenchy are going for a song."

"Wang?" Kate's forehead wrinkled.

"The designer. Vera Wang."

Her sister considered the remaining pastries. "Not to worry. Great resale shop up the road. Second Hand Rose. You'll love the dress I found there last weekend with Chili and Sarah."

"You're going to wear some other woman's wedding gown?" This wasn't what they'd planned as little girls, whispering under the covers at night.

"Sure. You'll love it." Kate shoved her chair back. "Let's hit the ladies room and get that tar off your foot." The little sister who'd hung on Mercedes' every word had just kicked her to the curb.

Stunned, Mercedes followed Kate around counters left like abandoned ships.

The bathroom was spacious and hadn't changed a bit. In grade school, they'd all crowd in front of the wide mirror and experiment with lipsticks from Dressel's Drugstore. Summer Tan and Peach Blush. Cotton Candy Pink and Sandy Beige. Then they'd stroll down Whittaker to the Swirly Top, their glistening lips smiling at the boys sprawled around picnic tables. But that was when Michiana Thyme was crowded with shoppers who smelled like coconut oil. Remembering how she used to jump up on this counter, Mercedes felt every one of her thirty years when she heaved herself up.

After dampening some toweling, Kate got to work on her foot. "This stuff is stubborn." Dabbing turned to scrubbing. Mercedes smiled, remembering Finn's comment about her pink toes. "Probably will come off with nail polish remover. That's all right, Kate. I'll try it when I get home."

Drawing back, her sister nodded. "Just give it to Mom." She tossed the toweling in the trash can.

"What's the deal with her anyway, Kate?"

Propping her hip against the counter, her sister turned thoughtful. Foreboding swept Mercedes' stomach. "From what Dr. Kumar says, she's had a series of small strokes, resulting in some memory loss. He called it cardiac dementia. She's a little scrambled, Mercedes."

"Permanently?"

"Time will tell. Does it really matter? She's still Mom."

Someday, Mercedes wanted to live in Kate's world, simple and satisfying—at least from what she could see. Growing up, she'd smoothed the way for her younger sister. Explained the facts of life. Now she longed to rip one page from Kate's book and fold it into her pocket for reference. "Kate, I saw you take the frozen peas out of the oven after Mom put them there yesterday."

"She gets confused, Mercedes."

"Aren't there tests just so we'd know what we're dealing with?"

Crossing her arms, Kate gave her a level look. Suddenly they were back in high school, arguing over who would mow the grass. "Look, I don't want to upset Mom with a bunch of medical tests. It's not like she has a job to go to every day. She's at Breezy Point for as long as she can safely be there."

Her sister had issued a warning. Blushing, Mercedes couldn't meet Kate's eyes. "I'm sorry I suggested selling Breezy Point last spring."

"Suggested? You practically had a For Sale sign out at the road."

She ran a shaky hand across her forehead. "I was just in a bad place."

"I know that now. Don't worry about it."

The pity in Kate's voice made Mercedes uncomfortable. "I'm fine. Really. You've got things wrong."

But she couldn't fool Kate, who took a deep breath while Mercedes' own chest tightened. "Any idea how long you plan to stay?"

"Don't really know." Sliding off the counter, Mercedes checked herself in the full-length mirror. Finn had seen her like this? She dabbed at her smeared eye makeup and finger-combed the tangled blonde hair. Did it matter? Her lightheadedness said maybe it did.

"What kind of work are you interested in?" Kate gave her an assessing glance. "This is a small community. Not much work around here."

"I know that. I'll do anything." Mercedes had to stay in motion.

Kate's brows knit together. "Is everything all right? You still have your condo in New York?"

"I, ah, divested it." Word choice made all the difference. She'd learned that in PR. "Divested" sounded a lot better than foreclosure. Better than bankruptcy.

Kate whistled. "Whoa. Bet that went for a pretty price."

Swallowing hard, Mercedes shook her head. "Not really. I'd taken out a second mortgage to keep the company afloat."

"Right, you told me you'd lost clients."

"The recession. You know. My accounts dried up." She didn't know who made her feel worse...the clients who had to close their doors or her own employees who lost their jobs.

"I'm so sorry, Merc." Her sister's hug surprised her. They'd never been an emotional family.

"I'll get through it," she mumbled against Kate's shoulder.

"I know you will." Her sister's faith in her made Mercedes' throat swell.

She pulled away. "Anyway, I'm here and I hope to pull something together to get back in the game."

"The game?" Kate blinked.

"You know. New York. I need a stake to start a new agency. I'll get it somehow."

"I see. Right."

There was no way Kate could understand, and Mercedes wasn't going to spell it out. The past year had been total humiliation. Giving her staff the news that they were now unemployed had felt worse than a public flogging in Times Square. "I'll figure it out, Kate."

Flipping off the light, her sister followed her back into the office. "I know you will Mercedes, but remember I'm here to help." When she reached her desk, she picked up a magazine. "Here's the latest copy of *The Beacher*. There might be some jobs listed. Would you consider working in a shop or something like that?"

Mercedes took the white tabloid that had been around since she could remember. Just then the door opened behind her and Kate looked up. "Did you forget something, Finn?"

Not again. Turning, Mercedes clutched her jacket around her. "Where are your dogs?"

"With friends." Finn exchanged a look with Kate. "I'm here to set up your computer system." An old dinosaur of a computer sat on the desk. It matched the room perfectly.

Kate met Mercedes' eyes. "Did I mention that Finn is our..."

"Gull Harbor's computer expert," Finn said.

Kate's eyes widened.

"Of course," Mercedes said. "You used to live in the computer lab. I remember how you took care of presentations for assemblies, including pep rallies before the games." He'd been their go-to guy.

Finn nodded to *The Beacher* clutched in her hand. "Going to catch up on all the local news?"

"She's looking for a job," Kate said before Mercedes could get a word in.

"What do you have in mind?"

She rolled the crisp pages of *The Beacher* into a tighter cylinder. "Anything. I'll do anything." This was no time to be proud.

"My sister might have something for you. She mentioned recently she needed some help." Mercedes didn't miss the shock on Kate's face.

"What does she do?" Not that she could be choosy.

"Lindsay cleans the summer homes. A few grades behind us in school so you wouldn't know her."

"Okay, well..." Mercedes tapped *The Beacher* against her palm. So it had come to this. What other options did she have?

"Just think about it." Finn whipped out a card and handed it to her. "Give me a call if you think you'd be interested."

"Thanks. I'll be in touch." *Touch?* The thought of touching Finn Wheeler took her breath away. Definitely time to leave. "I'm going to take off, Kate. Looks like you've got work to do."

"Nice seeing you, Mercedes." Finn's eyes twinkled.

"Thanks for your help." Trying to salvage some dignity, she swept up her shoes and padded barefoot to the door. She looked back over her shoulder. "See you later, Kate."

"Later." Kate gave her a thumbs up.

Turning toward the door, Mercedes hoped the back slit hadn't ripped indecently high. Were they both staring in horrified silence? She closed the door behind her and exhaled. As she picked her way down the grimy stairs, she thought about the elevator in the high-rise building where she had her PR firm. Classical elevator music. Gleaming mahogany walls. The uniformed doorman.

Bursting into the bright sunshine outside, she laughed.

~.~

Finn enjoyed the back view of Mercedes' upper thighs. She'd always had great legs. He'd lived for the moments her little blue skirt flipped up when she cheered at the games.

"Thanks for coming to her rescue," Kate said as the door closed. "It's not often that Mercedes needs help."

"Happy to oblige." Finn had a serious crush on Mercedes Kennedy all through high school, not that it had mattered. Back then she was a cheerleader and way out of his league. Now? Game on. She wasn't wearing a wedding ring.

"And you say Lindsay c-cleans summer homes?" Kate sputtered.

"Mercedes said she'd do anything, right? It's not like Lindsay runs a strip joint." If Mercedes worked for his sister, he might see her more.

Staring him down, Kate shook her head. "Now, Finn. Can you really see that?"

"Don't sell your sister short. Mercedes always had a lot of spirit." He hesitated for a moment, thinking about her bare left hand. Time for a reality check. "So, her husband is back in New York?"

Kate's lips tilted. "Mercedes isn't married, Finn. And the word is your last Chicago woman didn't work out."

"Chicago woman," he sputtered, cheeks burning. "You make me sound like a heartbreaker."

"Ah, huh. Why did you tell her you were our computer man? That's not really true."

He squirmed. "I'm not a tell-all kind of guy."

"I know but still." She threw him a side glance. "You're too modest."

Back to the matter at hand. "Now, what is it you need here in the office? A hot spot and phone hookup?"

But while he worked with Kate, his mind wandered to her sister. The golden gleam of her hair in the sunlight, her slim, leggy body in his arms. Yeah, he was looking forward to seeing more of her. He started working on the wires, snapping connections into place

Chapter 2

When Mercedes drove up to Breezy Point, her mother was
hunched over the hydrangea bushes. The green weeding bucket sat
next to her, a sun-faded hat protecting her face. Gardening had
always been Alice Kennedy's therapy. Before her parents' divorce,
Mercedes often found her mom outside, jamming her trowel into
the ground or ripping out dandelions as if they'd committed a
capital offence.

Today her mother looked up, smiled and waved. Feeling upbeat
after running into Finn Wheeler, Mercedes turned off the car,
grabbed her handbag and shoes and got out. The grassy patch in
back of the house felt cool against her bare feet.

New York might thrive on change but here? Breezy Point
looked the same as always and today the white clapboard and faded
blue shutters felt comforting.

"Look at you. Going barefoot now that you're back from the
city, honey?" Setting her trimmer down next to the bucket, her
mom pushed herself to her feet and hitched up her aqua pants.
During her rehabilitative stay at the Gull Harbor Care Center
following her stroke, she'd learned the wonder of Internet
shopping from her roommate, Marie McGraw. Her wide range of
beige slacks had been taken to Goodwill. Turquoise and purple

now ran riot through her closet.

Holding her shoes up, Mercedes studied the red soles. "I landed in a tar strip on Whittaker. That street needs resurfacing, not patching."

Her mother reached out. "Let's see if I can get that off."

Mercedes gladly surrendered the heels. Stain management was one of her mother's many strong points. The back screen door squeaked when she opened it, and a wave of chocolate greeted her. "You baking something?" Mercedes followed her mother inside.

"Yep, one of your favorites." Whisking off her hat, Mom fingered her blonde curls.

But she rarely indulged anymore. Mercedes peered inside the oven. "Chocolate chip zucchini cake?"

"Yep. You got it."

"Loaves?" The fragrance of chocolate posed a real threat to Mercedes' size two.

"I like to give them away. Cole loves them." Opening the cupboard under the sink, Mom rummaged around until she found her cleaning supplies. Mercedes slipped off her jacket, hung it over a wooden chair and sat down. She set her heels on top of the morning paper, open on the kitchen table. Taking a soft cloth, her mother worked some kind of cream into the shoe. "Did you see your sister?"

Nodding, Mercedes reached for some grapes in the bowl. "She was hard at work." But Kate wasn't the person occupying her thoughts. No, her mind was on the tall, dark-haired man who swept her up as if she were one of the cottonwood tufts floating in the summer air.

"Did you like her office?"

"It needs some work."

"Probably so. Selling the building took a while, as I recall. Guess no one wants a shop with pretty clothes anymore, especially beach wear."

"It's the economy, Mom. A lot of people don't have money for vacation clothes."

"Well, now it's Kate's office. Kind of nice that she's right on Whittaker."

You would have thought that two-block stretch was Fifth Avenue the way her mom's face glowed. Or was she just happy that Kate, her youngest daughter, had come home and now planned to settle here? "Maybe someday it will be office space. Right now it looks more like an empty shop." She sniffed the air. "You think that chocolate chip zucchini bread is done?"

Her mother leapt up, her chair banging back against the wall. "Oh, my goodness." Grabbing two hot pads from the counter, she opened the oven and tested each loaf with a toothpick. Mumbling to herself, she whisked the pans to the wire racks on the counter. Mercedes' stomach growled. This craving for sweets was so not her. Getting up, she made herself a cup of coffee in the machine, her gift for Mom last Christmas.

After turning off the oven, her mother went back to working on the shoes. "You seeing anyone, Mercedes?"

Since her stroke, her mother's mind often flipped from one topic to another. "Yes I am. Stephan. Stephan Forbes." His name had such a ring to it.

"That's nice. And what does Steven do, dear?"

"He prefers Ste-PHON, Mom. Not Steven." Stephan had a fit when people didn't pronounce his name correctly. "He's in commercial real estate."

Her mother's lips formed a perfect O. "Your boyfriend is a high roller. Isn't that what they call it?"

Mercedes laughed. "Maybe. The recession changed all that. I think he's still rebuilding his business." *Maybe that's why I haven't heard from him for five days.* She didn't like being ignored.

"Anything serious?" The teasing note in her mother's voice was new. Alice Kennedy had always avoided personal conversations with her daughters.

"Hard to tell, Mom. We've been seeing each other for a while. Almost a year."

"Really? I don't recall you mentioning him."

"I didn't want to get your hopes up." *Or be pestered with questions.*

"I see." Handing Mercedes the shoe, Mom sat back. "Afraid that's the best I can do."

Mercedes turned the soft leather heel over in her hands. "How do you do this? Now all I have to do is attach the tip, and I'm back in business."

Her mother's hand shot out. "I have just the glue."

Digging around in her purse, Mercedes found the rubber tip. Coming home had its advantages, especially when a mom was there to take care of you. In five minutes, the shoe looked like new.

Mercedes could forget about the tar but not the incident. Her chest tingled at the memory and she fingered a pearl button on her blouse.

"Back to work." Grabbing a spatula, Mom loosened the sides of the chocolate chip zucchini loaves. Then she spilled them out onto the racks. Sweet-scented steam filled the room. The August heat bore down, and Mercedes jumped up to turn on the overhead fan. Outside, locusts cut the air with their high, sharp keening. "Going to be a hot one today."

Her mother blotted her forehead with the dishtowel. "Going swimming?"

"Maybe. Haven't been down to the beach yet." Mercedes listened for the soft shush of the waves on the shore.

"So I noticed." Her mother gave her a searching look, and suddenly the old Alice was back. No pulling the wool over her eyes. "Might as well take advantage of it, right? People pay plenty to rent a house on this beach. What's the point of me hanging on to Breezy Point if..."

But she stopped. Did her mother remember? Only a few months earlier Mercedes had urged her to sell off the five lots that made up the family home. Thinking back, Mercedes blushed. Apologizing to Kate that morning felt like an overdue confession. What good would it have done if Mom had sold, and Mercedes had used her share of the funds to shore up her business? She would have thrown good money after bad. Thank goodness Kate called a quick halt to Mercedes' plan.

"Maybe I'll take lunch down to the beach." No Manhattan pushcarts here with falafel or spring rolls.

"I'll make it for you. Turkey on rye?"

"That would be really nice, Mom."

"Glad to have you home, Mercedes. Don't forget this cake is here. A warm slice is always nice. Isn't that what we used to say?"

"Oh, I don't eat sweet stuff, Mom. Too fattening." She licked her dry lips.

"Maybe you should, honey. Why, you're getting downright skinny"

"You should talk." Her mother's sinewy embrace snapped Mercedes back to Finn's muscled arms. Lean but firmly muscled.

Mercedes kissed her mother's forehead. "When did you change your hair color," she asked, her nose tickled by the blonde curls that had once been iron gray.

"In the nursing home. Phoebe, Kate's friend, came to the care center once a week. She colored it for me. Told me I looked foxy. Imagine that."

"I think she's right."

"Phoebe told me change was good." Her mother plumped her pert hairdo with her hands.

"Maybe Phoebe's right, although change sure isn't easy." This past year, Mercedes had been through enough change to last a lifetime. "I'm going upstairs to find my old swim suit."

Her mother opened the refrigerator. "I'll work on that sandwich."

An hour later, Mercedes walked north along the shore in her old, green bikini. In high school, she'd been a size eight so today she had to knot the sides tighter over her hip bones. Feet splashing in the cool water, she chuckled over the morning's adventure. If she were in New York, no one would sweep her to safety when her shoe got stuck. They'd walk by, not wanting to get involved.

But Finn had acted immediately. The man had handled her with unsettling confidence. Her entire body came awake, remembering. Feeling disloyal, she shut down those feelings fast. After all, she had Stephan. They'd been using the L word for some months now. What was the point of dating someone exclusively if she didn't love him, right? But Stephan didn't send this heady rush through her body. Now, what was this about? Seemed like she questioned everything these days.

While she splashed through the shallows, the tiny ridges of sand massaged her feet and helped clear her head. Although she'd covered herself with sunblock, she felt the unrelenting noon sun. Thank God she'd worn a hat. The last thing she wanted was freckles. Overhead gulls cawed, diving into the waves to scoop up lunch. Children wielded plastic shovels while their parents lounged in nearby beach chairs. No familiar faces. Probably summer people, like the folks Finn's sister worked for.

Her steps slowed. Reaching down, she grabbed some flat stones from the bottom of the lake and winged them over the water. Was she really going to clean houses? She'd seen that look in Kate's eyes, daring her. Some May days, they'd stand knee deep in the icy water until one of them gave up and dashed out screeching, legs red from the cold. Usually, Mercedes held out the longest.

Turning on her heel, she headed back to the green and white webbed chair she'd left at the water's edge in front of Breezy Point.

She plopped down, stretched her feet into the cool water and reached for the phone in her tote.

Stephan's phone rang and rang until his voicemail came on. She always teased him about his radio talk show voice. But as she listened this time, she felt irritated. Why didn't he pick up? She left a message. "Just me calling to see how you are." But wasn't he the one who should be concerned? "It's sunny here…" Since when did he give a damn about the weather? "Wondering how your business is going. Love you."

There it was. That love word. But he didn't come on the line, and she shoved the phone back into her bag.

The breeze died and the day turned sticky. For a while, the sun drained her of all energy. She could be in high school again, working on her tan for prom. Those days seemed long ago and impossibly carefree. After a while, the black flies descended, leaving itchy bites. Pushing up, she waded into the water and swam to the sandbar. No flies out there and she bobbed on the gentle waves, turning toward the west. On a clear day, she could see the faint outline of the Chicago skyscrapers. Today clouds obscured the horizon. Maybe she'd take a drive into Chicago one day. Stroll up the Magnificent Mile. But why? She couldn't afford to shop.

She shivered, goosebumps forming on her skin. Once back on shore, she welcomed the hot dry sand. Grabbing her old Cinderella beach towel, she patted herself dry and sank back into the low beach chair. Suddenly hungry, she unzipped the small, insulated pack and took out the sandwich. Alice always stacked the turkey so thick you could hardly get your jaw around it. Chewing thoughtfully, she loved the softness of the baby Swiss cheese and the sting of the Dijon mustard. Maybe she'd even eat the second half. But she didn't want to get careless. Her usual self-control took hold and she sealed up what was left.

Popping open a can of soda, she let the bubbles fizz on her tongue and closed her eyes. The rhythm of the waves and the cry of the gulls took her back to the long summer days when she'd stretch out on the sand with Kate and their friends. Back then she was dating Chuck Lindner, but he wasn't the man on her mind today. And neither was the man who didn't answer her phone calls. Finally, she folded up her chair and climbed the stone steps back up to the house.

Late that night after her mom had gone to bed, Mercedes tiptoed down to the kitchen and unwrapped one of the loaves of chocolate chip zucchini cake. Slicing off a thin sliver, she took it out to the porch and ate it slowly, rocking on the wicker swing.

So Stephan wouldn't answer the phone? She knew someone who probably would.

~.~

Sunlight filtered through the birch trees as Mercedes pulled her car up in front of the blue cottage on Apple Lane. No curbs in Gull Harbor. Guests parked on the edge of the front lawn. Breathing in the scent of pine and lake, she turned off the car. What did a girl wear to clean a summer cottage? Tiola, her housekeeper in Manhattan, had worn a black uniform.

Lindsay had been brief during their phone conversation.

"Shorts and a top. The kind of stuff you might throw away tomorrow. I wouldn't wear open-toed shoes if I were you."

"Of course not." Mercedes' cutoffs and pink T-shirt would have to do, along with her old walking shoes. And her hair? Stephan would tease her no end about these pigtails. But she still hadn't heard from him.

Grabbing her purse, she climbed out of her black Mercedes. She'd endured a lot of teasing about having a car with her name. Made perfect sense to her.

Ducking under an arbor, she took the steps into a screen porch and rang the bell. Somewhere inside a vacuum snarled. When no one appeared, Mercedes wiped her shoes on the welcome mat and stepped inside. The main room held comfortable-looking rattan furniture with blue and green cushions. Beach posters hung on the walls. Ear buds stuck in her ears, Lindsay Wheeler was doing battle with the vacuum. The overhead fan mussed the long bangs framing her frown. Like Mercedes, she wore cutoffs and a tank top.

Mercedes stood there, wondering how to get her attention. Glancing up, Lindsay jerked and screamed. One swipe and her ear buds went flying. The vacuum sputtered to a halt. "Sorry, I didn't hear you."

"I rang the bell but..." Mercedes waved a manicured hand in the direction of the vacuum.

Fixing her with gray eyes very much like her brother's, Lindsay folded her hands on top of the handle. "So you came."

"Yes, I ah, told you I'd be here."

"Just meant glad you could make it. This isn't a glamorous job."

One flick of Lindsay's wrist and the vacuum cord snapped from the outlet.

What had she been told about Mercedes? "I didn't think it would be." They faced each other.

Lindsay's eyes fell. "Sorry. My brother tells me I'm abrupt. He's probably right. The business is growing, which is good. But I'm having a hard time handling it all." Her shoulders slumped while she rolled up the vacuum cord.

You haven't cornered the market on that one.

"Let me show you the laundry room. That's where most people keep their cleaning supplies, unless you have them. I usually bring my own, just to make sure." She glanced pointedly at Mercedes' empty hands.

"You didn't tell me I needed anything."

"Guess I didn't." Turning, Lindsay led her through the kitchen and into a back laundry room where she picked up a bucket. Plopping it in the sink, Lindsay poured some noxious chemical into it and turned on the hot water. "Have you ever done any cleaning?"

"My sister and I had our chores growing up. You know, swept the front steps, mopped the kitchen floor, scrubbed out the toilets."

"Toilets?" For the first time, Lindsay's lips quirked up. "You scrubbed toilets? Seriously?"

"Yes, I did." Irritation tightened Mercedes' throat. She knew *how* to do it but never thought she'd ever be doing it again.

Still smiling, Lindsay turned off the water so fast, the pipes shuddered. "Come on, I'll show you around." She whirled from the laundry room, and Mercedes followed her back into the kitchen.

"Usually I work from the top down, counters to floor, before I use the mop." She motioned to a mop propped in a corner.

"Sounds simple." The mop looked a little ratty and belonged in the Harbert Antique Mall. Cripes, she'd used one like this years ago.

Lindsay began ticking things off on her fingers. "First get the towels out of the washing machine and stick them in the dryer. Guests are supposed to start them before they leave. You should find a pile of used sheets in the middle of each bed. If not, you have to strip the bed yourself. Sheets go in the washing machine. The dishwasher is usually running unless the guests are lazy. Most owners have that in their contract. So you just empty it."

Was this cottage air-conditioned? Mercedes' forehead was dripping, and her underarms dampened while Lindsay took her through the drill. "Owners like everything to be shipshape when the new tenant arrives. Usually we have about ninety minutes to do that."

Should she be taking notes? "How many bedrooms do most cottages have?"

"It varies. Maybe two or three. Lately I've been getting the bigger homes right on the beach. Totally different story there. They can have four bedrooms easy and at least three baths." When Lindsay's voice wobbled, Mercedes didn't know what to do. "Which is why I'm looking for help."

The wicked witch of the west had morphed into a lost little girl. Mercedes knew the feeling. She fought a weird impulse to hug her new boss. But too much emotion in the corporate world had often been interpreted as weakness.

"Follow me." Lindsay hitched a thumb toward the bedroom area.

The first room was small and cramped with two twin beds shoved together. No lump of used sheets sat in the center of the beds, and Lindsay fisted her hands on her hips. "Sure, they lounge at the beach for a week but can't even strip their own beds at the end?" Whipping off the light blue blankets and sheets, Lindsay worked on one bed, anger rippling from her in waves. This was a girl on the brink.

Mercedes took the sheets off the other bed. "Who writes the contracts?"

"The owners. I try to get them to add my suggestions but it's their house. No one wants to lose a renter." Lindsay balled the bed sheets against her stomach as if it ached.

Tempted to walk right out the door, Mercedes bit her tongue hard and followed Lindsay back to the laundry.

"Then there are the bathrooms." Lindsay rolled her eyes. "Showers. Toilets. Sand everywhere."

Freezing her cheeks, Mercedes refused to let disgust show on her face. The next fifteen minutes she followed Lindsay around, wondering what the heck she was doing here. "Each owner gives me a key… You listening to me, Mercedes?"

The tone sounded familiar and she blushed. Had she actually talked to people like this in the past? "Sorry. Yep, I'm with you." How had her employees felt?

Lindsay sucked in a breath.

"How many of these cottages do you clean every Saturday?"

That little-girl-lost look filtered over her features again. "Five, but some of the rentals turn over on Fridays. Spreading it out helps a little. Lately more people have started calling me. I can't afford to turn anyone down or they'll contact someone else."

Mercedes knew the feeling. She'd dealt with that every day in her agency. "Anyone else offering housekeeping services in this area?"

"Sure. It's a perfect part-time job, easy to work it into waitressing. Some girls work at Rosie's Breakfast Club, Barney's or the Mangy Mutt too. You know, trying to make ends meet."

"Yes, I do know." For the first time since she'd arrived, Mercedes felt some kind of kinship.

But it didn't look like Lindsay was feeling the love. Her eyes turned iron gray as she pulled some ticketed keys from her pocket. "Like right now? I got four homes waiting for me and no time to do them all well."

"Want me to take two?" Had she really said that?

The doubt clouding Lindsay's face hurt. Did she really think Mercedes wasn't up to the task?

"Hate to throw you to the wolves." The keys jingled as Lindsay tossed them from one hand to the other. "But yeah, I'd really appreciate if you could take two."

Mercedes wanted to rip those keys from her hands.

Lindsay studied the tabs. "Do you have GPS? The addresses are on the keys."

"No problem. Got it."

"The one on Meadow Drive keeps cleaning supplies in the laundry room. Buckwood Trail? Under the kitchen sink, mop is in the closet. I'll come by to check when I'm finished." She dangled the keys like a challenge.

Mercedes grabbed them. "Fine. See you later." These homes were going to sparkle if it killed her.

By the time she reached the first house, she was plenty pumped up. Her tennis shoes caught on the stone steps when she took them two at a time. Inside, the place looked ransacked. Toys all over the floor, breakfast bowls left on the TV stand. Sand gritted underfoot as Mercedes ran from room to room to size up the job.

Lindsay had been kind. Only two bedrooms and a stacked washer/dryer in the hallway. Following the directives, she moved the towels from the washer into the dryer. After grabbing the sheets from the bedrooms, she stuffed them into the washer and added soap. The hum of both machines was music to her ears.

Leaning her head against the cool metal, she took a deep breath. Good God, could she do this?

Of course she could. She steeled her stomach and straightened. After some exploring, she found the cleaning supplies. Sprays and bottles were packed into a plastic carrier that she supposed every cleaning lady needed. Dishes were clean in the dishwasher. She'd leave them for a bit. First, she'd empty all the trash.

Grabbing a large white plastic bag, she dashed from room to room, emptying the wastebaskets. The sand that crackled underfoot was getting on her nerves. Didn't anyone hose their feet off outside? Her mother would have had a fit if they dragged in all this sand. After dumping the trash, she gathered up the toys and threw them into a toy chest. Looked like the renters had fun. Gladiolas past their prime drooped from a vase on the kitchen table. The refrigerator held a few soft drinks and some beer. Should she pitch them? She'd have to ask Lindsay about that.

For a second, she stood in front of the open refrigerator until the freezing air made her skin prickle. How amazing that she would ask another woman for permission to do something. Grabbing the cans and bottles from the frig, she stomped a pedal on the metal trash can and tossed them in. The crash of metal and glass brought great satisfaction.

Then with a giant heave, Mercedes yanked the bag from the can and trotted outside to the large green garbage can. Back inside, she lined all the wastebaskets with fresh bags. A sense of urgency drove her. She had a ton more to do.

Bathrooms were next. After attacking the shower stall, she moved to the sinks and toilets. She'd hated doing chores when she was in high school. Her mother had been a perfectionist. Now she sprayed, scrubbed and wiped with confidence. She'd been trained by the best.

In the closet, she found the wet Swiffer and pads but with one swipe of the linoleum, she could feel the sand scratching the floor. "Crap. I forgot about sweeping." Slamming the mop to one side, she grabbed a broom and dust pan from the closet. Next time, she was going to bring ear buds. Make the work go faster.

Next time? Her stomach seized into a tight knot.

But what choice did she have?

Maybe she needed something stronger than a broom for all this sand. Heaving a vacuum from the closet, she started on the floors and then went to the rugs. She hadn't seen braided rugs like these in ages. Taking them outside, she slapped them against the porch railings. Sand flew and she left the rugs on the railing to air. Buoyed by her success, she went back into the kitchen, grabbed the mop and started swinging. This was her job and she was on it, fueled by the energy that had vaulted her to the top of her field in New York.

The crash nearly sent her through the ceiling.

"Oh, no! Please, no." Turning, she clasped the mop handle to her chest. Gladiolas and glass littered the floor, along with foul smelling water. This day had gone to hell in a hand basket, as her mother always said.

Chapter 3

Standing on the front porch of the cottage on Meadow Drive, Finn studied the black Mercedes convertible. Only Mercedes Kennedy would have a car that matched her name.

The sound of breaking glass spun him toward the house. The front door was ajar and he headed straight for it. "Mercedes? Everything all right in here?" Skirting the wicker furniture, Finn made his way back to the kitchen.

Mercedes knelt on the floor, scooping up flowers and broken glass. At least she was wearing plastic gloves. Was she crying?

"Mercedes?"

"Finn." Rubbing her eyes with her wrists, she didn't look glad to see him. "I had an accident."

Sunlight beaming through a window caught bright shards of glass. "Hold on. You'll cut yourself. I'll get a broom."

Nodding, she pointed. "In the closet." The defeat on her face stabbed him through the heart. This was the girl who'd rallied the school with her Victory Stomp that shook the bleachers.

While he swept up the mess, she blotted the water from the linoleum with paper towels. Eye makeup ran down her cheeks. "What happened?"

"I wasn't watching what I was doing," she huffed. "That's what happened."

"Hey." Leaning the broom against the counter, he helped her to her feet. She wouldn't look at him. Her lower lip trembled and his stomach flipped over. She looked cute but miserable. "Don't be so hard on yourself, okay?"

"What are you doing here?"

Backing off, he grabbed the dustpan and pitched pieces of glass into the garbage.

"Just driving by." No way would he admit he'd stopped to say hi to his sister but was really looking for Mercedes. Lindsay had given him the address, all the while scolding him. "She'll probably still be there. Finn, I don't know why you sent her my way. Does Mercedes Kennedy ever get her hands dirty? I need real help here." His sister's eyes had glistened. Must be the day for tears.

"How did you know I was here?" Suspicion darkened Mercedes' green eyes.

"Who else has a Mercedes SL 550 convertible? You were driving it the other day." He kept his voice calm. Not the time to sound like a stalker. "How's the first day on the job?"

"Probably my first and last day." She studied the mess in the trash. "How will I ever replace that vase?"

"Clancy's flower department."

"You think?" Her face brightened.

"I know. Clancy's never lets me down. I buy my mom flowers there all the time."

Mercedes chewed her lip. For a second he was back in chemistry class, watching her puzzle over a formula. No lipstick today, but her lips were plenty distracting without it. She glanced at the vacuum. Laundry was whirling in the washing machine, and she was probably far from finished. He backed away.

"Look, I'll dash down to Clancy's right now. How much longer will you be here?"

"Forever?" Her crooked grin gave him hope. "Maybe an hour, if I'm lucky."

"Fine. No problem."

"You don't have to do this, Finn."

"I want to, okay?" He'd be a hard-hearted idiot not to help ease the pain in her eyes. Besides, he wanted to score points with his high school crush.

Once on Red Arrow Highway, he let the Bentley fly and reached town in record time. The only grocery store in Gull Harbor, Clancy's was jammed. Most vacationing families arrived on Saturdays. First, they might stop at Nacho's vegetable stand outside of town but eventually everyone wound up at Clancy's. The area was in chaos when he arrived. Cars angled for parking spots in the hot sun. Bypassing them, he pulled into the library lot across the street.

The flowers were to his right when he entered the store, and he grabbed one of the clear vases from a shelf. For a second he studied the bouquets of roses. Not yet. Buying flowers might be a little over the top. He joined the checkout line.

"No flowers for this vase?" Haley asked when he paid.

"Not this time. My, ah, mom just needs a vase." He'd known Haley's family for years, and this town was a gossip mill.

When he banged back into the cottage, Mercedes was heaving that vacuum around as if it were the enemy. Her face lit up when he proudly produced the vase.

She turned off the vacuum. "Thanks so much, Finn. First you get me this job..."

"Where you'll be wildly successful."

"Oh, I doubt that." The look she gave the vacuum could turn a marshmallow to stone. "Then you save me from making a fool of myself on the first day."

"Mercedes, you could never be a fool."

Silent, she gnawed at the corner of her lips. Damned distracting and he stood there like a goof. "Guess I'll clear out. Let you work."

The washing machine buzzed and she jumped.

"Your laundry's done, Mercedes," he said softly.

She pulled on the pink t-shirt, clinging to her body. "I know that."

But he couldn't leave. "You could be sixteen again with those pigtails."

Looking wistful, she ran her fingers down one of them. "Sixteen only comes once."

"Not for the boys who remember."

Her head snapped up and his cheeks burned. Then she smiled. "You're a sweet guy, Finn Wheeler. I am definitely not sixteen, but thank you." This was a lady desperately in need of some cheering up. When she dashed a hand over her damp cheeks, the makeup fanned out like blackbird wings.

"How about driving up to the umbrella auction tonight in

Harbert?" He threw it out like live bait.

She blinked. "The what?"

"Remember those big umbrellas in front of the shops near Harbert? Have you driven past since you got home?"

She wrinkled her nose. "No, but I kind of remember them. They still auction them off every year?"

"Tonight, in fact. Wine and cheese."

"That sounds like a date." A red flush shot up her cheeks. "I'm seeing someone."

Of course she was. Wasn't going to stop him. "This isn't a date, Mercedes. Just a drive up the road to see some umbrella art I think you'll enjoy."

She chewed at the end of one of her pigtails and heat hit his groin like a red hot poker. "I really shouldn't."

Right, you really shouldn't tease me. "It's for a good cause. Benefits the Gull Harbor Care Center."

Her attitude shifted. "No kidding? My mother rehabbed there after her stroke. I even went to their Memorial Day barbecue. Good people."

Was a yes coming his way?

Casually, he scanned her bare left hand. He'd been right the first time. She wasn't wearing and engagement ring. How serious could she be about this guy? Time to play another card. "You can bring your mother. She might enjoy it."

He'd struck a nerve. Her indecision dissolved. "Oh, Finn. She'd probably love that. We haven't been anywhere since I got home."

"Is that an enthusiastic yes?"

"I guess so." Her smile was slow in coming.

Relief made him laugh. "Pick you up at five thirty?"

Pushing a wisp of hair from her forehead, Mercedes glanced at a seagull clock on the wall.

"Don't worry. You'll have plenty of time to get prettied up."

"You think I need it?" She frowned at her cut-offs and form-fitting shirt. Sexy as hell but apparently she didn't think so. "Okay, you win. Umbrella sale. Got it."

"Auction. Charity auction."

"Whatever." She gave him a nudge toward the door.

"You're pretty when you blush."

"What?" Her full lips fell open.

"Later." Backing down the front steps, he almost tripped. She shook her head, laughing at him as she closed the front door. Twirling the keys around his fingers he whistled all the way to his car. After all, he was a patient guy.

And mothers loved him.

~.~

When Mercedes told her mother about Finn's invitation, she acted like a little girl invited to her first birthday party. "Oh, isn't that wonderful?" The sweet enthusiasm made Mercedes feel guilty. After all, she'd almost turned Finn down. Her mother had gone through a lot this spring with her stroke. Now Kate was busy with the wedding and her new job, so that left Mercedes. Had she been too wrapped up in her own problems? Attending an umbrella auction sounded about as exciting as watching paint dry. But not for her mother.

"What should I wear?" Mom pondered out loud while the rhythm of her rocking chair picked up speed.

They were both chilling on the front porch after a quick meal of egg salad sandwiches. Mercedes lounged in the wicker swing while her mother rocked in the bentwood rocker. Kate stuck her head out the door. She was living at home until the wedding, although they hardly ever saw her.

"You two have fun in Harbert, you hear?" Dressed in a pale blue sundress, Kate looked gorgeous and her green eyes glowed. Had she been this thrilled ten years ago when she married Barry Bankoff? Maybe it took time to find the right husband. Barry had been Kate's college sweetheart, and they'd grown apart before his disastrous affairs that led to their divorce.

"Oh, don't you worry about us." Their mom waved her away. "I might just buy an umbrella."

Kate threw a warning glance at Mercedes. "Now you be careful. I've heard those umbrellas go for over a thousand dollars. This isn't just another outfit on the shopping channel, Mom."

"Don't worry," Mercedes broke in. "I've got this, Kate."

Then Kate's eyes softened. "Hey, Mercedes, you okay? You look tired."

How ridiculous. "I cleaned two cottages today, top to bottom, the way we used to wash down Breezy Point on Saturdays. Probably smell like a truck driver." She pulled on her pink *Say Yes to Michigan* shirt. "Can't you smell the cleaning products?" Her back was killing her and she'd chipped two nails, even though she wore rubber gloves.

All this for minimum wage.

Kate sniffed the air. "All I smell is the pine trees."

"Right. Everything that gets counters and floors clean today smells like pine or lemons. It's an unwritten rule." It felt good again to be a family, laughing together.

The rumble of Cole's truck sent Kate flying to the back door. "See you later," she called back.

The silence on the porch was punctuated only by the creaking of the rocking chair.

Now her sister was the one dashing out on a date. For the flash of a second, Mercedes felt left behind. She looked up to find her mother's eyes on her.

"Your turn will come, Mercedes."

Great. Now she felt twelve years old. "I know that, Mom."

"Why, you succeeded in anything you ever took on, honey. Cheerleader voted homecoming queen. You've always made me so proud." Her mom smiled while she relived Mercedes' past.

How could she explain? The soothing rhythm of the lake drifted up to the porch. Mercedes closed her eyes, letting it wash over her, but in the end she just felt empty. She missed the honking horns, the soaring skyscrapers. Too much silence brought her face to face with failure.

"All these years, I've lived here and never been to the umbrella auction. Thought it was more for the tourists. Who did you say this man is who's taking us?" A delighted smile took years from her mother's face.

"A boy I went to school with." Mercedes sent the swing in motion with a restless foot.

"I see. And his name is…" Mom wrestled a small notebook from her pants pocket. She was always scribbling things down. Mercedes' heart broke the first time she saw the crumpled pages.

Closing her eyes, Mercedes rocked her head back in the swing. "Finn Wheeler. The brother of the woman I'm doing some work for right now. He was my chemistry partner in high school, but I didn't really know him."

"That's nice, dear. A local boy."

Pulling in a deep breath, Mercedes grabbed her phone and checked the time. "He'll be here at five thirty."

"Oh, good heavens, Mercedes. I have to get prettied up." Jumping up, her mom headed inside, Mercedes right behind her. Climbing any steps took time and Dr. Kumar wanted their mom to do it unaided. Biting her lip, Mercedes coaxed her mom sideways up the stairs, one step at a time and clinging to the handrail.

When five thirty came, she was sitting with her mother at the kitchen table. The back door was pushed open so she could watch the long road leading to the cottage. Mid August and darkness seemed to come earlier each day. Her black wrap-around sundress with the cap sleeves felt tight around the waist. She fidgeted. "I'm gaining weight." Tearing at the ties, she loosened them.

"Oh, my goodness, Mercedes. You're way too thin." Her mother waved away her concern. "How could anything be tight on you?"

"I like being slender." In New York, she never ate breakfast.

When she tried that here, her mother plopped a bowl of oatmeal in front of her. Somehow, she got it down. The brown sugar made it palatable, and she didn't want to hurt her mother's feelings.

Now she had to pay the price. If she kept eating Sarah's pastries, none of her clothes would fit, and she couldn't afford a new wardrobe.

Not pleased with herself, she swept back the blonde hair that had grown past her shoulders. What had happened to her crisp, professional hairstyle? One of Kate's new friends had a salon in town. Phoebe. Was that the right name? Mercedes pictured a crowded salon with rickety chairs and cracked mirrors edged with kids' photos. Perm solution and hairspray would cloud the air. She couldn't hope for anyone of Serge's caliber here in Gull Harbor. A ball of disgust formed in her stomach. Maybe she'd end up with a ratted bubble and look like Rizzo from *Grease*.

For now, it would have to do and she knotted her hands in her lap. No way could she afford a quick trip to Chicago. Besides, who would she see around here? Although certainly Stephan would come for Kate's wedding. Once he called, they could settle that. She fidgeted with the tie at her waist.

"Do I look all right?" Her mother wandered into the bathroom off the kitchen and stood primping in front of a shell-edged mirror. Because Mom couldn't climb stairs at first when she came home, Cole had transformed the unused pantry into a cute little powder room.

"You look pretty, Mom," she told her mother, dressed in an aqua top and pants, shiny purple beads forming a gladiola on the front of the blouse.

Coming out of the powder room, her mother looked panicked. "Where's my pocketbook?"

"Right here." Mercedes plucked it from a chair. "It's okay, Mom. Nothing to be nervous about."

"For heaven's sake, I'm not nervous." Looping her white pocketbook over her arm, Mom sat down. "After all, we're just going down the road."

She couldn't fool Mercedes. Her mom was super excited, and Mercedes' own heart kicked up when tires crunched on the gravel outside. She jumped up and walked to the door.

Fanning her fingertips across the screen, she remembered how Finn's heart seemed to thud against her own the day he rescued her. How foolish. She scrubbed her fingers on the rough surface but couldn't shake that feeling. And it wasn't just her fingers reacting.

The falling sun released shadows under the pines and birch trees edging their small parking lot. Fireflies flitted in the darkening pockets. Finn waved as he unfolded his tall frame and stepped from what looked like a black Bentley. In New York, men shouldered their way through crowds with brash conviction. Not Finn. One hand in his pocket and the other carrying flowers, he ambled toward her. His deep set eyes were shadowed by the setting sun.

He'd brought her flowers? Her stomach turned squishy. Maybe she was hungry. Maybe deprivation wasn't the way to go.

When had the shyness that kept him in the computer lab

morphed into an easy-going confidence? In high school, Finn Wheeler had been invisible until he slid in next to her for chemistry class. But he sure seemed to recall a lot about her, which was very unsettling.

As he loped toward her, the rolled-up sleeves of his blue oxford shirt revealed corded forearms. In his hand was a bouquet of purple flowers. Athletic legs stretched long and tan below khaki shorts. The Dockers without socks immediately registered as a sexy touch.

Finn Wheeler. Sexy. Who'd have thought it?

Last summer she'd gone with Stephan to visit Mandy and Brett Barclay in the Hamptons. Stephan's socks and loafers clearly marked him as a city boy. Tonight Finn was all laid back and beachy as he sprang up the back steps. "Thought you might like these." He held out the velvety purple gladiolas.

"Oh, you didn't have to do this." Pushing open the screen door, she took the flowers, feeling her own blush.

He grinned. "After today, I thought you might need them."

She held the door wider. "Come on in and meet my mother. Mom, our ride has arrived."

"Flowers! Purple gladiolas." Mom ran one hand over the front of her top. "My goodness, they match my outfit."

"So they do."

"Aren't you thoughtful. A man who brings flowers." Her mom beamed up at him. "Oh, Stephan, I've heard so much about you."

Finn's eyes veered to Mercedes, and she buried her nose in the blooms, as if gladiolas had a scent. How embarrassing was this? At least he knew she really was seeing someone. Had Mom plucked that name from the notes in her hand?

Chapter 4

"Mom, this is Finn Wheeler. We knew each other in high school."

Her mother's smile folded like a paper fan. "Sorry, dear. Sorry." She crammed her paper back into her purse.

"That's okay." She hated the confusion on her mother's face. "High school was a long time ago."

"Finn is it?" Peering up, Mom adjusted her glasses.

"I answer to anything, Mrs. Kennedy."

"Me too. Call me Alice," Mom said with a giggle.

Not missing a beat, Finn took Mom's hand. He flashed her a smile any woman would welcome. Mercedes wanted to hug him. "So nice to meet you, Alice."

The sun came though their white curtains, and she could swear a halo outlined his dark hair. Clearly Mom was charmed by Finn, and Mercedes' own stomach was fluttering. Taking the flowers to the sink, she filled a pan with cool water and left the gorgeous purple blooms soaking until later.

"Ready?" She turned back to Mom and Finn, feeling like she was about to step onto a roller coaster.

"Just one thing." Finn swept her nose with a thumb and came away with yellow nectar. "Now we're ready."

But Mercedes didn't feel at all ready. Her nose tickled from his touch and the evening ahead felt dangerous. Finn held out an elbow to her mother, who took it with a charmed smile.

While Mom was ushered down the stairs, Mercedes locked up. She caught up with them in time to see her mother's pleased smile when he opened the door of his stylish, black Bentley. She'd taught her daughters to appreciate gentlemanly courtesy and so far, Finn checked all the boxes.

Mercedes was feeling pretty satisfied herself as she sank into the soft black leather seat. She'd made it through the day. Pathetic, but she felt like running out with her pompoms and cheering. Maybe "Hold that line!" or "First and ten, let's do it again!" Lindsay Wheeler might be hard to work with but today Mercedes had done all right. Well, except for the broken vase.

Her new boss had stopped by just as Mercedes was finishing up at the second cottage. Looking frazzled, Lindsay whisked through the rooms. She ran a hand over the kitchen counters, checked the floors and plumped pillows. The main bathroom brought her to a halt. "You turned the toilet paper into a point?"

"Like a fine hotel. Not unusual." Mercedes blushed.

"Really? Guess I've never been to a *fine hotel.*"

Mercedes choked back a retort. Lindsay looked exhausted.

But she didn't want to think about Lindsay tonight or her new job as they drove up Red Arrow Highway in the soft summer air. Mercedes had no clue what this umbrella auction was but she was out of the house. Finn smiled when she cracked open a window and rested her head back on the seat. A cool evening breeze flowed though the car, banishing the heat. In the backseat, her mother hummed a tune that sounded like "Some Enchanted Evening."

"Where in Harbert is the auction?" Mercedes asked.

"Paul's Woodshop always hosts the event, just up ahead past Lakeside."

Mercedes remembered the cluster of antique stores that marked Lakeside. Not that she'd ever had time for antiques...or umbrellas. "Do you go to this auction every year?"

"Of course." He grinned. "Don't look so surprised. The proceeds always benefit a local cause."

Finn was a man with principles. She liked that. In New York, she'd attended an endless stream of benefits that had been more about business for her and Stephan than philanthropy. Together, they'd sipped champagne at the Fricks Collection Young Fellows Ball, danced at New Yorkers for Children Spring Benefit and rubbed elbows with artists, fashion designers and celebrities at the Whitney Art Party. She'd always picked up a few contacts and so did Stephan. They worked the room, discretely leaving cards with the right people.

The right people. Where had all those business connections been when her business floundered? Mercedes studied her nails, the pink polish chipped from scrubbing.

In the backseat, her mom's head swiveled. "What do you suppose they sell in all these shops?"

"Everything. You've been in them before." The Frisky Frog, Local Color Gallery or Wine and Whimsy beckoned with charming signage and sparkling windows. Then it hit her. How could any vacationing mother enjoy shopping with kids in tow? Not likely.

Marketing strategies had always come naturally for Mercedes. An idea flared to life. She gripped the door handle so tight her hand hurt.

"Everything okay?" Finn shot her a concerned glance.

"Yes, fine." Would Kate be open to the plan? Mercedes' hand throbbed. Her younger sister seemed pretty territorial about her PR role in Gull Harbor. She'd have to present this carefully.

"How did everything go today?"

"Today?" Breathing Finn in, she fell into a serious brain fog. Soap had never turned Mercedes on until he leaned closer. Stephan preferred expensive colognes and had a heavy hand.

"I mean, after I left the cottage."

"The cottage. Right." Mercedes tried to concentrate but ended up counting his eyelashes. "You mean the gladiolas?"

"Ah, huh." When he blinked, she lost count.

She swallowed hard while her mother kept humming. "Thanks for picking up that vase for me. You didn't tell your sister, did you?" The thought knotted her neck.

"Of course not." Finn looked offended.

"Sorry, Finn. I'd like to forget the whole thing." She'd never let Lindsay Wheeler get to her. Not at minimum wage.

Finally, they reached Paul's Woodshop along the left side of the road. Cars spilled from the small parking lot to line Red Arrow. In the field next to the parking lot, rows of chairs had been set up in front of a small stage. What looked like food on long tables drew clusters of people. Tiny white lights had been looped through the bushes and trees.

Her stomach churned. What was she doing here? This looked and felt like a giant yard sale. She felt out of place and awkward. Wistfully, she recalled elite affairs where uniformed doormen checked engraved invitations. The ballrooms would be festooned with impossibly elegant floral arrangements, balloons bobbing against the high ceilings, trailing glittery ribbons. Women wearing the latest fashions preened on the arms of tuxedoed men, there to see and be seen by the right people.

"Oh, just look, Mercedes. Those tiny lights. Aren't they something?" Her mother's delight reminded Mercedes how jaded attendees could become at the Manhattan galas. Shrieking and laughing, this group seemed to be cutting loose.

Finn cut his speed and parked. Together they strolled toward the gathering. Mercedes' Manolo Blahnik sandals sank into the grass and she treaded carefully. She couldn't afford to ruin another pair of shoes.

The colorful umbrellas displayed on the lawn resembled giant moon flowers. From beach scenes to mermaids, flowers and penguins, the designs were whimsical and fun. Kitschy but charming. "These would cost a fortune in New York." She ran a hand over the painted canvas.

"Do you have a favorite?" Finn asked, touching her elbow.

She glanced over the group, but her mind remained rooted to her tingling elbow. "Probably the mermaid."

"Really? Interesting."

Her mother drew closer. "Remember the story, Mercedes? *The Little Mermaid?*"

Life had been so simple then. "Sure do. I wanted to be a mermaid when I grew up."

"The mermaid had long blonde hair just like hers," her mother explained for Finn's benefit.

"Like this one?" He considered the bare-breasted mermaid poised on a rock, her strawberry blonde hair spilling over one shoulder.

Her mother studied the umbrellas. "I've seen these before. Kate was driving. I think she was bringing me home from the care center. Right, that's it." When her mother's mind snapped back into place, hope sparked in Mercedes' heart.

"How about some refreshments, ladies?" Finn asked. "Looks like they're serving wine."

"Oh, yes, white," Mercedes and her mother said together.

"Be right back." Finn headed off, turning more than a few heads.

"Such a nice boy." Her mother looked to her for agreement.

"Yes, he always was nice." Absent-minded. That's what she remembered about Finn Wheeler. Had his head in a cloud and often slid into class late, t-shirt untucked and glasses sliding down his nose.

"Well, look where that got him."

What did her mother mean? Mercedes almost asked but so much of what Mom said seemed random, spun out by some electrical impulse firing in her brain. When one of her friends called out, Mom waved back.

If it weren't for her mother, Mercedes wouldn't be here. In

New York, black was considered safe and chic. Here in Michigan, her tailored black sundress felt out of place next to women whose clothing bloomed with summer flowers. Returning with their wine, Finn easily fell into small talk with her mother. Turned out his own mother, Rose, had gone to school with Alice. Gull Harbor was like that. Everybody knew everybody.

"Do your folks still live here?" Mercedes asked. So many older people had left Gull Harbor for warmer climates.

"Yep, still in the same house. Rose and John babysit for Lindsay. They won't move away from their grandchildren."

So Lindsay had children? She looked so young.

"That Rose was always so sweet." Her mother joined the conversation but her voice trailed off when she came upon the next umbrella. "Will you just look at this?" She ran one of her veined hands over the huge sunflower.

"They should present the designs to a manufacturer. Might be a market for these in other areas of the country." Mercedes could picture one of the brilliant designs outside the glass windows of her condo. The wrap around terrace had been a selling point, and her heart still pinched at its loss. Although she hadn't been home that much, owning a Manhattan condo had been an achievement. But she had to move on.

Finn had circled back to the refreshment table for french bread and brie. Mercedes sipped the woodsy chardonnay slowly to make the two hundred calories last.

Her mother drifted off to visit with some old friends. Finn returned with a full plate of appetizers, and suddenly they were alone. Just the two of them and the food. A double temptation.

Setting his wine on a table, Finn offered her the plate of brie and bread. "Your mom seems to be having a good time."

"Thanks for inviting her...us." She shook her head at the appetizers.

Finn stopped chewing. "You really wouldn't have come without her?" Now she'd hurt his feelings, and he'd been so darn nice.

Her sandals shifted in the grass. "As I said, I'm seeing someone, Finn. But Mom needed some time out. It was sweet of you to offer." The scent of fresh bread teased her. So did Finn's thoughtful smile.

She closed her eyes. Following her usual mental trick, she imagined sinking her teeth into the bread. Felt the soft texture beyond the brittle crust. Then she did the same with the cheese. The buttery brie would cling to the roof of her mouth. She'd flick it off with her tongue, taste and swallow.

Usually that visualization technique worked. Tonight? She stayed hungry.

"Hey, you okay?" Finn nudged her with an elbow.

Her eyes flew open. "Yep. Fine." Her mouth felt dry and her stomach growled. She wanted the damn bread.

Finn ate with abandon. Only one hunk of brie left. He popped it in his mouth and eyed the buffet table. Mercedes' eyes traveled to high cheek bones and a strong nose. When had Finn Wheeler become a Greek god?

"Come on. Let's get a refill before the food is gone." Taking her elbow, he steered her toward the buffet table. She balked. He tugged and glanced down at her feet. "Hey, are you stuck?"

"Think I'll stay here." She stationed herself near the mermaid umbrella.

Putting down his food, he took out his phone. "Let me take your picture."

No use to protest, the snapping began. Trying to be casual, she draped one hand over the painted canvas and hung on.

"I'll send these to you." Finn checked the shots and smiled. "So, you really like that mermaid?"

"Love her. It." Glancing over, she saw with horror that her fingers cupped the poor mermaid's breast. She was groping the art. Snatching back her hand, she formed a fist. "Weren't you going to get more f-food?"

Wearing that mischievous smile, he whispered, "Relax. Lighten up, Mercedes."

Heat crackled up her neck as she watched him leave. Attractive women reached for Finn as he passed. With his jaunty stride, the man was serious eye candy. She smiled when he brushed off the clinging women.

Soon he was back and the torture by fresh bread continued. She couldn't take much more. Tossing a chunk into his mouth, he turned to look at her mother, still secure in her pack of old pals. "You're a good daughter to come home and help your mother recover. She seems to depend on you."

Mercedes ran a fingertip along the rim of her glass. "Well, it's my turn. Kate was going through a divorce last spring when Mom needed help. I was really tied up, so she came from California and stayed for the summer."

"Only for the summer?"

She shrugged. "Right. Until she ran into Cole. Old habits die hard."

"I'm all for that."

What was he talking about? Eyes dropping, he offered her the plate of tasty temptations.

"No. I said no." Her voice came out shrill. With some effort, she dropped the tone. "Cheese is fattening, especially brie."

"Mercedes, you're thin as a rail." When Finn's eyes did a sweeping figure eight she almost felt it on her skin. "Since when do you worry about your weight?"

"Doesn't every girl try to stay in shape?" Sinking her heels firmly into the grass, Mercedes fought for balance.

"You look fine to me. More than fine. Almost good enough to..." And he bit into the french bread.

"You're crazy." She upended her glass.

"And you like it." Finn was flirting and Mercedes was enjoying it, but she had no comebacks. Even when she pitched new clients, she'd never felt this nervous.

"Look, it's a beautiful night and we're just having fun, right?"

Dropping her gaze, Mercedes studied her pink toes in the black peep-toe sandals. Her mind flipped through her Rolodex of party conversation.

"So you like the brie after all?" She raised her eyes to his twitching lips.

Good God, she was shoveling it in as if she hadn't eaten in

weeks.

He held up the empty plate. "Should I get more?"

"No. This dress is tight enough, thank you."

His gray eyes swept her like a stormy wave. "I like your dress. And I like what's in it."

She sucked in a breath. They went back to chatting about the blasted umbrellas until her stomach stopped the cartwheel thing. Like a sponge softening under water, the tension of the past few months released.

"Are you having a good time?" Finn asked at one point.

"I'm having a great time." The realization surprised her.

He rocked back on his heels. "That's good. No, that's great."

Laughing, they shared a goofy smile. He was the same but different, and she liked it. She scanned the crowd. "Do you see my mother?"

"Relax. She's right over there with her friends." He pointed and then dropped his hand to her back, comforting as a hair dryer on an icy cold morning.

A lake breeze filtered through the trees and lifted his dark hair. "Can't you just go with the flow?" he asked.

"With you, I seem to," she murmured.

"I'm flattered."

"I'm terrified."

She felt his laugh in the pit of her stomach. His hand slid slowly from her shoulder down over her bare arm, like he was memorizing the curve. "Do we need all the answers right now?"

Looking up into the night sky, she frowned at the multitude of stars that never appeared above New York. "I just like to know what's coming, that's all."

"Ah, a girl who has a magic calendar for the future." Finn chuckled. "Wasted time in my book. The future's going to get here. Right?"

"Is everything that simple for you?"

He pitched his empty plate into a nearby trash barrel. "Not really. I just put up a good front. I think you do too."

Strangest conversation she'd ever had. At the gallery openings with Stephan, they talked about form and design, color and the artist, contacts and business possibilities. Nothing personal, she now realized. She'd never discussed her mother with him. He'd never asked.

"How long has your dad been gone?"

"I had just left for college when my parents divorced, and my dad died a couple years after that."

"Guess I'm lucky that my parents still have each other."

"Trust me, you are."

Finn moved closer. Up close and personal, that was Finn Wheeler. "Why don't you tell me all about your boyfriend?"

"You are out-outrageous." She'd almost told him he was out of line.

Insolent merriment danced in his eyes. "Come on. You know I'm just a simple Gull Harbor boy. So, you been seeing each other a long time?"

"Maybe a year or so." *Not that it's any of your business.*

"Think you'll marry him?"

The breath whooshed from her body. "Okay, that's it. Stop." Was she holding up her hand like a traffic cop?

While he pursed his lips, Finn's eyes did the talking. The words she read in those smoky gray depths stirred something deep inside. "Ooookay, why don't you tell me about your work in New York. Safer subject?"

"Much. " Sadder too, not that she'd admit that to Finn. "I had a public relations firm. Kennedy and Associates."

"Had? Past tense?"

"Yes. I had to close shop." Telling her twenty-four employees still brought a lump to her throat.

"Sounds impressive. So what happened?" Under that endearing shock of hair, his forehead knit into a frown as if he were trying to figure out a complicated chemical reaction.

"The recession happened." Enough. Time to change the subject. "You think I passed muster with your sister today?" Every time she thought about Lindsay and the damn toilet paper, she felt like crunching pretzels.

"I'm sure you did fine. She's happy to have help."

"She doesn't seem happy." Mercedes clapped a hand to her lips. "Sorry."

"You're right but the truth hurts. She's young to be a widow. I don't know how long it will take until the hurt and the anger go away."

Mercedes couldn't imagine.

"You two look like you're up to trouble." Her mom's arrival came as a reprieve.

"I admit it. I am up to trouble, Alice," Finn said with a saucy grin. "And your daughter better be ready to handle it."

"Oh, my." Her mother's eyes sparkled. "Should I allow this, Mercedes?"

"Probably not." She loved this new, playful side.

He nodded toward the rows of chair. "Maybe we should stake our claim before it's too late." They filed into a row and sat down. The bidding started. While hands jabbed the air, excitement spiked. But the nervous energy coursing through Mercedes had nothing to do with the auction.

One hour later after Finn had dropped them off and she'd helped Mom upstairs, Mercedes huddled on the screen porch with her phone. On Saturday nights, she was almost always with Stephan. But he didn't answer. The beep pierced her ear and she left a message. "Hi, it's me. We haven't talked in a while. Give me a call when you have a chance, okay?"

Phone in hand, she sat in the darkness, watching the moon ripple across the water below. The fact that Stephan didn't pick up on a Saturday night should have bothered her more.

Chapter 5

The next night Kate and Cole came for Sunday dinner, along with Cole's little girl Natalie. Prissy, Cole's Great Dane, trotted in with them.

"What's with the dog?" she whispered to her mother.

"I babysat for Natalie while Marie finished her rehab."

"With that huge dog?"

"Why, of course. Now shush." Mom broke away to give Natalie a hug.

The Harlequin Great Dane could have been a show dog. When Mercedes stroked the dog's back, Prissy turned to lick her hand with a massive tongue. "What a beautiful dog. You never see anything like this in New York. No room for them."

"Prissy, sit," Cole commanded.

Licking her chops and panting, the Great Dane did as she was told. Mom rewarded Prissy with a good scratch behind the ears. Mercedes wished she had a camera. Growing up, the only pets they'd had were the goldfish, Archibald and Agnes. One time their father brought a puppy home from his favorite bar. "You take that thing right back," their mother told him. "I have enough on my hands." The unsaid *with you* had hung in the air.

Now she fawned over the dog like a long lost friend. "Prissy and I have an understanding, don't we?" The dog closed her eyes in ecstasy, pointed ears flicking forward under Mom's fingers.

Dashing into the living room, Natalie called back, "Alice, got any new books?"

Never call an adult by his or her first name. Their mother had drummed that into them. Now Mom laughed, following Natalie into the living room. "Right there on the TV stand. I picked them up at the secondhand bookstore in town. Kate told me what to buy."

Chuckling, Kate gave Mercedes a hug and whispered, "Do you believe it?"

"Never in this lifetime."

"At first, the two of them were like oil and water this summer," Kate continued. "But Mom needed someone to stay with her when she was released from the care center. I was busy at my flower stand. Cole didn't have anyone to watch Natalie until his mother-in-law Marie came home from rehab."

"A match made in heaven." Standing in the doorway, Mercedes regarded her mother and Natalie with interest. Alice would make a great grandmother. How soon would that be?

The new Alice Kennedy looked cozy enough to read bedtimes stories and fix hot cocoa. The old Alice? She'd been crusty and dictatorial. Watching her mom cozy up to Natalie was like watching a Hallmark movie.

Cole drifted outside to start the barbecue. "Why don't you and Natalie catch up," Kate told her mother. "Mercedes and I will help get dinner on the table."

"Oh, my. Got to take advantage of that one. Come on, Natalie." Mom beckoned toward the porch and they disappeared, Prissy right behind them.

"That's a horse, not a dog." Mercedes pulled lettuce from the refrigerator along with asparagus spears and potatoes. Everything felt off kilter. "The chicken is on the bottom shelf, Kate."

Working with the marinated chicken breasts, Kate chattered happily about the wedding. While she snapped off the ends of the asparagus spears, Mercedes tried to recall Kate's marriage to Brian Bankoff. He didn't take to Gull Harbor so the couple had rarely come back for holidays or a summer vacation. He was a Boston boy, born and bred. No small towns for him. Her mind veered to Stephan. Would he have the same reservations? Finished with the asparagus, she poured water over the bright green spears and set the pan on the back burner of the old Sears stove.

It might not matter if Stephan didn't care for Gull Harbor. She didn't intend to stay here any longer than necessary. Although she was enjoying the eccentricities of her hometown, she yearned for the big city sophistication. After all, she'd worked hard to get there.

Setting the chicken aside, Kate dug around in a drawer and came out with a paring knife. "I'll work on the radishes and onions we brought."

"Green onions." Mercedes regarded them with curiosity. "Haven't had those in forever."

"Cole loves them."

Her sister's proprietary tone made Mercedes smile as she went back to the potatoes. After rinsing them and blotting them dry,

Mercedes cut them into chunks and doused them with olive oil for roasting. The two sisters had fixed dinner together a million times growing up but today felt different. Now Kate was cooking for her man, and Mercedes felt like the odd person out. Kate opened up the refrigerator and peered inside. "I could go for some white wine. How about you?"

"Second shelf down. Think I'll take a pass for now."

Kate gave her a questioning glance and pulled out the chilled chardonnay. "You feeling okay?"

"Absolutely. Just think I'll stick with water." She'd been good last night, drinking only the two-hundred-calorie glass of wine. But those chunks of bread? Finn had caught her off guard. Must have been his gray eyes. Or the hand that touched her elbow and stroked her arm. A shiver coursed through her.

"How did it go last night at the Harbert Auction?" her sister asked, uncorking the wine.

"Mom seemed to enjoy it."

Kate poured herself a hearty glass, sipped and smiled. "What about you and Finn?"

Grabbing the head of Boston lettuce, Mercedes began to tear leaves into the small pieces that were key to mindful eating. "There is no me and Finn, Kate. You know that."

"Oh, I beg to differ." Her sister gave a hearty chuckle. "After all, I saw you two together. The chemistry in my office was as thick as the ricotta in the cheese crowns."

Clutching her stomach, Mercedes moaned. "Don't even mention those. That's where it all started."

"What started?"

"I keep a tight eye on my weight."

Kate didn't look happy. "Mercedes, you could stand a little more weight on those bones."

The lettuce leaves tore so easily in her fingers. "That might fly here but not in New York. Single-digit sizes and I'm not talking about size eight."

"Doesn't sound healthy."

Cole burst through the back door. "Grill's going nicely. Anybody got a cold beer in here?" With his pirate dark hair and broad shoulders, Cole Campbell was one good-looking man. Easy to see why her sister had fallen for him. Again.

Giving him a quick kiss, Kate said, "Beer is in the fridge and chicken's on the counter. Both waiting for you."

"Like you?" Sweeping Kate into his arms, Cole nuzzled her neck. "All I want is right here."

Really? You have to do that right in front of me? She was happy for her sister but some days it was hard, like trying to peel potatoes.

"Cool it, dude who is almost my husband." With a glance in Mercedes's direction, Kate gently pushed Cole away. Mercedes felt like a peeping Tom.

But Cole wasn't the man on her mind. No, the strong arms reminded her of Finn. Ditto with the broad shoulders. Grabbing a tomato, she sliced it for the salad.

"Give me some space here, Cole." Kate pushed the pan of chicken toward him. "I'm a woman with a mission. We have to fix dinner."

Cole left and Kate turned her attention to a cucumber for the salad. "So, Mom was okay last night?" Kate asked.

"I guess so. She saw some old friends."

Kate stopped slicing. "She's changed, hasn't she?"

"A little." Mercedes nodded. "Yep. Remember Grandma Minnie after her stroke?"

"She was one ticked off woman, swatting us for the slightest thing."

"Maybe she was just frustrated, Kate." Mercedes had felt so sorry for Grandma. "Mom's gotten sweeter, I think. Not a bad trade, right?" Laughing together felt a heck of a lot better than the bickering in high school. Kate would borrow Mercedes' eye makeup and forget to return it. One of them would leave the milk out and then blame it on the other sister. So petty, now that she thought back. At this age, none of that mattered.

"So you don't wear makeup anymore?" She studied her sister's healthy glow and felt a flash of envy.

Kate arranged the lettuce, tomato and cucumber salad on one of their mother's aqua Fiesta platters. "Who has time for makeup? Besides, Cole likes me this way."

Oh, Lordy. Mercedes could hear her friends who worked in the New York cosmetic industry groan. But like Stephan, she'd heard nothing from Brittany or Jackie.

"With the wedding right around the corner, I suppose you're crazy busy. Told you I'd help out." No word yet about getting their dresses. Maybe they'd all wear towels and bikinis since the ceremony was on the beach. She swallowed a rogue chuckle, reminding herself that she didn't get to call the shots on this one.

Lifting the lid, she checked on the asparagus. "I was relieved to see so many shops still open along Red Arrow Highway."

"Some have turned over but most are still there."

Now might be a good time to pitch her idea. "Seems like they close around seven o'clock every night."

"Makes sense, right? Everyone's beat from the beach."

"Probably true, but how do young mothers shop with kids?" Wiping off the counter, Mercedes dangled her question and watched Kate's expression change.

"I have no idea. Can't imagine taking small children on a shopping trip." She shuddered.

"Might be fun to have an event that includes all the businesses from Gull Harbor to Stevensville. Ask the shop owners to keep their stores open until midnight."

She could sense Kate's shock. "Midnight? How many people you think would come out?"

"Package it. Call it Midnight Magic. Or Moonlight … something."

"Madness. Moonlight Madness. Shopping so late would be crazy, right?" Kate was smiling as if she liked the idea.

"Moonlight Madness. Who could resist that?" Mercedes' mind leapt from one possibility to another. Squeezing out the sponge, she left it on the side of the sink. "A grand prize giveaway. Coupons from stores. Special Moonlight Madness pricing. Maybe a scavenger hunt."

While they got dinner ready for the table, they brainstormed.

The few times they'd been home together in the past, they didn't talk about their work. Today that seemed ridiculous. A lost opportunity fueled by two competitive sisters.

"You girls look like you've been having a good time," their mother commented when they sat down at the table twenty minutes later. Mom's family had been ahead of its time. Long before the open-living concept became wildly popular, Breezy Point had been one large room. Dining table on one end and living room stretched along front windows that opened to the screen porch and the lake. Now the whole room smelled like grilled chicken. Stretched out at their feet, Prissy panted, eager for any morsel sent her way.

"Trust me, we cooked up more than food in that kitchen tonight." Mercedes smiled at Kate and then turned to Natalie. "Will you be going back to school soon?"

"Yeah. But I'd rather be staying here with Alice."

"Your Grandma Marie loves having you with her," Cole cautioned his daughter. He'd built a small cottage for his mother-in-law on his property.

"I know that, Dad." Natalie gave him the look. Kate might have to take a strong hand with that one in her teens. Word had it that Samantha, Cole's ex-wife, lived in California. She'd just upped and left one day, wild as the wind.

While they passed the platters of food around, the conversation turned to the wedding. Following the comments zipping across the table like the salt and pepper, Mercedes had eaten half her meal before realizing it. For the first time in ages, her stomach felt full.

She sat back.

After dinner, Kate and Mercedes did the dishes together.

"We really should get Mom a dishwasher for Christmas, Mercedes." Kate pushed a hank of hair from her eyes with a soapy hand.

"Sounds like a great idea." Mercedes would worry about the cost later. By that time, she intended to have some kind of company up and running.

Through the white, lace-edged curtains, they could see Cole cleaning the grill outside while Natalie tossed a Frisbee for Prissy to snap up in her huge jowls. On the front porch, Mom cheered them on. The sense of family surrounded them, close and comforting.

Kate had it all. Mercedes told herself Kate had earned all this. Her divorce from Bryan had been painful. But restlessness rippled through Mercedes, like waves on a windy day.

She'd always expected to be married by age twenty-five. But when she moved to New York following graduation, her life took a different direction. Until last year, she'd felt satisfied with her accomplishments. Then her business failed. When loneliness took hold in the middle of the night, she wondered about the choices she'd made.

Kate stacked the clean plates in the dish strainer, while Mercedes dried them one by one. They worked in silence for a few minutes. "Feels good to make dinner with you, big sister," Kate said when every dish had been washed.

Mercedes smiled and placed the last plate in the cupboard. "I know just what you mean."

"Thought we'd go up the road to Second Hand Rose next week to buy bridesmaid dresses. Chili's got her heart set on hot pink. That okay with you?"

Cringing, Mercedes bit her tongue. Three weeks to go and they were going to march into this used clothing store and pick out dresses. How insane was this? But this was Kate's day, and Mercedes wasn't going to ruin it. "Fine with me."

Throwing her arms wide, Kate laughed. "Isn't the whole thing crazy?"

"Right. Crazy. Crazy cool, little sister." Hooking an arm around Kate's neck, Mercedes gave her a quick kiss.

"So good to have you home," Kate whispered. "I want to share all this with you."

"Me too." One final squeeze and Mercedes sighed before pulling away. Shaking out the damp dish towel, she hung it on the handle of the Sears oven to dry. Then she ran her fingers through her blonde hair. "If I don't get something done to my hair soon, I'll go crazy. It's getting out of hand."

"Your hair was long in high school, remember? It was beautiful." Leaning one hip against the counter, Kate studied Mercedes' hair.

"For work in the city, my bob worked really well."

Her sister didn't look convinced. "You miss New York?"

"The city, yes. The work? Sometimes. At the end it wasn't fun." The shocked expressions on her employees' faces would stay with her a long time. She'd failed them. "Tonight felt a lot better just tossing ideas around. I don't miss the tense sessions in the board room with clients that weren't easy to please."

Her sister's face brightened. "Maybe we can flesh out, what was it, Moonlight Madness? Do you think we could get the promotion ready for Labor Day?"

"Sure, whatever it takes." Kate would go along with this? Mercedes almost giggled with relief. The past few months had left her with the bitter taste of failure. Maybe Moonlight Madness would change all that—at least for one night.

Following Kate onto the porch, they cheered Cole and Natalie on during a Frisbee contest.

"My, that was fun," her mother said with a yawn when they were locking up later.

"Guess you like having us around, even when we get underfoot."

Mom turned. "Mercedes, you're never underfoot. I love having you here."

Her throat thickened. "But I'm thirty, Mom." What mother expects a grown daughter to come back home? Mom's illness had given her a free pass to stay for a while. At least, that's how Mercedes saw it.

"I don't care if you're fifty-five or sixty as long as you're happy."

"Oh, you sweet woman." Her mother felt so small, so frail when Mercedes wrapped careful arms around her, chin resting on those springy curls. "I'm glad to be here, Mom."

Pulling away a bit, Mom said, "You girls are always written on my heart, Mercedes." And she outlined a little heart on her blouse with one finger, the way she had when they were small. For the first time, Mercedes felt this was home. A visit that could help her pick up the pieces.

After seeing her mother safely up the stairs, Mercedes took her phone out to the porch. The moon glittered on the water below, and an owl hooted deep in the woods. August heat hung almost liquid thick. Flipping on the overhead fan, she sank onto the porch swing. Even in the dead of winter in New York, her terrace had been one of her favorite places. She'd fed on the lights of the city. Michigan was the complete opposite, so quiet and still. She pressed a direct dial button.

After three rings, Stephan picked up. "Mercedes?" He sounded surprised.

"Yes. Did you get my messages?"

"No. But it's been busy. Another opening up in a Tribeca gallery." His yawn indicated just what he thought of it. "So what have you been doing?"

His voice grated on her, so polite and impersonal. Of course, she couldn't tell him about mucking out people's cottages. He'd think she'd lost her mind. "I'm checking out the real estate market here."

"No kidding? I suppose there are a lot of high-priced properties, right? Chicago people and all that."

"Of course. But not like New York. Not Manhattan valuations."

"Well, you can't expect that."

Did she imagine the condescending tone? Silence fell. She

waited for him to tell her that he'd come to Kate's wedding. No way was she going to press him. But she really wanted him there so she'd have him as an escort to keep her head on straight. Things had gotten out of kilter recently. She didn't do well with unexpected kinks in her plans.

Stephan said nothing. In fact, it sounded like he was typing on his computer.

Her patience shredded. "Have you booked your flight for my sister's wedding?"

She heard rustling paper as if he were checking his calendar. He cleared his throat. "When would that be again?"

She wanted to scream. "The weekend after Labor Day. Early September."

"Oh, right. Let me check some flights. Are you inviting people who matter?" He laughed. This had always been their private joke. They liked to rank events according to which people would be attending. Tonight it didn't feel funny.

"I haven't seen the guest list, Stephan."

"Well, give me some time."

No *I've really missed you, Mercedes.*

No *I can't wait to see you.*

Her heart shriveled. They'd been dating for a year and he didn't know if he could make it? Yep, she could be standing there alone in the sand, watching her sister marry the love of her life.

Oh, she already knew what his answer would be. Getting a last-minute airplane ticket was always costly. They were getting down to the wire. Her empty stomach convulsed. "Well, I won't keep you."

If she'd been sitting at her desk upstairs, she'd move some paper around. She could out-office him any day of the week. But only the dry sound of the leaves overhead filled the night air.

"Sure. I'll let you know about the event, okay?"

Event? He was stiff-arming her.

"Sure that'll work. There are some people I want you to meet." She dangled that last line. It had always worked.

Maybe not this time. They said good-bye.

Rocking the swing with one foot, she flipped through the photos on her phone. Finn had sent her some that day. She opened them and paged through. When she got to the shot of her with the mermaid, she broke into laughter. Laughed until she cried.

Chapter 6

Not a single privacy booth in sight. Standing in the doorway of Phoebe's Place, Mercedes felt no hope. Kate's friend ran a hair salon that let it all hang out. Literally. For all the world to ogle. What other options did Mercedes have? Her hair hung past her shoulders, clinging to her neck in the August heat. Three black chairs ranged along the left wall with shampoo bowls in the back. Hair dryers blasted two older women discussing their bunions in loud voices above the din.

The old-fashioned contraptions reminded Mercedes of vintage TV shows. So did the worn green and black linoleum. The entire place felt like museum material. At Jean Paul's in New York, clients were discreetly escorted to a private booth. Gull Harbor? Apparently, having your hair done was a group experience.

"Hey, girl. Come on in, Mercedes." Phoebe beckoned to her with a hair dryer. Not every woman could wear mauve hair, but on Phoebe it looked good. "I'll be finished here in a sec."

"So sorry I'm late." Mercedes had been balancing her checkbook. A lost cause. She sank onto an overstuffed loveseat in the front.

"We're on beach time in Gull Harbor. Nobody's ever late." Phoebe pointed an elbow to a clock where every number had been replaced with a sailboat. "I'm just finishing up here with Joanne."

A pretty woman with chestnut hair looked pleased as Phoebe wielded the hairdryer and a styling brush. Mercedes had only flipped through two magazines when the hair dryer clicked off and Phoebe waved her over.

Sliding into the black vinyl chair while the other client checked out, Mercedes eyed Phoebe's styling products. None of the brands looked familiar. High-heel slides flapping against the soles of her feet, Phoebe hurried back to her station. "You can hang up your purse right there, hon." She pointed to a hook. Her brown Gucci bag looked strangely out of place under an ad for Breck shampoo. The actress in the ad had been dead for years.

"Didn't you just love her? I'm big on retro decor." Snapping out a black plastic cover-up, Phoebe tied it around Mercedes' neck and studied her in the mirror.

"Just a bob," Mercedes told her. "Chin length. Crisp. What do you think?" That last question might be dangerous.

"Will you just look at this?" Phoebe scooped up handfuls of Mercedes' hair. "Some women would kill to have hair this thick. And you want to cut it off?"

"Trimmed. I didn't have time for a cut before coming home." No need to mention that she also didn't have the money for Jean Paul's. Hadn't for quite a while. At least one inch of her dirt brown roots was showing. She'd gotten creative about teasing her hair over the top.

"Want to jazz it up a little bit?" Phoebe threw her a mischievous smile in the mirror.

Mercedes froze. "I don't think so, Phoebe. What did you have in mind?"

"Maybe a pink stripe to go with your bridesmaid dress? Sarah told me all about your shopping trip."

Mercedes sighed, thinking of the dress hunt two days earlier. "I wanted black."

"Black?" Phoebe's surprised tone said it all. "Isn't that for funerals?"

"Not in New York." But Mercedes' voice faded off. She wasn't in New York anymore.

"Bet you girls had a blast that day, right?"

How could she explain the horror of the shopping trip? Three days earlier, Kate had joined Sarah and Chili at Second Hand Rose. Her skin crawled when she eyed the racks jammed with used clothing. "Just try on whatever makes you happy," her sister had thrown out, flouncing around the small shop as if it were Saks.

While Chili chose a mauve satin gown with deep ruffles, Sarah settled on a shell pink dress with elbow-length sleeves and a full skirt. By that time, Mercedes' empty stomach was burning with acid. She flipped through the hangers slowly, trying not to touch the clothes. Sarah and Chili both looked so thrilled with their selections, but nothing on the rack appealed to Mercedes. While it may be trendy to have dresses that didn't match, it didn't feel right. This wedding was becoming a hodgepodge, a term her mother always used. Kate was eyeing Mercedes with the same expression she'd used in high school when Mercedes refused to wear jeans her mother had picked up for her at Sears. Even in middle school,

Mercedes had stood her ground, angling for designer jeans

"Oh, Mercedes. Too many choices for you?" Never shy, Chili broke into her thoughts. "Here, I will help you, *amiga mia.*" Mercedes' uneasiness turned to full blown alarm when Chili grabbed a strapless cocktail dress. Sparkling with pink and silver sequins, the bodice topped a skirt layered with wide ruffles. *"Posibilidades, no?"*

Possibilities? Not really. She'd never worn anything so frilly, not in New York anyway. Her sister's hands were fisted on her hips. Mercedes felt a twinge of guilt. She didn't want to ruin Kate's wedding day.

"Looks interesting." Feeling like she was jamming her hand into a blender, Mercedes fingered the soft fabric and eyed the flashy bodice. No dainty cap sleeves, no straps. She'd be tugging at the dress all night.

"Let's try it on." Not a woman to be ignored, Chili had maneuvered her through a narrow hallway into a spacious fitting room. With several hooks on the wall, this felt like the old Filene's Basement. She'd only gone to Filene's once. "Come out when you're ready," Chili threw over her shoulder, yanking the curtain shut. With a sigh, Mercedes stripped and stepped into the dress. Turning toward the mirror, she was grateful for the side zipper.

A pink flush coloring her chest and cheeks, Mercedes gaped at her reflection. The dress was a little big on her but maybe her mother could fix that. Wide ruffles swishing softly against her thighs, this little cocktail number looked fabulous. More cleavage and leg than she ever showed, but the dress left her wondering.

Maybe this sexy, kittenish girl was the woman Mercedes always wanted to be. Out front, Chili and Sarah called to her. Slipping into the black slings she'd brought, she walked out. "What do you think?" Jaws dropped when she pirouetted in the three-way mirror.

"Gorgeous. Why didn't I try that on?" Chili laughed.

"Mercedes, you look so pretty," Sarah said.

"Who is this woman?" howled Kate, eyes wide. "Sexy. Gorgeous. But do *you* like this dress?"

Mercedes almost didn't recognize herself, the woman grinning shyly in the mirror. "I'll take it."

The memories of that shopping day were still fresh in her mind while Mercedes watched Phoebe fuss with her hair. Would a severe blonde bob go with that dress?

Lifting a length of Mercedes' hair again, Phoebe wiggled her eyebrows. "What do you say to a pink stripe?"

In the mirror, Mercedes saw herself open and close her lips, like a fish washed up on shore. "No pink hair," she finally squeaked out. "Not today."

"Okey-doke." Phoebe gave a pert nod. "How about some layers?"

Mercedes closed her eyes. "Okay. Why not?" Might be good to switch things up for Stephan at this wedding. Sure felt like his interest was waning.

"When did you get back in town?" Phoebe asked when she returned with a bowl, dabbed her brush into the color and got to work.

"A couple weeks ago."

"Bet your mom and sister were glad to see you."

Were they? "I think they are."

"So you're here to help with the wedding?"

Mercedes winced. "Everything's taken care of. Kate has her own ideas."

"You don't say." Phoebe's earthy chuckle suggested dark secrets. "I'm so happy for her. Cole Campbell, one of Gull Harbor's hotties. Everybody adores that man. And your sister? The town needed a flower shop and with Chili's help, Kate stepped up to the plate. Now she's going to promote Gull Harbor. She's a gem."

"So I see." It felt strange to have someone gushing over her younger sister. Then it hit her. Kate had probably endured this all through high school. Had she gotten tired of hearing about all Mercedes' accomplishments? Maybe it was pay back time. Now Kate had landed a man the whole town "adored." That couldn't be jealousy pinching her heart. Since Mercedes already had Stephan, what did it matter?

But did Mercedes have Stephan? Even more important, did she want him? The Gull Harbor women seemed so passionate about their men, with none of the New York restraint and discretion. Uncertainty rippled through her. Was she crazy about Stephan?

Phoebe put her bowl and brush to one side. "Let's just get you settled. While your color sets, you can read up on all the movie stars." Leading her to the front, Phoebe pointed to chair and handed her a magazine. The plastic cover-up crinkled as Mercedes surrendered to the chair. Sitting in plain sight with foil-wrapped hair felt unnerving. Cars whizzed by on the highway, the floor rumbling under the occasional semi. Telling herself no one could see her anyway, she turned to the magazine. Photos of actresses ducking into New York clubs made her homesick. The bright lights, busy streets, the city that never sleeps. She had to get back there. Closing the magazine, she slid it onto a side table. Her head nodded while she waited for her hair color to set. She'd been staying up too late, reading every New York blog she could find, gorging on scraps of city news.

But New York was not in her dreams when Mercedes nodded off in the chair. No diesel fuel or fast food stands made her pinch her nostrils. Instead, she breathed in Finn's fresh soap and ran from him, laughing as he chased her around an auction umbrella. Elvis and Wiggy yipped at his heels and her own heartbeat spiked. In the dream, Mercedes wore her bridesmaid dress. The ruffles floated in the evening air that cooled way too much of her skin. She felt exposed and stumbled. Finn caught her. "Mercedes," he murmured, burying his face in the warm crook of her neck. His lips brushed the soft skin above the bodice. Slowly he worked his way up to her neck. She'd never felt such surrender. Her hands cupped his head, drawing him closer. "Oh, Finn," she whispered before his lips found hers. He tasted like everything she'd ever wanted.

Mercedes jerked awake from her nap with a sore neck and drool dripping from her chin. The magazine had fallen from her lap to the floor. Appearing in front of her, Phoebe gave her a curious look. "Let's get you shampooed."

Good grief. Had she said Finn's name out loud?

"Right, right." She scrambled to the back of the salon.

Switching to the shampoo chair, Mercedes leaned her head back against the cool rim of the bowl. Chattering all the time, Phoebe turned on the spray. Her words flowed around Mercedes like warm water, or like Finn's arms in the dream she tried to remember but needed to forget. She had to shut that dream down fast. Instead, she concentrated on Phoebe's strong fingers that soon had Mercedes feeling like a wet noodle. Jean Paul never did it quite like this. He always complained about the Manhattan traffic while he worked or the lack of a good restaurant near his salon.

Jean Paul had been more like an extension of her workday. Hardly relaxing, she now realized. Phoebe was a vacation, massaging her scalp while tossing out town tidbits.

"Are you married, Phoebe?" Mercedes asked.

The hairdresser's smile went south. Mercedes winced when Phoebe's fingers dug in. "Divorced two years ago. Best decision I ever made. That Harley just streaked off into the sunset. But honey, I kept mine." As her laugh rolled through the salon, it wasn't hard to picture Phoebe straddling a rumbling Harley.

"How about you, Mercedes? Got a special somebody?"

"He's back in New York," Mercedes murmured.

"Aw, bet you miss him."

"Um, sure." Did she?

"He's coming for the wedding, right?"

"Probably." Their plans felt uncertain, a condition she'd never tolerated. Stephan was being strangely evasive. She should feel more upset about that.

The conditioner Phoebe lathered into her hair smelled like apples. Some of her happier childhood days had been picking apples with her parents in orchards along Red Arrow Highway. One whiff of the conditioner loosened her shoulders and wrapped her in those apple orchard days of the past.

"You can sit up now, hon."

The towel Phoebe wrapped around her hair was soft and fluffy. Mercedes practically floated out of that chair and followed the hairdresser to the front. Phoebe was not a woman of few words, and this morning Mercedes was happy to listen to her story about a summer trip to Sturgis, South Dakota, for a Harley rally.

"I bought some new leathers, you know?" Phoebe patted her full hips. "Wanted to look good with all those hot guys. Setting my sights, if you know what I mean."

"Right, of course." Mercedes felt mesmerized while Phoebe told her about a place called One Eyed Jack's Saloon.

Giggling, Phoebe pointed to a picture taped to the mirror. "Don't you just love that selfie I took with a bison?" In the photo, Phoebe was dressed in a big hat, sunglasses and a tight, leather jacket that probably made breathing difficult. One arm looped around the neck of a long-horned beast that two men appeared to be holding down.

"That's something," Mercedes agreed. *Something scary.*

"One heck of a good time, I tell you." The shears kept snipping while Phoebe chattered. "Everybody thinks Mount Rushmore's a big deal but it was kind of tame after that bison...and the men who were giving me a hand, if you get my drift."

"I think I do." Mercedes swallowed a shocked chuckle.

Squirting gel into her palms, Phoebe rubbed them together before running her fingers through Mercedes' hair. Felt good to be pampered. No wonder older women came here once a week.

"Phoebe, what would you think if Gull Harbor had a Moonlight Madness sale the Saturday of Labor Day weekend?"

"Tricky title. What is it?" Phoebe kept snipping.

"All the shops and restaurants would stay open until midnight. And you'd have special offers. Do you think the owners would go for it?"

Phoebe considered the plan. "Could be tons of fun, hon. We need something different around here, that's for sure."

Mercedes' confidence grew. "Kate and I were talking about doing special flyers you can give to your customers. Ignacio and Chili would probably hand them out at their vegetable stand. Clancy's and Dressel's Drugstore would go along with it, right?"

"I don't see why not." Phoebe grabbed the hair dryer. "Sounds exciting."

"I know it's last minute, but we want the summer to end with some event to spur business going into the fall."

"Hey, girl. I like the sound of that." Phoebe lifted her voice about the whirr of the dryer.

Mercedes felt so proud that this was her idea, her contribution. If Phoebe went along with it, probably the rest of the businesses would too. When Phoebe clicked off the dryer and set it down along with her brush, Mercedes scanned her station for the hair straightener. She didn't see a flat iron in the place.

"Now for my final special Phoebe's Place touch." Standing between Mercedes and the mirror, Phoebe made fists in her hair. The pinching and tugging on her roots made Mercedes nervous.

"So what do you think?" Phoebe stepped back

"Good God." The blonde who faced her in the mirror was a total stranger. Soft curls framed her cheeks and whispered against her neck.

Just when she sat there gasping, Lindsay Wheeler sauntered in with two little girls. With her bouncing ponytail, she looked so young. For a second, Mercedes' attention was diverted as Lindsay approached the desk. Finn's sister seemed to be all business, even with her daughters. Although Lindsay shared her brother's chestnut hair, the girls were blonde.

But back to Mercedes' own hair. Where was the damn straightener?

Hands clasped to her chest, Phoebe looked like she might cry. The last thing Mercedes wanted to do was hurt her feelings. "Phoebe, it's terrific. Real...different and I, well, I just don't know what to say."

The concern left Phoebe's delicate features. "You are one hot mama with that hair style. Maybe next time you'll want some colored highlights." The cape crackled when Phoebe whisked it off.

"I'll have to think about that."

Turning to Lindsay and her daughters, Phoebe clapped her hands. "Who is getting a haircut today? Rebecca or Susan?"

"Both of us!" They shouted together.

"Now girls, let's keep it down." Lindsay rolled her eyes at

Phoebe then came to a stop right in front of Mercedes. "My, oh, my. That's a great look. Different, right?"

"Everybody meets in my shop," Phoebe trilled. "You two know each other?"

"Yes." Mercedes' answer was a whimper. Would Lindsay tell the world that Mercedes helped her clean cottages?

But Lindsay merely nodded, a hand on each daughter. "Now, Phoebe, we need shoulder-length hair for school. Mommy doesn't have much time in the morning."

The older girl protested and Lindsay's lips tightened. "Rebecca, I don't have time to put french braids in your hair every day." Her voice rose at the end. For a second, Mercedes actually felt sorry for her. Being a single mother must be hard.

Rebecca and Susan viewed Lindsay with solemn eyes. Maybe they realized their mother was teetering on the brink.

Mercedes stepped toward the desk where Phoebe waited with a pleased smile. The price was incredibly reasonable, and she gave Phoebe a generous tip, using one of the credit cards that hadn't been maxed out. Outside, she put the top down on her car. Today the scarf stayed in the glove compartment. The sun felt warm, but not sweltering, with a few clouds somersaulting across the bright blue sky. Maybe her curls would straighten out by the time she got home. On the drive back to Breezy Point, Mercedes put a call in to Stephan. After that crazy dream, she needed a reality check. He didn't pick up.

Turning onto Lake Shore Road, she slowed down. One quick glance in the rearview mirror told her that her curls were still bouncy. How amazing. What did it matter that they were a bit tangled? She ran her fingers through the snarls and the curls sprang back. Was it possible that her flat iron had crushed natural curls from her hair? Maybe the new do would be a time saver.

Birch trees and pines towered overhead and blue morning glories twined over a split rail fence. Orange tiger lilies ran riot along the road. The vivid colors rivaled the gaudy neon of Times Square. She slowed down. In Manhattan, the tall buildings obscured the sun and the only greenery came from pots. Here sunlight sifted generously through the trees and cottages were framed by lush bushes of blue hydrangeas. Walking along the side of the road, a family laden with buckets and floats headed to the beach. Their life looked so normal, so routine.

How Mercedes wished she could relax into this summer. Just flop back on one of those floats, drift on the water and be mindless. But her busy mind wouldn't let her. Nope, her thoughts strained ahead like a racehorse reaching for the finish line. She needed some plan that would take her back to Manhattan where she belonged.

When she pulled into the parking lot, her mother was tying up the tall pink hollyhocks, heavy with double blooms. "Why, don't you look sassy." Her mother drew closer for a better look.

"Do you like it?" She slammed the car door shut. "I probably look ridiculous."

Eyes squinting, her mom came closer. "No, you don't. You look different. Prettier if you ask me. "

Mercedes snorted. "I don't know how to take care of a hairdo like this." Just touching those curls made her crazy.

"Didn't Phoebe sell you one of those combs? You know, the ones with the long teeth?"

When she shook her head, she felt the curls bounce. "I'll pick one up at Dressel's Drugstore. Other customers were coming in." She wondered what kind of hairdo Lindsay Wheeler got. Probably something practical, from what she'd said to her daughters.

Her mother followed her into the cool kitchen, the air moved by the overhead fan Cole had installed. "Do I look ridiculous?"

"Sometimes change is good, Mercedes." Her mother wasn't giving up. "Your curls were so cute when you were a toddler. I think you look pretty."

"But I don't know what to do with this." She pulled out one kinked strand.

Her mother's raised eyebrows said she didn't agree. "That'll be the day when you don't know what to do, Mercedes Kennedy."

"I'm going into Clancy's to get some cleaning supplies. Some of the cottages turn over on Friday so I'm going to work tomorrow, Saturday and Sunday."

"That Lindsay, she's really got her hands full doesn't she?"

"She stopped at Phoebe's salon this morning with her two daughters. Lindsay lost her husband in Iraq."

"Yes, I know. Poor thing." Taking out a pitcher of iced tea, her mother set it on the counter. Mercedes took out the tray of ice cubes.

"Awful. I can't even imagine." Mercedes filled two glasses with ice and tea.

Mom took her iced tea in both hands. "The war is terrible but the men's service is beautiful. They're true patriots. The comfort people in this town offer each other? Well, that just goes with Gull Harbor. That's beautiful too."

"I guess you're right. But the families pay such a high price." Mercedes thought of Sarah, who must miss Jamie terribly.

"Why don't you take a rest, honey?" Her mother peered at her with eyes that saw everything. "You look tired."

"Oh, I already had my nap for today." Her cheeks blazed, thinking of the dream she'd had sitting in Phoebe's chair. "Think I'll head for Clancy's."

Her drink snug in the cup holder, she drove into town. From time to time, she slid a piece of ice into her mouth. The day was heating up. Good thing she'd put the top up and turned on the air conditioning. But it wasn't the hot weather melting the ice in her mouth. No, it was the memory of a dream that wound its way around her heart.

Chapter 7

So it had come to this. Mercedes, who once swore by her Hermes handbag, now gripped a purple plastic cleaning caddy. But she felt proud of her range of supplies. She'd researched every niche product available to avoid noxious fumes. That's just who she was. When Mercedes Kennedy took on a project, she did it right. But the caddy weighed her down, in more ways than one.

Of course, she had to charge the supplies to her credit card. Who knew sprays and creams could be so expensive? But she was equipped for her new role. Wearing cutoffs and a pink tank top, she'd stuffed her new curls under a pink and blue bandanna. She even wore sweatbands on her wrists, the kind the tennis players wore as they pounded the courts under the grueling sun. Time to get serious. No more smirks from her new boss.

Lindsay's car was out front when Mercedes rang the bell of the small white frame cottage on Whispering Pine Road. Just like last time, Lindsay didn't hear her. A vacuum growled in the background. Mercedes walked in. This time when Lindsay didn't jump when she glanced up. Instead, she frowned and turned the vacuum off. It snarled into silence.

With one sweep of gray eyes so like Finn's, Lindsay took her in. Her lips twitched when her gaze reached the head scarf. Mercedes must look ridiculous. Her shoulders slumped.

"Looks like you're all set." Reaching into her pocket, Lindsay pulled out a cluster of keys.

Mercedes straightened. "How many cottages this time?"

Lindsay burst out laughing. "Honestly, Mercedes. You're such a trip. You'd think I was giving you a list of homes to paint instead of four cottages to tidy up."

Tidy up? Did Lindsay have any idea how her back and knees ached after her last cleaning gig? But right now, this was the only game in town. Dammit, she was going to do a good job, no a *great* job, if it killed her.

She checked the addresses. How long would it take to upload them to the GPS in her car? "Why don't we have a race? See who can finish faster today?"

Lindsay's eyes narrowed with suspicion. "This isn't a sprint, Mercedes. It's a marathon. My reputation rides on whether or not we do a good job. Remember to do the baseboards and the drains. That takes time." Then she smiled. "You're on."

Tennis shoes skidding in the sand, Mercedes ran back to her car. Her fingers fumbled as she uploaded the addresses and studied the map on her GPS. She'd start with the house farthest away and work in. Gunning it, she tore out and headed for Willow Road.

The cottage drowsed in the early morning sunlight when she pulled up in front. Its pink siding was set off by huge blue hydrangeas. She breezed past them, purple caddy in hand. Once inside, she set her carrier down and raced to the first bedroom for the bedding. She found the laundry room in the back and jammed it full of sheets from both bedrooms. Were all washing machines this small? After dumping in a liberal amount of liquid soap, she slammed the top and pressed a button.

Opening the dryer, she silently thanked the renters who'd started a load before leaving. Snapping out the warm plush towels, she folded them neatly, the way Tiola did it. Leaving the pile of fresh towels on top of the dryer, she raced from closet to closet until she found the broom. Sand crunched underfoot as she swept it from the corners before running the vacuum. She ran a hand over her damp forehead. Not even ten o'clock and she was sweating bullets.

Finished with the floors, she emptied the dishwasher and then started on the bathroom. How many people had stayed here, twenty? After donning sturdy rubber gloves, she scrubbed the shower, the sink and the toilet. Would Lindsay laugh when she found the pointed end of the toilet paper? A girl had to have standards. With a wicked smile, Mercedes creased a sharp point.

She was swabbing the kitchen floor when the washing machine began banging around like some prehistoric animal needing release. Horrified, she dropped the mop and ran back to the laundry room. Good God. Sudsy water had flooded the floor, and she slipped as she skidded into the room. The washing machine had vibrated away from the wall. Panicked by the mess, she slapped at the buttons until it stopped.

Whatever made her think she could be the cleaning queen? Body limp, she fell against the machine. Sure, she could make a hostess point on a toilet paper roll. But basics like washing clothes?

Tiola had done that for her. This laundry room felt like a foreign country in rebellion.

But she couldn't give up.

Grabbing a mop, she began to sop up the water. *I will do this. I can do this.* She was mid-swish when she heard the front screen door creak open and whap shut. Flip flops slapped toward the back. Was Lindsay coming to check up on her? Mercedes leaned on the mop and waited.

"Mercedes? You back here?" Finn. But Mercedes' relief was quickly followed by horror. She was a sweaty mess.

"Hey, girl. What are you doing?" Leaning in the doorway, Finn looked disturbingly fresh in khaki shorts and a white t-shirt. "Whoa. What have we here?"

"I-I think their washing machine is broken."

Flipping the top open, he peered inside. "Too many clothes in here."

"Sheets," she supplied.

He grinned. "If washing machines get too full, the water goes all over."

"And you know this because...?"

Finn looked adorable when he blushed. "Okay, this happened to me one time. Huge mess. At least this floor isn't carpeted."

"No kidding." She glanced at the water all over the floor. "I thought it would save time. What an idiot I am."

Coming closer, he cupped her chin. "Now stop. You know that's not true."

When she looked deep into those gray eyes, she believed him.

The hand dropped from her chin, and his flush deepened. "You won't save time doing it this way, Mercedes. But it was an honest effort."

"Lindsay and I are having a race."

"Really?" He sounded delighted. "How many cottages do you have?"

"Four. I'll probably be here until midnight." Why had she even suggested this?

He held out a hand. "Give me two."

She was touched. This guy was so sweet. "I guess you know the drill."

"Trust me, I've done it before."

How amazing. "So you help your sister out sometimes?"

"Sometimes." He waggled his fingers. "Give me your phone and two of the keys."

She dug them both out of her pockets.

After tapping some buttons on the phone, he handed it back. "Call me when you're finished. And no more overloading the washer, okay?"

"Don't worry. I've learned my lesson."

When he got to the front door, he turned to face her. "Oh, and Mercedes?"

"What?"

"I like the curls." He winked and the breath caught in her throat. The screen door closed behind him, and Finn whistled as he went down the stairs. Watching him get into his car, Mercedes slowly twirled one of the curls around her finger. Warmth unfurled inside. This man touched her in secret places. How could she shiver and burn at the same time?

But back to work. She snapped on the old plastic radio on the kitchen counter. The Rolling Stones set a fast, throbbing pace. She was going to win this competition or else, especially with Finn taking two of the houses. That gave her time to pay attention to details. Their mother had been particular and her demands, so irritating years ago, came back to Mercedes now.

The August heat spiked as she worked. How she appreciated the effort Tiola had put in back in New York. Of course, her condo had never gotten this kind of use. Did any of these homes have central air? She clicked on the overhead fan in the main room. As she vacuumed the floors, she wondered about Finn. She'd been really upfront with him about Stephan. Was he determined to be her friend...or what? The "or what" both bothered and excited her.

She was struggling to pull on a fitted bottom sheet when it hit her. Stephan would never help her mop a floor or make a bed. He'd come up with some excuse. A phantom phone call. An emergency trip to the drugstore. Mercedes flopped on the bed and watched the fan whirr above her. But she couldn't waste time. Not on Stephan. She felt a slow anger building and vaulted from the bed.

The next house on Tulip Lane had three bedrooms. This time she walked through the entire place before starting to work. She made two equal piles of sheets and then put one into the washer. After the water stopped filling, she lifted the lid to check. Plenty of space to swish around, and she eased out a sigh of relief. No way did she want to risk an overflowing washer again.

How was Finn coming? But as she searched the closets for the vacuum, she figured he was fine. The man had an eye for detail. Back in high school, the details had to do with formulas and chemical reactions. She knew she could trust him.

As she slapped the rugs on the back railing, she wondered if Finn had dated anyone junior or senior year. She'd never seen him at prom. Had he even gone to the football or basketball games? Questions about Finn Wheeler and his sweet, gentlemanly ways circled in her mind while she swept and mopped, scrubbed and sprayed.

The people who owned this cottage had a binder on a wicker desk in the kitchen. On the cover was scripted "Our Home." She flipped it open. In addition to restaurant menus, the couple had included information about appliances, garbage pickup and anything else that seem to make sense. Closing the binder, she got back to work. The binder of information had given her an idea. Check-in was four o'clock so she had to hurry. How would she ever have gotten this done without Finn's help?

The last load of sheets finished just as she was wiping down the counters in the kitchen. Every floor had been swept and mopped. She'd arranged the clean rugs on the floors. After a final tour through the house, she collected her container of cleaning supplies and locked the door behind her. Outside the sun was shining through the birch trees. Somewhere nearby, a woodpecker was persistently hammering on a tree. She could do this.

The Tulip Lane cottage sat about one block from the beach and she could hear the waves, so restless today. Exhausted, she longed to feel the sand between her toes, feel the waves cool on her skin. Chucking her carrier into the trunk, she called Finn. "How's it going?"

"Just finished." He sounded breathless. "I'm all hot and sweaty."

The image weakened her knees. "Me too." She collapsed against the hot metal of her car, picturing the T-shirt clinging to his broad back and firm chest. Or maybe he'd taken his shirt off? She grabbed the door handle.

"Mercedes? You still there?"

She cleared her throat but not her mind. "Of course."

"Okay. Check with Lindsay. If you won this crazy competition, I think you owe me something."

Her fingers tightened on the phone. "What would that be?"

"A drink at the Mangy Mutt tonight? As a friend."

"Done." Strictly business.

Ending the call, she phoned Lindsay. "How's it coming?"

"You can't be finished."

Mopping her brow with one of her wristlets, Mercedes smiled. "But I am."

Silence hummed on the other end of the phone. "I'll do a sweep through but I'm sure everything's fine." Lindsay didn't sound convinced, and Mercedes chuckled all the way home. She put the top down on the convertible and cruised down Red Arrow in wicked euphoria. The air tousled her curls and she didn't care. Instead, she imagined she was Phoebe, not asking permission or bowing to anyone.

By the time Lindsay called her back, Mercedes was relaxing on the porch with her mother, sipping lemonade.

"I guess you win." Disbelief echoed in Lindsay's voice. "The places look great. But you forgot to turn the toilet paper back at two of them."

Shoot. Mercedes had forgotten to tell Finn about that detail. "I was in a hurry."

"Uh, huh." Lindsay didn't sound convinced. "Say, Mercedes. Phoebe told me about Moonlight Madness. Are you in charge of it?"

"Kate is. Want to participate?"

"Any publicity helps, but I don't know what I'd offer."

Was Lindsay asking her for help? "Why don't you give out coupons? A special discount on your services?"

"But then I'd earn less. I might sweep in more business than I can handle."

"But you have me now, right?" What was she saying? Lindsay's silence told her she'd been taken by surprise too. "I mean, if that's all right with you."

Down below, a sailboat cut across the lake, slim and sleek. How Mercedes wanted to be out on that boat, the sun on her skin and the breeze in her hair as she tacked back and forth.

"Sounds fine to me." Lindsay's acceptance jarred Mercedes back to reality. "I appreciate your help."

"Maybe Phoebe will let you leave your coupons at her stop along the highway."

"Good idea. Thanks." The appreciation caught Mercedes off balance. Had she misjudged Lindsay? Maybe she was just proudly independent, like Mercedes.

"You're welcome."

"Was that Lindsay?" her mother asked after she ended the call.

"Yes, we had this stupid contest today. But I won." Amazement tweaked her smile wider.

"I'm so proud of you, Mercedes." Her mother set her glass down on the white wicker side table. "You came home and jumped right in. Kate told me about Madness in the Moonlight, or whatever you're calling that thing when people shop at night."

"You've always been so proud of me."

"You bet. You gave me good reason."

Oh, if only she knew the details. How lucky that her mother had been spared the outraged phone calls from vendors, the heartache of laid off employees. Bankruptcy made a lot of enemies out of former friends. "Gosh, I wish it would cool off." Mercedes fanned herself with one hand. The locusts were at it again, razoring the hot summer air with their song.

"Oh, honey, fall will be here before you know it."

Autumn. The season had always brought a flurry of activity in New York. She gloried in wearing the latest fashions when she met with clients. She could almost smell the soft woolens and feel silk blouses and soft cashmere sweaters.

But not this year. The excitement rising in her chest like the escalator in Saks shuddered to a halt. This year she'd be shopping in her closet.

Below them, the waves slapped the shore, bringing back more carefree summers. She jumped up. "Is Gator still in the boathouse?"

"I believe so. Kate hasn't moved her things to Cole's house yet. She doesn't want to jinx the wedding." How good it felt to laugh together.

"Since I'm going out tonight, I think I'll get in a quick kayak run now."

"Going out?" Her mother's eyes brightened.

"Just meeting an old friend at Mangy Mutt." But Mercedes felt a telltale flush work its way up her neck. If she mentioned Finn, her mother would ply her with questions.

Mom picked up her glass again. "You need to have some fun, Mercedes. You always drive yourself so hard." Maybe mothers always look out for you, no matter how old you get.

Ten minutes later she was in the dim boathouse that smelled of wet wood, wrestling with the two-seater green kayak her sister had named Gator. Grabbing the plastic handle on the front, she dragged it down to the beach. The sand was warm under her feet as she trudged toward the water, shoulders pulled back from the weight.

Why hadn't she come down here sooner? This beach was a treasure. She realized that now that she was cleaning houses for guests who paid plenty to use it for just one week. Laughter rose from the family in front of a cottage a few lots down. Zipping on the lifejacket kept in the kayak, she snapped the paddle together and pushed the boat into the water. Leveraging herself up over the side, she slid down into the seat. Perfect. The paddle felt familiar in her hands as she began to stroke.

The day was fading from the sky, the sun picking up speed in its descent. Since this was Friday, many of the families would be going home tomorrow. Maybe some of the newcomers would even be staying at the cottages she'd clean tomorrow. Swinging her arms from left to right, she paddled straight out past the sandbar and turned north. Fewer people dotted these beaches where the houses were huge and the beach frontage wide. Some families had left their sun tents up, sand toys clustered under the shade.

Unlike many of the glassed-in mansions that could be found along Lake Shore Road, Breezy Point looked more retro, a sleepy relic from the 50s. Her mother liked it that way. As she kept dipping her paddle into the water and pulling, Mercedes couldn't believe all the homes under construction. Hammers rang out and saws whined. Workmen were busy with open porches and bedroom wings. Four or five bedrooms were becoming more common in the mega mansions. The afternoon sun bounced off the glass, which had been tinted for the sake of privacy. She even spied some pools high on the dunes. Was that ridiculous or what? She had mixed feelings about all the change and wondered what role Cole Campbell played in all this.

When she reached his house, she noted the huge deck he'd added, which would hold the reception, according to Kate. This was going to be the most casual wedding ever. She longed for jacketed waiters in an exclusive club, where ice sculptures highlighted the appetizer table and chairs were adorned with silk net bows. But she wasn't the bride.

She'd attended a lot of weddings with Stephan. But they'd never talked about marriage. Setting her paddle across the bow, Mercedes let the kayak drift. She adjusted the bill of her baseball cap and pulled her ponytail tighter. The sun heated her arms and thighs. Maybe she should have worn a shirt over her bikini. The heat and the waves slapping the boat lulled her into daydreams.

When they were growing up, she'd take this kayak out with Kate and they'd talk about the future. Exciting careers after college, jobs that would take them away from their small town where nothing much ever happened. Handsome husbands and perfect children. What had happened to all that?

A speedboat roared past and the waves grew steeper, a dangerous place to be in a kayak. Grabbing her paddle, Mercedes turned the prow into the waves and headed back. The air had turned cooler by the time she pulled Gator onto the shore in front of Breezy Point. Time to take a shower and get ready to meet Finn at Mangy Mutt.

Just for a drink. That's all it was, right?

Chapter 8

Saturday night and the Mangy Mutt looked packed, a line of waiting customers snaking out the door. Mercedes remembered when the place was called Surf Gardens. Back then music would float from the second floor patio. Like every other teen in town, she couldn't wait to join the older group, dancing and laughing under the colored lights strung across the patio. A fire destroyed the place a few years back. Apparently, someone bought it and made the necessary renovations.

Mercedes had to park about a block away. August was always crazy in Gull Harbor, not that any of the merchants minded. For a lot of Chicago families, August was the time for the final trip to the beach before school started. For the locals, the month marked the serious slow down in their businesses.

Finn had texted her that he would be waiting at the entrance. She didn't see him in the line. The kayaking hadn't helped her back, and her arms ached. Still, she felt pretty good about beating Lindsay, although Finn had made that possible. Lindsay would skin her brother alive if she knew. Sand crunched under her wedge heels as Mercedes walked toward the crowd of people. The stylish, black cloth shoes that tied at her ankles were made for Manhattan's streets, not sandy Gull Harbor.

Families with tired children stood patiently in line. Inside, the large waiting room looked jammed. She didn't see Finn until he poked his head out the front door and waved. So he'd gotten here early. "Pardon me," she said, making her way through the crowd. Unlike New York, the people parted with a smile not an angry snarl.

"When did you get here?" she asked. Her skin heated when Finn touched her arm, maneuvering her inside.

"Just got here. Evening, Bambi." He nodded to the girl at the registration desk.

Looking like she was about eighteen, she batted her eyes at him. "All set, Finn?" More fluttering of those eyelashes.

"Yep." He turned to Mercedes. "Up top okay with you?"

"Terrific." He must have been here for ages to get a table on the open deck upstairs.

"Follow me." The girl pranced toward the steps.

On the way, a gigantic corkboard on the wall caught Mercedes' eyes. "That looks like Wiggy and Elvis." She pointed to a pair of Jack Russells pinned in the center of a collage of dogs, all kinds, all sizes.

"It is. Everyone sends in pictures of their pets."

"How great is that?" Skimming the photos, she found Prissy, Cole's Great Dane. "What a great idea."

Finn's hand in the small of her back urged her forward. Backache forgotten, she felt a pleasant heat loosening every muscle as she followed the girl up the steps ahead of them.

"We could have sat at the bar," she murmured as they stepped onto the wide, breezy deck with black patio umbrellas and metal railings. She hated to take up a table when they were only here for a drink. She turned toward the lake. The fantastic view made short work of her guilt. "Will you just look at that?"

"Which is why we're not at the bar."

Glancing around, Mercedes felt overdressed. Her black knit top and khaki pencil skirt might suit Manhattan but seemed too formal for Gull Harbor. Bambi led them to one of the metal tables overlooking the harbor just one block away.

Finn pulled out a chair and Mercedes sank onto it. "Mind telling me how you managed to score a table on the rooftop deck?"

Shrugging, he gave her a mysterious smile. "Sometimes there are advantages to being a local."

A waiter arrived. The service here seemed outstanding. "Let's start with a drink." Finn handed her a menu with a dog screened back behind the listings.

Start? "I'll have a Cosmo," she told the waiter.

"Want to live dangerously?" Mischief sparked in Finn's eyes. "Try the cucumber cooler."

She eyed the drink menu. "Guess it couldn't have any more calories than a Cosmo."

Finn leaned closer. "This isn't about calories, Mercedes. This is about having a good time."

Pen poised, the waiter discretely studied the street below.

She swallowed. "Sure, bring it on." Maybe it was time to do things differently. The work today left her muscles aching, and she'd totally enjoyed it.

The waiter trotted off. "Finn, you're staring at me." His lips tweaked up.

"Maybe I like the view."

"Let's watch the sunset." She nodded toward the horizon.

She felt his deep chuckle in the pit of her stomach. "I forgot how bossy you can be."

"Hey, that's not nice."

"Then I'm sorry." When Finn said that, she believed him.

She settled back with a sigh. He had a point. The oldest child could be like that, or so she'd heard. Time to decompress, so she focused on the sky turning pink where it met the lake. "I haven't seen a sunset since I got here, not even from our porch."

"Too bad. You're missing one of the finest perks this area offers."

He was probably right. "No one talks about the sunsets in New York. The buildings are too tall."

"Still missing the big city?"

Mercedes nodded. "I lived there for ten years and it's in my blood now. It's...home, I guess." But as she said the words, she wondered.

"So you're only staying here until what, the end of August? Like the summer people who just breeze in and then leave?"

She played with a cocktail napkin. "Oh, I think I'll be here longer than that."

The drinks arrived, filled with ice and floating a cucumber slice on top.

"To summer reunions." Finn clicked his cooler against hers.

"To old friends," she said pointedly.

"Whatever." As he sipped, Finn's eyes held hers, so mysterious. Or was the falling darkness just throwing shadows?

She felt relieved when his attention shifted to the food menu. "What looks good to you?"

"You said drinks," she reminded him, nudging the menu away.

He grinned. "Yes, said the spider to the fly."

This man could make her crazy.

"Come on, Mercedes. I didn't want it to sound like a date, okay?"

"Because it's not."

When he pursed those full lips, she wondered how they'd feel on hers. Taking a deep sip, she gulped down an ice cube that brought on serious shivers.

At least, she thought ice was the culprit.

Her stomach growled, and she decided Finn was worth breaking her diet.

The waiter arrived. Her eyes fell to the menu and she picked the first thing. "Fish tacos?"

"I'll take the same. Fish tacos for two," he told the waiter.

"What? No burgers?" she asked after the young man had walked away.

"Would it surprise you that I'm a vegetarian?"

She leaned closer. "Nothing would surprise me about you. Remember, I don't know the adult Finn Wheeler."

"Maybe we should get to know each other. You know…as adults." His eyes dipped to the deep v in her top and goosebumps rose on her chest. "I'm not as weird as I was in high school."

"Who said you were weird?" Did he know the other kids had called him Goofy because of those ears?

"You kidding? Just about everybody." His forehead puckered.

The man was so open and honest that she had to laugh and Finn joined in. Their voices entwined as if they did this all the time, a couple sharing private jokes.

A couple? She snapped her jaw shut.

"Am I kind of weird?" His eyes glowed in the dim light.

"We'll just see," she teased. "High school was a long time ago."

"Maybe, but I never forgot you." The joking tone was gone.

She propped her chin on one hand. "Really? What was I like in high school?" Did she really want to hear this?

Finn stretched his long legs out to one side. "Insanely busy. Always running to a meeting. You must have belonged to every organization in high school."

She erupted into laughter. "Right. Except National Honor Society."

"I had that covered." He grinned self-consciously.

"Right. You were the g–." Good Lord, she'd almost said the geek word and he knew it. "Sorry," she said softly.

He shook his head. "No apologies needed. I knew I was a geek in residence. Totally tied up with computers."

"And it paid off for you, right? Now you have an IT business." She thought back to the day that he'd helped Kate set up her office.

"Yes, yes I do." He glanced away but she had no time to

wonder what nerve she'd hit. The food had arrived. The mixture of fish and vegetables crackling on the plate turned her stomach. She hadn't eaten anything this substantial in a while.

"Dig in." Finn snapped his napkin onto his lap. "You okay?"

She could not look at him. "My stomach's been acting up lately."

"You should have mentioned it. Don't worry, Mercedes. I'll finish what you can't eat." He tugged her plate away. How could she explain this was about calories not a stomach virus? "How about some chicken noodle soup?"

Before she could say a word, the server appeared. "Rustle up some chicken noodle soup, would you, Andrew?"

"Sure thing." He bustled away.

"Geez, you must come here a lot. I didn't even see chicken noodle soup on the menu."

"Restaurants always have stuff in the back. I spend quite a bit of time here."

Dusk had fallen, softening Finn's chiseled features. What a perfect evening. She shifted her attention back to the harbor where boats were pulling in for the night, their white hulls gleaming through the gathering darkness. The air caressed her face, warm but not muggy. If she closed her eyes, she could almost imagine she was sitting out on her Manhattan terrace.

But then she wouldn't be with Finn. And right now, this was where she wanted to be.

The soup arrived, complete with oyster crackers. Suddenly ravenous, she dipped her spoon into the wide noodles and large chunks of chicken. She'd never tasted soup like this. Finn made short work of the tacos. By the time he finished, her bowl was empty and the oyster crackers were gone.

"You feeling better?"

"I'm fine." In New York, she visited the Metropolitan Museum to clear her head. The expression in Finn's eyes was familiar. She'd seen that look in the eyes of people appreciating great works of art.

What was happening here? "Do I have something on my mouth? Like a spare noodle or a cracker crumb?" Mercedes dabbed her lips with the napkin.

Finn slowly shook his head. "Nothing. I like your hair that way." His eyes raked over it like a comb.

"Really? I don't." She ruffled one hand through the mess. "I just can't get it to flatten the way it used to be."

Tilting his head to one side, he smiled. "Your hair was long and curly in high school."

"You noticed?" *And you remember?*

"Of course. You sat next to me."

"Just that one class."

Blushing again, he rattled the ice cubes in his glass. "And math. I sat in the back. You sat near the door with Chuck in that class."

"Right. I guess I did." But she didn't remember and broke the gaze.

Finn's jaw shifted. "So why don't you tell me about this man you're dating."

"What? Stop with these questions." Still, they flattered her. "Are you my big brother now?"

He shook his head slowly. "Trust me, I will never look at you the way I look at Lindsay."

The intent in his eyes left her speechless and sweaty.

"Come on, Mercedes. I'm just asking a simple question."

She swallowed hard. "What do you want to know?"

"I want to know exactly what my competition is." He was serious. And he was waiting.

How could she describe Stephan? Words like *tall, businesslike* or *confident* tumbled in her head.

"What is it about him that attracted you?"

"His confidence," she said easily. "He's a guy who knows what he wants."

"Interesting. And he wanted you. That makes two of us."

"Pardon me?" What was going on here?

Finn did a slow, sexy blink. "Come on. Don't tell me you're surprised."

"Of course I am." Her lips felt numb. "You said this was a friendly drink."

"Only because I wanted you to come tonight."

"Well, here I am," she whispered.

"And I'm glad. Are you?" The metal table felt small and intimate. His hand moved. For a second, she thought he'd run it down her arm—the way he had at the auction. For a second, her arm trembled in anticipation.

But he fell back. With a sigh, Finn thrummed his fingers against his drink. She wondered if they felt cold. "Wh-what else do you remember?" she stammered. She had to break this crazy mood.

"Think back."

She drew a blank. "Right. To what?"

"That day." One eyebrow lifted. "You remember, right? Under the bleachers."

"Oh, right. Of course I do." The guys gave Goofy a lot of crap in high school. She'd ended it one day. Amazing how simple it had been back then. Another round of drinks appeared, and she took a deep gulp to cool her parched throat. "We've been here a while. Don't you think we should give up the table?" But she really didn't want to leave.

"Soon." His eyes flicked to the horizon. "I love to watch the sun go down from up here."

"Great vantage point." But she was having more fun looking at him.

"We should go up to Weko Beach some night," he said.

"Do the veterans still play taps from the sand dunes?" How many times had she snuggled with someone in a car at Weko Beach, while those taps echoed off the dunes.

"They sure do. They had a really nice service there over Memorial weekend." Had the dimming light darkened his eyes? "I took Lindsay and my parents. The day started with a service at St. Mary's church. You know, for the families of veterans. Then there was a parade and at night, we all went to Weko."

"Quite a day." And so sad. "Tell me about Lindsay's husband."

Finn expelled a breath. "Rich was the kind who'd help you paint your garage. They were high school sweethearts. He was one of the first guys to go overseas. The first bad news."

"How did Lindsay take it?"

"She was expecting Susan when we got the word."

Mercedes couldn't even imagine. "But she seems so strong."

"Lindsay's got that attitude but underneath? She'll be missing Rich for a long, long time."

The realization came swift and strong. Mercedes wanted that kind of love. Hours could pass without a thought for Stephan. She socked back another mouthful of cucumber cooler.

In New York, the war was ever present. The Ground Zero monument wouldn't let them forget, and no one wanted to. They all carried that day in their hearts. And it was no different back here in Gull Harbor. Was Rich one of those smiling soldiers Sarah had posted in the bakery? Mercedes understood the heartache behind Lindsay's angry frown.

"Want to walk down to the beach?" Finn pushed back his chair.

"Don't you have to pay the bill?"

"Already did."

When? Maybe she'd had too much to drink. Watching her step, she followed him down the stairs and out onto the sidewalk. It took a bit to wiggle through the crowd still waiting for a table. "The guy who owns this place must make a fortune."

Turning, Finn scanned the restaurant with approval. "Yep, he does."

Walking down Whittaker, she gave herself to the warm breeze whisking over her bare arms and legs. When she hit some uneven pavement, she took his arm. The two drinks had made her giddy, and she'd didn't want to do a face plant.

"Have you been beaching it much since you got here?" he asked.

"Today I took my sister's kayak out. The beach looks the same but the houses? Lots of renovation going on."

"The development is good for the town. The old cottages can't stay the same." Did his voice hold a tinge of regret?

"Things change."

"Not everything, Mercedes. Some things never change."

~.~

Finn had questions. What had happened to the girl who threw herself into activities with wild enthusiasm? The Mercedes on his arm felt closed off. Shut down. "So what's next for you? Labor Day's almost here. You say you're staying for a while. How long?"

The shake of her head sent relief rolling through him. "Oh, Finn. I don't really know but I have to get back to New York. The sooner, the better. Got some loose ends to tie up."

"Like your boyfriend?" She didn't act like a woman who was crazy about another guy.

Mercedes was studying her shoes as she walked. Those pretty pink toes winked up at him. "I left more than a relationship behind. I want to go back for business reasons. Prove I can do it. But I need a stake to do that."

"So you'll start another business there?" This didn't sound good.

"That's the plan."

Well, he wasn't a quitter. They'd reached the benches that edged the inlet. "Should we sit down?"

"Sure." Mercedes sat down and crossed her long legs. Her tight skirt edged up, making it hard to watch the horizon. Settling against the wooden slats, she moaned, which went right to his groin.

"What is it?"

"Just my aching arms and back." Mercedes glanced over with a rueful smile. "I could never be a cleaning women for a living."

He chuckled and extended his arms along the back of the bench. "Just temporary...for both you and Lindsay."

The bench angled toward the setting sun. Motors throttled back as boats drifted in to dock in their slips for the night.

"It feels so peaceful down here." She shivered, giving him an excuse to settle one arm around her shoulders.

"I guess the boyfriend's coming for the wedding? I'll get to meet him."

"What's all this interest in him?" Her face tightened.

"Nothing." Finn didn't want to freak her out and squeezed her shoulder gently. "Just want to make sure he's good enough for you."

"Why?" Her green eyes looked so puzzled.

"I told you. I like to size up my competition." He'd let it go at that.

"I can't tell if you're serious or not."

"Trust me. This is my serious side. Do you doubt me?"

She tilted her head. "Yeah, the teachers liked that serious side. They didn't hear the cracks you made under your breath, or they would never have cut you so much slack."

"That's crazy," he muttered, feeling his face flush. She was right.

"You'd come in late to chemistry, glasses crooked and hair bunched around those crazy ears."

"Not the ears again." He tugged on one in irritation.

"Sorry, Finn. I thought your ears were cute." Right now, they were burning.

"Anyway, Mr. Daley looked the other way. Never gave you a detention."

He snorted. "Maybe that's because I helped him de-bug his PC all the time."

"No way." Her shock made him laugh.

"That class was a waste. I knew I'd never use it."

Her wary expression was back. "You took great notes."

"For you."

"Aw, Finn. Really? That's so sweet."

She really had no clue. For a second, she was the girl back in chemistry class, grateful for notes that dumbed down a class she found difficult. "You were so smart, Finn. The rumor was that you created the scheduling program."

"That was more than a rumor."

"And you never took credit for it?"

"Why would I?" The conversation had taken an uncomfortable turn. He'd rather play with the soft curls at Mercedes's neck. She didn't seem to mind. "The guys already considered me a nerd."

"I can't figure you out. I never could." She tilted her head, smiling so sweetly.

"Talking about high school is boring. That's all in the past."
Except for you. "Mercedes, you never laughed at me. "

"And you remember all that?" Her shoulders relaxed.

"Of course I do." Back then, he'd hated it but used the teasing to motivate himself. He'd succeed and prove everybody wrong. And he did. "That's why I was in the computer lab all the time."

"So long ago." When the sun set in Gull Harbor, it brought a certain stillness. "Isn't it peaceful here?"

"A lot more peaceful than New York, I would think."

"You have no idea."

"Actually, I do. I go to New York for business. Hate it with a passion. Can't wait to get home."

"Really? I wish I'd known. We could have met for..." Was she going to say *dinner*?

"You probably didn't need someone from your past showing up." How he'd agonized over that decision. Whenever he began to Google Mercedes Kennedy again, he knew his current relationship was over. "I figured you were married with kids hanging on your skirts, that kind of thing."

"But I'm not." She sounded so forlorn.

His arms tensed. He wanted to wrap them around her.

Mercedes was studying him. "Okay, why are you giving me that look?"

He drummed his fingers on the back of the bench. "Sometimes I can't figure out who you are."

She bit her lower lip. "Me neither. Sometimes."

Forget restraint. "Oh, pretty girl." Her hair felt so soft when

Finn gently cupped the back of her head.

"I like that crazy thing you're doing with your fingers." She scrunched up her shoulders like a little girl and smiled. That did it.

Finn could hear the hitch in her breath when he dipped his head. His lips settled over hers, and they opened like he'd touched a magic spring. Kissing Mercedes felt like coming home. He took his time with his tongue. So did she.

"Oh Finn." Soft palms shaking, she cupped his face and searched his eyes. Then she let her head fall back with a sigh of surrender. His lips found her neck, long, luminous and smelling fabulous. "What perfume are you wearing?"

"Spellbound."

The name made him chuckle. "Well, I am."

"Sure. Right."

Dead serious now, he silenced her with a kiss that felt torn from his soul. Could she sense his ten years of longing? Tasting like cucumbers and chicken noodle soup, she moaned again. All sanity disappeared over the dark sand dunes.

"Get a room!" A voice called out from a passing boat, its motor chugging in the channel below.

They broke apart. God she was gorgeous. Oh so gently, he ran a thumb along the delicate curve of her chin.

"Are we making a spectacle?" Mercedes gently pushed away but kept her hands flat against his heaving chest. "I sh-shouldn't be doing this."

His heart was banging like a brass band. "Shoulds are useless. At least in my book. What do you want? That's what counts." And he waited.

"You're a renegade," she whispered with a shake of her head. "Why did I never see that in you?"

"Because that's not what you expected, not from me."

"Maybe. I don't know." Mercedes got to her feet with a kittenish stretch. "I should go home."

"I'll walk you to your car." Finn stood and shoved his hands in his pockets.

On the way up Whittaker Street, she chattered about the Moonlight Madness deal in more detail than he'd ever remember. Her soft voice floated on the night air but he didn't hear a word. There were too many distractions. The way her hands fluttered when she talked. The full lips she licked once in a while. All too soon, they reached her car and he opened the door. That's all, although he wanted much more.

In the soft glow of a street lamp, she peered up. Was there a question in her eyes? "Good night, Finn. Thank you for dinner. Great chicken noodle soup." Her slow smile teased him.

"You're more than welcome." He gripped the top of the door before slamming it shut. "Later."

"Later?" Eyes wide, she glanced up.

Finn nodded. Oh, yes. There would definitely be a later.

Chapter 9

Not much had changed in Kate's office when Mercedes stopped in the following week. Papers were heaped in haphazard piles anchored by pop cans. Pink and yellow notes adorned the chipped desk, its missing drawer currently being used as a wastebasket. How did her sister work in such chaos? But Kate always got results.

Kate looked up when Mercedes came through the door. "Hey, this is a nice surprise."

"Just wanted to see how Moonlight Madness is going." Hard as it had been, she'd stayed out of her sister's way.

Snatching a sheet of paper from her desk, Kate waved it. "You won't believe how many shops and restaurants are on board. Looks like the sale will go all the way up to Bridgman. I need to get the flyers out." She patted a bright yellow stack of paper.

"I'll take them around." She grabbed a bunch. At last, something she could do.

"I'd sure appreciate it. You could even leave one in the houses you're cleaning."

"A flyer and a chocolate bar?" Working together brought back memories. While their parents were watching TV downstairs, Kate would sneak into Mercedes' bed at night to read Nancy Drew mysteries. If they didn't like the ending, they made up a different one.

Still, they were grown up now and Kate could be headstrong. "I hope you didn't mind my stepping in."

"Are you kidding? I'm crazy busy." The calendar taped to the side of Kate's desk had every square filled with scribbles.

"How's the wedding coming?"

"Fine. I think we've got it." Kate rarely admitted to needing help.

Mercedes studied one of the yellow sheets. The map pictured the highway with shops and restaurants in funky little illustrations. "Who did this?"

"Diana, my friend from the book group. She owns the Hippy Chick shop just off Red Arrow on Whittaker. You should join us."

A book group? Mercedes pictured dreary discussions about foreshadowing and character flaws. She'd had enough of that in high school. "Bad timing, I'm afraid. I haven't been able to concentrate since I got here, much less read."

"Might relax you." Kate's chair creaked when she sat back. "Everything okay?"

"Absolutely fine." Except she could not get Finn out of her head since last weekend. Even the map blurred under her eyes. "I'm just more of a doer than a discussion person."

"You're probably right." She could feel her sister studying her. "How is work going with Lindsay?"

"Interesting. She's really moody."

"She's a widow, Merc. Just think how that would feel."

But she couldn't. Mercedes couldn't even imagine how it would feel to be married. "Right. Anyway, the cleaning gig is just a short-term solution. But it's got me thinking." Tucking the flyer back into the pile, Mercedes straightened it.

"I can see the wheels turning. What's up?" Kate propped her feet up on the desk.

"Maybe later, okay?" Mercedes wasn't ready to share her idea. Her plans might infringe on Lindsay's business, and she had to work through that first. "I still have a lot of pieces to fill in. So, you're sure I can't do anything for the wedding?"

Smiling, Kate moved her hand so her diamond caught the light. "Nope, got it covered. Everything's perfect."

"I'm happy for you." And really, she was. But then why did her jaw ache from grinding her teeth?

Letting her feet dropping, Kate sat up. "Can't wait to meet your guy. Steven, right?"

"Stephan." Just saying the name brought a wave of guilt. Her evening with Finn had her rattled. She felt different. About a lot of things.

"Is this something serious, Mercedes?"

"What?" Dust motes caught her attention, floating in the morning sunshine.

"Stephan." Kate prodded her. "Looks like you're all dreamy so maybe this is the guy, huh?" It took Mercedes a minute to realize Kate was talking about Stephan, not Finn.

"Ah, I don't know." She kept straightening the flyers until they were a crisp clean wedge of yellow.

Face lighting up, Kate leaned forward. "Wait a minute. Does that silly smile have anything to do with Finn Wheeler?"

"What are you talking about?" Thinking of Finn's hands in her hair, Mercedes twined a curl around one finger.

"Oh, nothing. Finn's a friend of Cole's, you know."

She was dying to know what Cole had said. "Finn sat next to me in chemistry class. I really don't know him that well." But even to her ears, that explanation was getting old. "We met for a drink last weekend."

"Oh?" The word hung in the air, begging for more.

Well after all, this was her sister. "Kate, it started as a drink and ended up as dinner. Remember when Mangy Mutt was Surf City? We all wanted to be old enough to have a drink in the bar. That rooftop patio seemed magical, remember? The live music would pour over Whittaker Street and colorful lanterns bobbed up top, lighting up the night."

"Maybe it still is magical," Kate murmured.

Mercedes ignored the silly smile on her sister's face. "Whoever owns it sure did a great job. Nice branding. Pictures of dogs everywhere. The place was packed. Food's pretty good too, but you probably know that."

Kate's chair hit the floor with a thump. "You realize Finn owns the place?"

The pack of flyers slid through her hands onto the floor.

"No. He never said anything about that." Tumblers slotted together in her mind.

"Finn is very tightlipped. The way he wanders around town

with his two rescue dogs can be misleading."

Feeling blindsided, Mercedes dropped to the floor and began collecting the yellow sheets. Kate helped her. She fought the urge to ask Kate more questions. After all, this wasn't high school anymore. Why hadn't Finn been honest with her?

Mercedes was halfway to the door when Kate said, "Cole says Finn's got a thing for you."

A thing? She turned, mashing the flyers against her galloping heart. "Really?"

"Right, he thinks it goes back to high school."

"What else did he say?" Okay, so she had no pride.

"Nothing much. You know guys." Her sister had retreated into her pre-wedding cocoon, lost in the glitter of her diamond and the future that lay ahead.

"See you, Kate." As Mercedes streaked down the stairs and out the back door, she remembered how Finn had carried her in not too long ago. The knot in her stomach loosened and she smiled.

When she reached her car, she clicked it open and tossed the flyers in the trunk. She wanted to keep busy. Kate was moving ahead, creating a future with Cole. Within a year, she'd probably have a baby. Mercedes would be an aunt. The shiver of excitement surprised her. So did the gut-wrenching longing. For a second, she clung to the hot door handle.

Don't be ridiculous, Mercedes. Wrenching the door open, she dove onto the hot, supple leather, started the engine and punched on the air conditioning. What a perfect day to head up Red Arrow and hand out flyers. After all, this had been her idea and she could talk up the event. In public relations, you had to build bridges through personal contact. She was good at that, as long as it was business.

Her first stop was Hippy Chick. Was that Diana dragging racks onto the concrete apron in front of the store? The willowy blonde had disappeared inside by the time Mercedes parked and began sorting through the colorful skirts and tops rippling in the morning breeze. Then her hands stopped. When had she ever worn a long, fluttery skirt with beading along the hem? Still, she wanted to thank Diana for designing the flyer. When she yanked open the door, a bell jangled.

Although the sun beat down outside, the shop was cool. In the back, Diana was talking on the phone with quiet authority. Mercedes kept a respectful distance but couldn't help hearing. "All right, send us the size medium. What were the Chesterton revenues like yesterday?" Listening, she nodded her head and scribbled on a notepad.

Not wanting to eavesdrop, Mercedes glanced at the merchandise. Dressed in a pristine white top and khaki shorts, she was horrified by the busy prints, ruffles galore and oversize pockets anchored with buttons. Good Lord, were Chicago people buying this? In New York, black was the color of simple but sleek styles.

"Can I help you?" The voice at Mercedes' elbow made her jump.

"Diana?" She held up a flyer. "I wanted to thank you for helping with Moonlight Madness. I'm Kate's sister."

"Mercedes? Sure. I've heard about you."

"That sounds ominous." Her breath caught in her chest. What

was the word around town? That she'd come home without a job or any prospects?

"No, I didn't mean it that way." Diana held out a hand, cool to the touch when Mercedes shook it. "So nice to meet you. I'm glad to help. We need more promotion."

"You must have an art background."

Diana smiled mysteriously. "Let's just say my background is a mixture of many things."

Interesting lady. Dressed in a flowing, blue ikat skirt and flouncy, white top with Gypsy earrings, she was the opposite of Mercedes. Men no doubt found her fascinating. "Could I ask what your offer will be the night of Moonlight Madness?"

Diana ran her hand over the top of a rack, straightening hangers. "Thirty percent off all the skirts."

"That should work." Mercedes hated ten percent sales, a measly discount that barely covered sales tax.

"Want to try something on?" Mercedes felt horrified when Diana's elegant hands plucked flowing skirts from the rack. "Let's see, you must be a small. Extra small?"

"What? Oh, no." Too late, Mercedes clapped a hand to her mouth.

Diana's smile was replaced by a tight frown. She slid the hangers back into place. "At least, not right now," Mercedes said, not wanting to offend Kate's friend. "Today I have to work my way up Red Arrow with these flyers."

"Ah, huh. Right." Diana was no fool. One glance and she probably had Mercedes' number, from her tortoiseshell headband to last season's Jimmy Choo sandals. This woman didn't miss a trick. But Diana didn't realize that she was looking at the old Mercedes.

Who was the new Mercedes? She felt life shifting beneath her, like the bottom of a sandbar. Suddenly off balance, she sidled toward the door. "Ah, I should hit the road. So nice meeting you, Diana. And again, thank you."

"Stop in again when you have more time." The beautiful blonde's inscrutable smile followed Mercedes outside. For some reason she felt kinship with Diana. And she hadn't felt that with anyone since she hit town.

Of course, there was Finn. Sometimes she felt comfortable with him. Other times she felt edgy and incredibly turned on, if she were truthful. But she wasn't going to over-think this.

Getting into her car, she hit the ignition button, pumped the accelerator then slammed on the brakes. The Mercedes wasn't in reverse, and she'd nearly taken out Diana's rack of clothing.

Chapter 10

Elvis yipped at Finn's heels while he shaved. From time to time.
the male Jack Russell would dance over to Wiggy, curled in a
corner of the master bath. She ignored him, but he kept poking
her, wanting to play. Finally, Wiggy snapped back. Tail drooping,
Elvis retreated to sit at Finn's feet.

"When you figure out how to get her attention, let me in on it,
okay buddy?" Raising his chin, Finn skated the electric razor below
his jaw and smoothed a hand over it. He didn't want to cause
whisker rash, in case he got that lucky. Since the park bench last
Saturday, Mercedes had pretty much ignored him, answering his
texts in frustrating monosyllables.

"Wiggy, what does it mean when a woman won't talk to you?"
The dog twitched one ear but wouldn't look up at him. This felt
like a female conspiracy. Finn clicked off the razor and finished
dressing. Tonight was Moonlight Madness and he intended to track
Mercedes down. On the way, he could check the coupons he'd left
at Phoebe's for Lindsay. Saying goodbye to Elvis and Wiggy, he
locked the door and took the steps down to the garage. Hitting the
remote for one of the massive doors, he decided this was a red
Corvette night. He jumped in and took off, loving the low rumble
once he reached Red Arrow. Tonight he wanted to feel like Cool

Dude, not the Goofy Mercedes remembered.

Local Color was his first stop. A decent number of people were checking out the paintings and pottery from local artists. But Mercedes wasn't there. Quick glance, a few hellos, and he took off for Mario's across the road. A Moonlight Madness sign advertised special prices in the window. The place was packed and smelled of spicy tomato sauce and garlic when Finn came through the door. Working behind the counter in a full white apron, Mario looked up and waved.

"See you later." Finn took off. Back on the road, he headed north.

When he saw the black Mercedes parked in front of Phoebe's, he smiled. Bingo. At least he wouldn't have to drive all over to casually run into her. He'd had a good time with Mercedes at Mangy Mutt. In lots of ways, she hadn't changed. But the uncertainty that clouded her eyes sometimes? What the hell had caused that? Stephan or her business? The Mercedes he'd known wore her self-confidence as boldly as her cheerleading letters. But not anymore. That bothered him.

When he entered Phoebe's Place, the salon was buzzing with women. Phoebe looked over and waved. But his eyes went straight to Mercedes, who was studying a card with bright hair colors in the reception area. Her eyes lit up as if she were happy to see him. "Hey, Finn."

Finn leaned over her shoulder and the smell of her apple shampoo rolled over him. "The purple might work." He wanted to bury his nose in the soft curls. But the thought sent his body into overdrive and he pulled away. She was dressed in the little black sundress she'd worn at the umbrella auction.

"Would a green streak be too flashy for me?" Looking pensive, Mercedes fingered a curl behind her ear. A weird melting started in his stomach and worked lower.

"Does my opinion matter?" He wished it did. Her cheeks flushed in the prettiest way.

He liked looking at her. She was wrapped up in the color card so he could take his time. Frowning, she smoothed the hank of green hair with delicate fingers. "Of course your opinion matters." The melting in his body turned to a searing heat.

Her hands had been a major preoccupation during chemistry class. He had nothing else to do. Except for Mercedes, the class was a total waste but he needed the credit to graduate. He spent considerable time converting the concepts to notes she could follow. To her total amazement, she'd gotten a B in the class.

Back then, she'd been so close but felt so far away. Time could change everything and everyone. "A green streak would be very daring."

"You think?" Uncertainty wrinkled her nose.

"The color would bring out your eyes. Live dangerously, Mercedes."

"Right." With a twisted smile, she reluctantly laid the color card aside. "I did that already in New York. Look where it got me."

"It got you Stephan, didn't it?" God, he even hated to say the guy's name. But Finn had to see how deep these waters ran.

She adjusted her headband. "Stephan and I are not about living dangerously."

"So you're boring together? What's up with that?" He felt both relieved and puzzled. "Everyone needs to take some chances, Mercedes Kennedy."

Her green eyes clung to his like moss. Finn studied her peachy lipstick, how it made her lower lip so inviting. At least she'd never worn the bright orange other girls favored, just the softer peach. He thought of Mercedes like that. Softer. His own lips—and another part of his body—began to swell.

Under his dazed eyes, her smile flattened. "Maybe I'm finished with taking risks."

"Isn't that what life's all about?" He hated to see her discouraged. "Any time you're in business for yourself, you have to take some chances. Things don't work out? You just make another decision."

"Sometimes the chances involve other people. That's when it's hard." Her lips pressed into a thin line, as if she'd said too much.

"Are you talking about employees?" The guarded twitch of her head said yes. "It's every man for himself in business, Mercedes. There are a million ways to make a living today."

"You really believe that, don't you?" Her eyes widened.

"Yes, I do." Maybe she didn't agree with him but he wasn't going to lie. "That's the way it is."

"For you, maybe," she murmured, looking so darn helpless. He fought the urge to gather her into his arms and tell her everything would be fine. The old Mercedes Kennedy would give him a good swift kick. Now? Maybe not. Had her bad experience radically changed her?

Wandering over to the reception desk, he picked up one of his sister's coupons. The stack had been a lot thicker when he dropped these off so he felt pleased. He hoped Lindsay would see some benefit from this promotion. She'd been a little hesitant when he'd encouraged her to participate. "This whole Moonlight Madness thing is so last minute," she'd grumbled. "I have no time for this, Finn."

In the end, he'd found someone to design the coupon for her and took it into Michigan City himself to be printed. Since the death of her husband, his sister had been struggling. His folks were concerned about Lindsay and her little girls. "She's lost her spirit," their mother fretted.

Looking at her watch, Mercedes sprang up. "I'm going to hit the road, Phoebe," she called to the back. "Have to check on things up the highway."

"See you later, hon." Phoebe waved back.

Mercedes brushed past him, trailing apple shampoo mixed with that Spellbound she wore.

"Need company?" Like one of his mangy mutts, he followed her outside. "Why don't we ride together?"

She hesitated. "Okay. I guess."

"Why waste gas? We can compare notes on the way." He kept babbling as he opened the door of his red Corvette.

She looked from the car to him and back again. "My, my. You do have a lot of toys." Looking pleased, she sank into the front seat. He circled the car. For a second he was the Nascar driver who had just taken the lead.

"Just one shop after another?" He hit the ignition and put it in gear.

"Works for me." She snapped her seatbelt, and he was happy to see her shoulders settle. "Sometimes it just feels good to have someone else drive."

"Doesn't your boyfriend drive you around New York?" He really should stop this obvious obsession.

Her brow furrowed. "We take public transportation."

"I thought New York was all about taxis."

"He likes the feel of the big city." Mercedes tugged at one of her tiny pearl earrings. "Says the underground is more real."

Sounded like the guy was cheap but Finn wasn't about to say anything. He remembered how Wiggy had snapped at Elvis tonight. A man was smart to quit when he was ahead.

The first stop was Frisky Frog, a shop that had been here as long as he could remember. Three cars were parked outside. Considering this was ten o'clock in the evening, that was a lot. They went inside. "What's going on in here, Myra?" The owner knew his mother.

"Hey, Finn. The usual." Showing a shopper to the waiting room, she shrugged.

Mercedes picked a coupon up from the counter. "Fifty percent off on bathing suits." She frowned. The two remaining shoppers looked around and were out the door, Mercedes and Finn right behind them.

"You don't look happy," he said, opening her car door.

"Bathing suits should have been discounted after the Fourth of July. The Moonlight Madness offers should be different and amazing." Her eyes sparked.

"Maybe they didn't have time to plan," he said as he slid in next her.

"You have to think on your feet, Finn. Be ready to change strategy."

He didn't want to press the point. At least Mercedes and Kate were doing something to promote the local businesses.

Then it was on to the next shop, a place called Shore and More. Like Beach Togs, the store was full of summer clothing, along with some heavier sweaters and coats. Two cars were parked outside.

Inside, the owner was filing her nails at the register. "Hey, Anne Marie."

"Hi Finn. You buying something for Lindsay or your mom?"

"Not tonight." Women were in the dressing rooms from what Finn could see. Mercedes circled the shop, checking signs and tags. "What's your best offer tonight, Anne Marie?" He figured he'd ask so Mercedes wouldn't be the bad guy.

With a sigh, Anne Marie looked around. "Summer sale. The usual, you know." From the corner of his eye, he saw Mercedes open her mouth and then shut it.

"Have you had many people stop in?"

"Not really." Anne Marie yawned. "What do you expect for ten at night?"

By the time they got in the car, Mercedes looked like a balloon about to burst. "This isn't what Moonlight Madness was supposed to be about. This is a fun night of crazy sales. Buy one, get one free. Fun, not the usual end of season stuff."

"Hey, relax, okay?" He touched her arm. One glance made him bring that hand right back to the steering wheel.

She was fuming. "These owners just don't get it."

"Maybe you have to teach them."

"Oh, Finn, why is it so hard?" She dropped her head into her hand. She looked like a little girl deprived of Christmas and he hated it.

A few minutes later, he pulled into Ivy's Cottage, where cars crowded the small lot. "Will you look at this?" Ivy McCray often ate at the Mangy Mutt, and he liked her roll-with-it attitude. He always talked football with her husband Herb.

Mercedes' eyes bugged out of her head. "My goodness."

"My thoughts exactly." He edged his car into a small spot, jumped out and led the way inside.

"Come on in, Finn!" Waving the purple feathery thing around her neck, Ivy motioned them into the shop. " Do you like scavenger hunts?"

"Love them," Mercedes piped up.

Ivy handed them each a list. "Search for these five things and then get fifty percent off the one you just can't live without."

Mercedes scanned the sheet. "These are nice items. A toaster oven. Jewelry box."

"Sounds like chick stuff." He followed her to the back where women were comparing notes. Picking up what looked like an Indian piece of pottery, Mercedes turned it over in her hands. "You like it?"

"Wonder if it's original. Looks like something from New Mexico."

"Might be." Taking hold of it, he loved the excitement in her eyes. "Let me buy it for you."

But she wouldn't let go.

"Mercedes?"

"That's not necessary, Finn."

His grip tightened. "Humor me." If he told her his parents marked special times together with a small token, she'd freak out. He smiled just thinking about it.

"Are you laughing at me?" Hurt darkened her eyes.

"Not at all. Let me do this for you, okay?" Her hold loosened, and he carried the piece to the register as if he'd just scored the hidden treasures of Rome.

~.~

Mercedes didn't want to accept anything from Finn. She might be out of work but she had her pride. Still, his determination was touching and reminded her of how he'd shared his chemistry notes.

When they drove away from Ivy's Cottage, the bag with Finn's gift sat in her lap. She liked Ivy. The shopkeeper understood the Moonlight Madness idea and that was gratifying.

"Don't forget to drop me off at Phoebe's," she reminded Finn.

"Don't worry, I'm not going to kidnap you."

"That's silly." Staring out into the darkness, she fingered the bag. The evening had been frustrating but fun. Finn had taken the edge off her disappointment, whereas Stephan might have had her create a chart with goals and really make her feel like a failure.

"Maybe you need more silliness in your life."

She swung to face his profile. "What does that mean?"

His fingers drummed on the steering wheel. She wanted that hand on her arm, on her thigh, anywhere. The realization sent a hot flush sizzling through her. Finn tightened his hold on the wheel. "You seem so serious sometimes. Wouldn't hurt to lighten up."

"I hate it when people say that," she muttered.

Pursing his lips, Finn snapped on some moody jazz that filled the car like fine wine. The music massaged her the way Phoebe's fingers worked her during a shampoo. What the heck. This was the first Moonlight Madness. Some of the shops and restaurants had gotten the idea but not all. Maybe next year... But she couldn't think that far ahead. Next year she wanted to be back in Manhattan, not traipsing down a rural highway.

Weariness steamrolled her.

The engine rumbled and the low-slung car felt every bump in the road. She didn't care. Finn's silence felt comforting. Except for his questions about Stephan, she enjoyed being with him. Everybody knew Finn so she hadn't felt like an outsider visiting the shops. Watching him shift, she let her thoughts wander. His hands were probably good for a lot more than school notes. Mercedes had a vivid imagination. The mental images flashing in her mind seared her with blazing heat. Time to count the green markers along the side of the road.

She had no idea of the time when Finn pulled into Phoebe's

parking lot. The only car left, her black Mercedes was a silhouette in the darkness. Pulling up next to it, he cracked open the windows and turned off the Corvette. Crickets sang in the tall grass and moonlight bounced off the red hood. "So did you buy your car because it matched your name or was that an accident?" Leaning back, he studied her.

"Both," she admitted, resting her head against the window. "My dad always teased my mother about naming me Mercedes."

Only Kate knew that sad fact. Amazing, the things she shared with Finn.

"Why? I like your name." His left hand was slung over the wheel and the other propped his head.

"My mother probably found my name in a book. She's like that. My dad said she should have named me Buick or Ford."

"He was joking, right?" Finn's lazy smile sent shivers like fuzzy caterpillars inching down her back. The bright moonlight emphasized the strong lines of his throat. That neck came after high school, like the biceps and the thighs. Calling a halt, she gulped. Okay, she'd lost the thread of this conversation. "Your dad would never have called you Buick."

She was back on track. "My dad hated it when my mother 'put on airs.' He was funny that way." But there hadn't been anything funny about the arguments she tried to avoid.

"I don't remember your dad very well..." Finn's forehead wrinkled.

Her sigh rasped the back of her throat. "I think everyone in Gull Harbor knows about my father. How he hung out at

Sammy's, down near Michigan City."

"He never seemed like a bad guy."

"No, but the drinking and the lying were hard to live with. Irresponsible and undependable. Never made it home for dinner. When he did, he would slip out to his gardening shed in the back and drink. We could hear the tops pop from where we sat on the porch."

She'd led him knee-deep into painful memories. "Sorry. Didn't mean to lay all that on you."

"That's okay, Mercedes. Sounds like your dad didn't step up to the plate."

She sighed in agreement. "No, he didn't. I was almost never home. Only Kate was there with my mom. Maybe I should have paid more attention." The words lodged an aching wedge in her throat.

"Come here, pretty girl." Finn pulled her gently into his arms. It wasn't easy to bridge the buckets of the Corvette but she couldn't help herself. Tonight she wanted any comfort he could give. When she curled up in his lap, Finn wrapped strong arms around her. His gray eyes seemed to search her soul. "Don't cry."

"I'm just tired, Finn..."

"Don't talk either."

His lips felt familiar enough to be reassuring, new enough to be exciting. Finn kissed her like he knew she wanted it. Needed it. And she did.

While his heart beat strong against her, sensations exploded inside. Suddenly she was a girl racing down the beach and soaring like the seagulls. They angled their heads to get closer, tighter. Explored with their tongues, nipped with their teeth. Gasped for breath before sinking into another kiss. *More.* Her mind and heart needed more. His breathing became labored. The cool evening air had turned volcanic.

Desire took her like a riptide. The wrap around sundress slipped from her shoulders and his lips grazed her skin. "You are so soft," he murmured. Finn trailed kisses down her neck and over her shoulders, hesitating at the dip between her breasts.

Eyes burning, he stared her down. "Mercedes?"

"Please don't stop," she whispered.

"Really?" His eyes seared her.

"You taste so good, Finn. Please."

Mercedes' breasts tingled and she pressed closer, knees curling around his hips. High school came back to her, when she made out with Chuck Lindner in the dunes at night. But she wasn't seventeen anymore and this felt a lot better. Meant a lot more. She'd opened her heart and soul to Finn. He didn't turn away. She'd never risked that with Stephan.

His hands made her crazy. Later she couldn't recall if the mindless plundering lasted five minutes, fifteen or an hour. Whatever it was, it wasn't enough.

Finally Finn pushed back, scrubbed a hand through his mussed hair and swallowed hard. "Mercedes?"

"Uh, huh?" The tension in her body hurt.

"We have to stop."

Feeling every angle of his body under her, she pressed down to carry that memory. Then she came to her senses. They were sitting in a car, for cripe's sake, and close to Red Arrow Highway. Not that many cars were out this late. "Of course we should. After all, I'm dating someone." She tugged her dress into place, while her own words mocked her.

"Right and I don't want you calling me Steven."

"Stephan, not Steven. And I-I wouldn't." She'd never felt like this with Stephan. The realization sent her scrambling for the other seat.

Finn threw her a bemused smile. "You're not in love with him, you know."

"I never said I was." Her hands trembled as she smoothed her dress over traitorous thighs.

"No...because you aren't." Finn sounded pleased. His confidence both irritated and pleased her. Springing from the car, he came around. She was trembling. When he reached for her hand and pulled her from the car, she fell weak-kneed against him. Steadying her with both hands, he kept her at a distance. Why? Mercedes wanted to stamp her foot in frustration but she had her pride.

Besides, she had a lot to think about.

"See you soon." His words were more a statement than a question.

"Ah, huh." Lips throbbing, Mercedes fumbled for her keys. Somehow, she made it into her car. Driving away felt like leaving the scene of a crime. When she checked her rearview mirror, he was still standing in the darkness watching her. She nearly drove off the road.

All the way home, she prayed her mother would not be awake. Her cheeks tingled, probably rosy with incriminating whisker rash. Her smile cracked into a chortle, deep and earthy. What the heck happened back there?

When she reached Breezy Point, she eased open the door and closed it slowly behind her. Slipping her shoes off, she crept through the silent shadows. What a relief that her mother wasn't awake to see that the daughter who'd left that night had come back a changed woman.

Chapter 11

Mercedes closed her bedroom door and slumped against it. She knew what she had to do. In New York, Stephan had spent most Saturday nights with her. Lips swollen from kissing another man, she had to talk to Stephan. Needed a reality check. Or maybe she needed to make a confession. Guilt prickled through her. Her bedside clock told her it was too late to call. She'd get in touch tomorrow.

The sound of the waves rolling onto the shore below pulsed through her open windows. Tonight the rhythm felt erotic. Sinking onto the window seat, Mercedes dropped her shoes and pulled her knees up into her chest. Feeling feverish, she let the damp breeze bathe her skin. Heck, she'd welcome a bucket of ice cubes.

Smiling, she ran her fingers lightly across her skin. Goosebumps rose where Finn's lips had touched and she shivered. Tonight made no sense. She was a New Yorker now, home for a short time. Could she chalk up her behavior to Moonlight Madness? Had to be. Her craziness mocked her as she changed into the night shirt that said *Say Yes to Michigan*. Sleep didn't come easily.

The following morning she woke up determined to reach Stephan. They'd sort things out. The poor man must be so darned busy. No word yet about his flight from New York for Kate's wedding next weekend.

Mercedes dressed quickly, pulling on a wrap skirt and a black knit top. Piling her hair on top of her head, she jammed her feet into her black sandals and grabbed her Gucci handbag. Charging out the back door, she found her mother bent over the hollyhock beds. "Going out for a drive," Mercedes told her. No way did she want her mother to overhear her conversation with her long-distance relationship.

"All right, dear. See you when you get back." An aqua hat jammed on her head, Mom hummed to herself while she nipped off some of the faded blooms.

Sunday morning was usually quiet on Red Arrow Highway. Summer people liked to sleep late. Husbands might venture down to the Lithuanian bakery for pastries and the paper but that was about it. Mercedes headed into town, where she parked on a side street. Taking out her phone, she pressed the speed dial. The phone rang and rang before going into voicemail. Stephan must be sleeping late.

Starting the car, she pulled back onto the road and slowly drove past the Mangy Mutt, embarrassed when her lips tingled. Clancy's carried the *New York Times* and she stopped to grab one before they were gone. The bulky paper brought a settling sense of routine. On Sunday mornings, she always read the paper with Stephan. Now she laid it on the seat next to her.

She took her time driving back up Red Arrow. Her New York boyfriend wasn't the man on her mind. No, she was thinking of how Finn's tousled hair felt in her hands, the persuasion of his lips, the gentle, knowing hands. She couldn't go home, not yet. Accelerating past the turnoff for Breezy Point, she headed north, slowing at the shops they'd visited last night. She tried to remember Finn's each word, every expression, as if she were in middle school again, giggling with the girls at the Swirly Top. When her stomach growled, she stopped at The Blue Plate Cafe for a blueberry muffin. Back in the car, she wolfed it down. Heck with moderation.

Of course she had to drive up to Phoebe's Place, the scene of the crime. In the early morning sunlight, the parking lot didn't have any romantic appeal. Still, her body leapt to life as if this were a Caribbean beach. After driving aimlessly with a silly smile on her face, she headed home.

Weren't summers made for dreaming? Who would be the man of her dreams? Feelings churned in her chest like the sheets in the cottage washing machines.

"Have a nice drive?" her mother asked when she came through the kitchen door.

"Um, yes. Drove up Red Arrow Highway until I got to Stevensville." She laid the newspaper onto the table. "Picked up a paper."

Mom glanced at the *Times*. "You must miss New York."

Do I? Not this morning.

Her mother put two pieces of bread in the old toaster. "What do you think of that big new big store? Might just put Clancy's out of business."

But Mercedes hadn't even noticed a big store. "Only time will tell."

Stretched out on the sofa, she paged through sections of the paper and didn't remember a single word she read. She had to talk to Stephan. He was always the soul of reason, and he was coming soon. She could sort out her feelings. Plot them on her mental white board like the steps of a marketing campaign. Get back on track. Stop acting like a sex-starved maniac.

Kate and Cole were coming for Sunday dinner, which kept Mercedes busy all day. Peeling and slicing cucumbers paper thin, she soaked them with onions in vinegar water. Then she brought out the bunt cake mold and whipped up a chocolate chip zucchini cake. Cole was going to grill for them that night, so she marinated six chicken breasts in Italian dressing. Summer vegetables had come in. She planned to stir-fry julienned zucchini slices with onions and top it off with a spinach salad, one of Stephan's favorites.

A big man, he was a hearty eater. Oh, he tried to watch his weight, but that wasn't easy when she handed off so much of her own meal. If it were left to her, she'd be satisfied with a half carton of yogurt. Stephan often commented on her self-control. "Moderation in all things," he'd say.

Taking a break on the porch swing, she took another pass through *New York Times*, noting the fashions and reading. The news seemed as distant as the city, and she set the paper aside to listen to the cardinals flitting through the pine trees. A brilliant red female hopped from branch to branch, chirping for her mate. One foot on the floor, Mercedes rocked the swing to the rhythm of the waves below and day-dreamed.

But it wasn't Stephan she thought about while she drained the cucumbers later that afternoon and added scoops of sour cream. No, her mind was filled with a lanky, elephant-eared boy with a man's hands and kisses that knocked her senseless.

The minutes ticked slowly by that Sunday afternoon. No word from Stephan. By the time Kate came to the kitchen door that evening, Mercedes had a plan.

With Natalie close behind him, Cole inhaled. "Man, sure smells good in here." The scent of chocolate chip zucchini cake hung heavy in the air.

Dancing in behind him, Prissy immediately sniffed along the counter. The great Dane was so darned tall, she could snatch anything with one swipe of her gigantic tongue. Cole squeezed Natalie's shoulder. "Why don't you take Prissy out to the front porch?"

"Prissy's fine right here." Her mother scratched the huge Great Dane behind her ears. And Prissy? The dog closed her eyes, in total bliss.

"Chicken marinating?" Kate opened the refrigerator door.

"Yep. Even mixed up a pitcher of sangria," Mercedes said, joining her sister in front of the blast of cold air. "You can cut up the fruit."

"Got it." Picking up a knife, her younger sister sliced the nectarines and oranges into chunks and then popped them into the waiting pitcher. Mercedes added the red wine and the liqueur that gave her sangria a special zing. Mom and Natalie drifted off toward the porch with Prissy.

While Mercedes took a tray of sangria out to the porch, Cole started the grill. "Did you get any feedback on Moonlight Madness?" Mercedes asked Kate when she returned to the kitchen and they were alone.

"Went well from what I saw. People were excited."

A wave of satisfaction swept over Mercedes.

"You should be proud, Mercedes," Kate noted. "We didn't have time to do much about it this year but next year…"

Next year? Mercedes didn't plan on being in Gull Harbor next year. She felt Kate scrutinizing her. "What?"

Kate just shook her head and opened a bag of taco chips. "Nothing. So you only wear khaki and white?"

Running a hand over her pristine white top, Mercedes bristled. "I wear black once in a while."

Her younger sister erupted into laughter. " Right. I know." Kate was darned irritating today.

Taking a bag of shredded cheese from the refrigerator, Mercedes ripped it open to spread on the chips. The cheese flew everywhere and her cheeks burned. Kate stooped to help Mercedes clean up the mess. "Come on. Don't take yourself so seriously, Mercedes," her sister said, tossing the cheese into the trash. Mercedes opened another bag. Spreading the taco chips on a platter, she sprinkled them with cheese and nuked it in the microwave.

Kate reached for the platter. "I'll take those out to the porch."

"Before you do, can I ask you for a favor?" Mercedes asked

casually. "Can I borrow your phone for a minute? My battery ran out and I want to make a quick call."

"Sure. But don't be long or these will all be gone." With a swirl of her long sundress, Kate was gone. Taking the phone, Mercedes went into the powder room and closed the door. The sunlight beamed through the shutters but Mercedes was not feeling cheerful. Something just wasn't right.

One steadying breath and she pressed in the numbers. Only two rings and he picked up. "This is Stephan Forbes," he said in his business voice.

"S-Stephan, it's me." Mercedes could hardly get the words out.

She heard the rumbling intake of breath. In the background, a woman asked, "Who is it?"

It only took a second for Mercedes' shock to flare into anger. "So I guess this means you're not coming next weekend?"

"Um, I was going to call you about that," Stephan said in a stilted, impersonal voice. "I'm afraid I can't make that meeting."

Meeting? "So your new girlfriend is standing right there?"

He must've gone into another room because she heard a door shut. "I'm no good at long-distance relationships, Mercedes."

"It's only been a few weeks." Being dumped was a whole new experience. "You could have told me that before I left. We talked about this, Stephan." Hadn't they?

The line hummed with emptiness.

She pushed words around the lump in her throat. "So I guess this is it."

"Doesn't seem like there's any reason to continue." What a

pompous idiot. He was still in his business mode. Squeezing her eyes shut, Mercedes rested her forehead against the closed door.

Maybe Finn had been right. Mercedes didn't love Stephan and probably never had. The shock went through her like a thunder clap. He was an important part of the world that meant everything to her, and maybe that was all he'd ever been. Emptiness opened up inside like a huge unanswered question. "Fine. Goodbye, Steven." No Stephan. Not anymore. She ended the call. It felt good to have the last word.

As she stood there, phone pressed into her chest, a knock came on the powder room door. "Mercedes? Everything all right in there?"

She straightened, dashing a finger beneath each eye before opening the door. "I'm f-f-ine."

"The heck you are." Frowning, Kate pushed her back inside the small room. "What just happened in here?"

"Something stupid," she finally said, handing Kate her phone. "I tricked Stephan. He wasn't picking up so I used your cell so my number didn't flash up."

"And?" Kate's knuckles turned white while she gripped her phone.

"He had another woman there." Slumping against the sink, Mercedes felt her bravado melt away. "I thought we were a couple. How could I have been so wrong?"

"Oh, come here." Arms around her, Kate rocked Mercedes and handed her tissues. This was the weirdest feeling in the world, being comforted by her baby sister. Strange and wonderful. "I never met Stephan but he's not worth it."

"I know you're right but still..." She blotted her eyes. After all, she'd been obsessing about Finn all day. "This year I've lost everything. My business, my condominium. And now a relationship I'd counted on. What's wrong with me?"

Her sister gave Mercedes' shoulder a shake. "Stop that right now. Sometimes you have to let things go before your life can start again."

Mercedes blinked. "Oh, Kate. That's you, not me. You were always a girl who could make lemonade from lemons."

"And you were the girl who never *had* to make lemonade." Kate was chuckling and Mercedes hated it. "Your turn now so suck it up."

"When did you get to be so wise?" Mercedes blew her nose.

"Most of what I know I learned from my older sister."

By that time, they were both laughing. "This room is starting to feel small for two people."

Kate glanced around, an odd smile on her face. "Oh, I don't know. Let's just call it cozy."

There was a story behind her sister's smile. "Okay, spill. What happened in here?"

Kate' s lips twisted into a wicked grin. "Some day maybe I'll tell you. Right now, I could use some sangria."

"Me too." Relief flooded through her. She wasn't used to failure but could deal with it. That night she allowed herself to eat an entire chicken breast. She even cut herself a huge wedge of chocolate chip zucchini cake. Comfort food.

Those size eight clothes from high school in her closet and drawers? They were starting to feel comfortable. She ran her fingers around the waistband of her blue capri pants. Maybe her life was expanding.

Chapter 12

All eyes were on the bride, except Finn's. Standing on the dune, he studied Mercedes. She couldn't see him so he took his time. Those creamy shoulders above her sparkly top brought back gut-wrenching memories. He knew how it felt to graze that soft skin with his lips. And the short fluffy skirt? The breeze was playing havoc with the ruffles. He almost laughed out loud when Mercedes clamped down hard on the skirt with both hands. Her bouquet got in the way. Face pink as the sunset, she looked totally frustrated. Mercedes liked to control everything, even the wind.

Like most brides, Kate looked like she might cry as she walked toward Cole. But his daughter was having the time of her life, showering flower petals in front of Kate while the Great Dane tried to snap them up. Prissy was the real hero of the day, in Finn's eyes. He'd have to get a picture of the prancing dog in that crazy pink boa. That shot would definitely have a spot at the Mangy Mutt.

When Kate reached Cole, the whispering stopped. Except for the seagulls, silence settled along the shoreline. Cole looped Kate's arm through his. All the women grabbed for tissues but none of that sentimental stuff for Finn. He was a man with a mission, casually scanning the other guys. Which one looked good enough to be Mercedes' boyfriend?

Finn had googled Stephan Forbes of New York City and his business page came up. He was good looking. Finn would give him that. But the guy had snake eyes and Finn didn't trust him. And the way his business was described? A lot of corporate mumbo jumbo. Stephan was probably a jack of all trades, master of none. He wasn't good enough for Mercedes, and Finn wasn't about to cede the field.

The only man who looked like he might be Stephan Forbes was a tall blond wearing a sand-colored sport coat. But Stephan didn't have light hair in the photos online.

Back to Mercedes. Beaming at the couple, the minister began the ceremony. Trying unsuccessfully to settle the illicit feelings holding his body hostage, Finn felt a little sleazy. How bad was it to lust after Mercedes in her tiny dress during a solemn service like this? But he was just that whipped. That night of Moonlight Madness had been amazing and crazy. Damn. He'd held his future in his arms and she felt more than right. Convincing Mercedes, however, was going to be a full time job.

Maybe it had been the moon. He liked to think it was fate. Whatever. He had no regrets. He'd been the man she turned to, not Stephan Forbes. That night had been his and as for the rest? Sure, he wanted her like he wanted his next breath. Made him restless just thinking about the things he had in mind. His Dockers shifted in the sand, and he dug in his heels while the minister came to the vows.

Problem was, Mercedes had to want it too. She had to *need* him, the way he needed that next breath. He was prepared to wait, give her time. Back in high school, she understood his notes when she had time to consider them. She just needed time to process.

Watching Kate and Cole recite their vows, Finn was determined to be *that man* for Mercedes. How amazing that she hadn't married over the years. Maybe her career hadn't left much time for a relationship, except for losers like Stephan Forbes. Look where all that big city energy had landed her. The breeze lifted one of her curls. Mercedes played with it before smoothing her hair back along her arched neck. Heat burned a path through his body, and he bit back a groan.

Yeah, he was just that whipped.

Thank God the service didn't last long. The couple's vows were pretty innovative and along with the rest of the crowd, he chuckled. "I didn't know if Kate would come back to me," Cole said, slipping the wedding band on her finger. "But some things are worth waiting for."

Finn's stomach clenched. He knew just how that felt. But he had to play his cards right. No doubt about it, Mercedes had come home wounded. Had New York and her failing business made her doubt herself? The night of Moonlight Madness, he'd seen the girl she'd been in high school. The girl who took life on with a saucy, confident smile.

In two beach chairs in front of him, Mrs. Kennedy sat next to Cole's mother-in-law, Marie McGraw. Finn had heard a lot of stories about what happened to Samantha McGraw, Cole's first wife. Drugs were involved, or so they said. He was a lot better off with Kate.

The service ended and a collective sigh swept the group. The newly married couple kissed and the crowd applauded. Then everyone dispersed. Mrs. Kennedy teetered dangerously when she tried to stand up in the soft sand. Finn jumped forward. "Gotta watch it now," he told Mercedes' mom, bracketing her with his arms.

"I guess I do." She patted his hand. "Thank goodness you're here, Finn."

Outlined against the setting sun, Cole addressed the group. "Kate and I thank you for sharing this happy day with us. Please join us in our home for one heck of a celebration." The simple invitation was so like Gull Harbor. Of course, everyone there knew where he lived. Well, except for Stephan. Where was Mercedes' useless boyfriend? But the tall blond dude was making tracks to his car, and Mercedes was still talking to the other bridesmaids. Finn decided to leave, take care of a couple things down at the restaurant and then circle back to Cole's house.

~~

Standing on the spacious deck overlooking the lake, Mercedes fidgeted with her pink calla lilies. Mellow jazz poured from Cole's sound system and grilled food seasoned the air. Tiny white lights spangled the trees and laughter floated from the house. This was going to be a long evening. She hadn't seen Finn at the ceremony, so he must have decided not to come. Maybe he was having second thoughts... about a lot of things. She'd never felt so alone.

Stashing the flowers behind her, Mercedes sank deeper into the shadows. Cars were pulling up along Lake Shore Road, their headlights arcing through the gathering darkness. She would stay at least an hour. After all, this was her sister's wedding. Yes, the ceremony had been simple but had its sweet moments. What she'd give to have a man gaze at her the way Cole had looked at her sister while he said his vows.

Try as she might, she couldn't imagine Stephan in that picture. All the time they were dating, she'd imagined their future in her head. The picture included a sleek apartment in the city and a weekend place at the Hamptons. But apparently the relationship, if that's what they had, couldn't weather a separation. She felt both insulted and relieved. What now? The situation with Finn was complicated. And maybe it was all in her head, conjured up by desperation. How humiliating.

The wind rustled through the pine trees, carrying the scent of Lake Michigan. Closing her eyes, she tried to imagine this was the ocean and she was at the Hamptons. But it wasn't. The smell of this lake was as familiar and distinct as the shape of her own hands. She'd never trade Lake Michigan for the Atlantic Ocean. Gripping the edge of the wooden deck, she stared down at the glittery straps of her Jimmy Choo sandals. Tonight they felt out of place. How she wished she could find a consignment shop to sell some of these god-awful-expensive shoes. Did Second Hand Rose sell shoes? She'd never noticed.

With a toss of her head, she shook off that thought. After all, she'd need them when she returned to Manhattan. A woman was nothing in the city without her designer shoes.

People were spilling onto the deck from Cole's french doors. Crouching in the corner, she must look like the biggest wet blanket ever. Maybe she could slip away, walk home and return later for Mom. But how could she handle sandy Lake Shore Road in these shoes? Going barefoot wasn't an option. The darkness was too absolute once she got away from the houses. She could step on broken glass from a party or a nail left by a construction worker.

As more people crowded the huge deck, the noise level mounted. Champagne corks popped at the bar set up in the far corner. In a cloud of White Shoulders perfume, her mother sat down next to her, the blue silk dress from the shopping channel billowing around her. "You look pretty, Mom."

"You're next, Mercedes."

She glanced away. "Don't count on it."

Not to be brushed off, her mother leaned closer. "Where is that boyfriend of yours? The one from New York?"

Snapping off one of the black-eyed Susans that grew wild around Cole's deck, Mercedes pulled at the petals. "Stephan's not coming, Mom. We broke up." Not wanting to make a point, she hadn't mentioned it.

"Honey, I'm so sorry."

"It's okay. Really." *Loves me, loves me not.* Mercedes watched the petals fall onto the brown deck. Dropped by her boyfriend of one year? She should be devastated. But she wasn't and her mind slowly circled that realization. Finally, only a green stalk was left and she tossed it over the railing. Could she even picture Stephan here with the people she loved? It felt okay that he hadn't come. But it didn't feel okay that he'd dumped her. She still had a lot to figure out, much of which involved Finn. Just holding his name in her mind made her woozy.

Finn stepped from the darkness like an apparition. "You two look like you're up to something."

Her mother blinked up at him. "Oh, it's you again, Finn. Mercedes was just telling me her young man isn't coming."

Finn didn't waver. "That right?"

Primping her blonde curls, her mother got up. "I think I need a drink."

"Me too." Mercedes started to follow but Finn grabbed her arm.

"Hey, pretty girl. Not so fast."

She stayed put. Her mother joined Marie and together they approached the bar. Mercedes turned back to Finn. Her throat ached at the sight of him. "You're looking good tonight, mister." She wanted to run a hand down his crisp, white shirt with the sporty open collar. Feel the beat of his heart. "Your shirt almost glows against that navy jacket."

"Yeah but I'm overdressed, right?" With a shrug, Finn slid out of the jacket and folded it onto the bench.

"Hey, you looked good in that jacket."

Glancing around at the guys in polo shirts, he shrugged. "I hate to feel out of place. Had enough of that in high school."

"Really?" In chemistry lab, his endless supply of rock band t-shirts had added to his geeky mystique.

"Why isn't your boyfriend here?"

Might as well get this over. "Because he's found somebody else. Didn't take long, right?"

"Damn fool," he murmured with disgust that soothed her injured pride. "His loss is my gain."

So outrageous. Her skin prickled. "Oh, is it now?" When had he become so confident?

The spark in his eyes rivaled the tiny lights in the trees. "You don't exactly look broken up about your loss."

A waiter swirled past with a tray of champagne flutes. Finn scooped two up and handed one to her. The first gulp made her eyes smart. The second one uncoiled the tight spring in her chest. As long as this strapless dress stayed up, she was fine.

Lifting his glass, Ignacio Rodriguez called for everyone's attention, clinking a spoon on the side of the champagne flute. The crowd settled. Looking around, Mercedes realized Kate had built some strong ties in a short time by reconnecting with her high school friends.

"A toast to the perfect couple that found each other again after ten years, right?" He glanced over at Cole, who nodded, his arm tight around Kate's waist. "To Cole and Kate."

With cheers and laughter, everyone raised their glasses. Kate blushed and their mother teared up, reaching for the tissue tucked in her sleeve. Mercedes felt a little choked up herself. Maybe she was just tired from the recent melodrama. She upended her glass. The bubbly broke against the back of her throat, causing a coughing fit.

"Hey, you okay?" Finn patted her back and then let his hand circle, warm and comforting. "Maybe you need something to eat, pretty girl." Setting their champagne glasses on the railing, he took her hand, led her to the buffet table and handed her a plate.

She froze. The smell of fresh bread tempted her. She'd already downed more than two hundred calories with the champagne. But the dress still felt comfortable. Definitely enough room for the bread, brie, grapes and scoops of marinated vegetables Finn was loading on a plate.

"Here you go."

"Thank you." Her hand shook as she took the full plate. Thank goodness it was dark. Seated back on the deck bench, she nibbled while asking Finn questions. Picking up a grape, she popped it in her mouth and bit down. Juice and flavor exploded in her mouth. She'd forgotten how sweet a red grape could be. He was telling her about renovating Mangy Mutt when his voice trailed off.

"Everything okay?" Finn took her elbow. The touch of his hand ignited her. The man set her on fire like one of the torches flaming around the deck.

"Um hmm." She nodded. One touch did this? She tested a chunk of brie and was quickly seduced by its creamy texture. Reaching for another, it appeared that she'd passed some test. Finn smiled and picked up where he'd left off. "As I was saying, I decided on contemporary for the Mangy Mutt..."

Her stomach settled and she looked up to find Kate studying her. They smiled at each other like they were back in her bedroom at Breezy Point, playing "when I grow up." Back then they'd picture their weddings, the fine husbands and the houses where they'd raise their two children, although Kate wanted four. That was all within reach for Kate. How ironic. As the oldest, Mercedes had been the first to ride a two-wheeler, the first to practice kissing her pillow and the first to have a real date. She'd always expected to be the first to marry but that didn't happen. This was Kate's second wedding. Today that felt okay. Maybe many roads led to the dream. And maybe the dream changed as a girl grew up.

Finn had emptied his plate and they started to circulate, eventually bumping into Will Applegate with Diana. "Finn, have you met Will, the administrator of the care center?" Mercedes asked.

Finn's smile widened. "No, but I've seen you around."

"Sure. I've stopped in your restaurant." Will shook Finn's hand. "Nice place."

"Beautiful ceremony, wasn't it?" Diana turned to Mercedes, her hand hooked through Will's arm. Mercedes wondered when that had happened. Will and Diana made a striking couple. Another pretty blonde woman with cameo features stood nearby. Definitely looked familiar and then it hit her. "Miss Knight?"

She turned with a pert smile. "Yes?"

"From the high school, right? I'm Kate's sister. I never had you for a class so you wouldn't know me. Mercedes Kennedy."

"Right. Kate's big sister. She's so proud of you. I'm still at the high school. Kate joined my book group."

While Mercedes and Carolyn talked about changes at the high school, Diana nodded politely. Mercedes overheard Finn asking

Will questions about Gull Harbor Care Center.

"Were you inquiring for one of your parents?" she asked as they moved away.

"You never know. Looks like dinner is served." He nodded at the buffet table where white-coated waiters were tending several steaming serving dishes.

"Didn't we just finish eating?" Her hand went to her waist. The dress felt snug enough to stay up but with enough room for the ribs and chicken that made her salivate.

"Those were appetizers, girl." Finn flattened one hand on her back. She felt it clear through to her ribs, yet his touch was so gentle.

Yes, indeed, the appetizer course had been replaced with ribs and barbecued chicken. Taking her turn in the buffet line, Mercedes scooped up dainty amounts of food. This freedom felt so new, so reckless

"You on a diet?" Finn glanced at her plate.

"I watch my weight."

"You're thin enough." He ran a hand down one slim arm. Goosebumps rose in its wake.

Tables were set up throughout Cole's spacious house but Finn and Mercedes settled back on the deck with her dainty sampling.

"Watch it. You might ruin that fancy dress, Mercedes." Handing her a napkin, Finn eyed the plate balanced on her knees.

"I'll probably never wear it again."

"Why not? You look great in it. Beautiful and hot." He took a healthy bite of the wings dripping with barbecue sauce.

"Finn, the dress came from Second Hand Rose, and it kind of gives me the creeps. Some other girl wore this." Mercedes would have traded this fluttery skirt in a minute for a slim linen sheath.

Frowning, Finn sectioned a chicken breast into large chunks. "So you never wore hand-me-downs growing up?"

"No, I didn't. But my clothes were passed on to Kate." Had her sister minded? She'd seem delighted, now that Mercedes looked back.

"So you see? Think of it as making the best use of things."

What a novel idea. "Do you lend out your tools?" Was this a guy thing?

"You bet. With my name stenciled on them."

After the cake had been cut, Cole thanked everyone for coming. "But don't you even think of leaving. We're just getting started."

The music from the speakers swung from jazz to classic rock. Everyone danced and the deck vibrated beneath her feet. Even Natalie jumped around with one of Sarah's little boys. Cole led Mom to the dance floor and she beamed up at her new son-in-law. Seeing her dance lifted Mercedes's heart. She was only sorry that it wasn't her own wedding bringing her mom such joy. The next song was *Unchained Melody*, the most romantic love song ever.

"Dance?" Not waiting for an answer, Finn tugged her to her feet.

"Sure." She fought the urge to mold herself to his body. Uncertainty plagued her. Even though she wasn't with Stephan anymore, she was going back to New York. She didn't want to mislead Finn.

"What's this?" Swirling her around, he angled closer. "You trying to hold me off?"

"Don't be silly."

He looked pointedly at her stiff arms. "You're acting like that night of Moonlight Madness never happened. Why?"

"No crazy moon tonight, Finn." She kept her tone light and playful.

Maybe it was the unexpected breakup with Stephan, maybe it was her nervousness about Moonlight Madness, but she wanted to be careful.

"We don't need the moon, Mercedes." He cupped her hand against his chest. She felt the steady beat of his heart. Knew the feel of his sculpted lips, the touch of his hands, his heated breath. Her body arched toward him, defying her practical mind. "I'm headed back to Manhattan, Finn." She tossed the words up like a shield.

"Not tonight, right?" His eyes studied her. "Let's take this one step at a time."

She had no place to hide with this man. When Finn nuzzled her neck in the darkness, she turned toward his warmth. Finn sensed the change, kissed her cheek, and she weakened.

"Come on." Pulling away from the group, he led her down the stairway to the beach. The noise from the party dimmed. Their feet sank into the cool sand.

"Better ditch those shoes or you'll ruin them. Or are those throw-aways like the dress?"

"Jimmy Choos? Absolutely not." She carefully slipped off her elegant heels and left them in the sand. He parked his Dockers right next to them. "You ever wear socks, Finn?"

"Not if I can help it."

She turned from his sexy smile. Holding hands, they ran laughing to the water's edge.

"Will you look at that moon?" Finn pulled up sharp and pointed.

"Not full but it's cutting a path to the shore." A blazing cool light reflected across the water, its path fractured by the ripples.

Finn came closer. She held her breath when he ran his hands slowly down her bare arms. "Maybe we should be careful about the moon tonight. Not get too crazy?" He gave her that quiet smile.

She had to be honest. "Oh, Finn. I don't know what I want." The water lapped over her feet and she yelped. Summer was ending and the lake was turning cooler.

Lacing his fingers through hers, Finn nudged her onto the dry sand. "Maybe I should take the water side." They started walking along the shore, their bare feet leaving imprints in the sand.

"You're always so thoughtful."

His eyes twinkled. "Yes, I am. A gentleman from sole to crown."

She snapped her fingers. "What was the name of that poem?"

"*Richard Cory*. That discussion went on and on." He rolled his eyes.

"Were you in that class?"

"Yes, I was, Mercedes Kennedy. You didn't hear my insightful comments?"

"I'm sorry." She noticed Finn in chemistry because he sat right next to her. He'd been in math and English with her too? How embarrassing.

Coming to a stop, Finn turned her to face him. A cool breeze caught her curls but Finn brushed them back from her eyes. "What? You didn't know I was there?"

"I'm sorry." High school blurred in her memory.

"I sat two rows behind you so I could watch you."

Really? "You're kidding. So that's how it was?"

"That's how it *is*, pretty girl. Back then you were trying to impress another guy. Today? I watched you all through your sister's wedding." Finger gentle under her chin, he tipped her face up.

"Oh, Finn. You did?" Her stomach folded over like a warm July wave. "I thought maybe you didn't come."

"Of course I came. I enjoyed looking at you. You played with your hair all the time." Lifting a strand, he let it slip through his fingers.

"You shouldn't do that." Mercedes brushed his hand away.

"Why not? You don't have a boyfriend, remember?"

"Yeah, I know." Looking into his gray eyes, she felt muddled, so she closed her eyes. Felt his arms around her and melted.

When he kissed her, Finn tasted like barbecue sauce. "More, please." Mercedes cupped his face in her hands and settled into a deep kiss. The man felt and tasted so fine. She wanted more. Much more. Desire burned a path through her body. Finally Finn broke the clutch, drawing in a breath through set teeth. They swayed together in the sand.

"Oh, hell." He lowered his lips again with a deep groan. The teasing and tasting began, and she took and gave it all until they finally lost their footing, tumbling into the sand.

Laughing, they fell back. Sand cool against her back, she didn't care what happened to her hair or this dress. A million stars pierced the dark sky overhead and her head spun. Finn pulled her to him, his fingers tracing every bead on the bodice, every ruffle on the short skirt. But when his hand dipped under the hem, she clamped down. "Wait. Let's be sure."

His playful expression turned serious. "I'm a big boy, Mercedes. And I know what I want."

"Oh, Finn. Can't you see?" She hated the hitch in her voice. "I'm not ready."

Blowing out a breath, he carefully smoothed the dress over her legs. Did he think she was a tease? Her stomach tightened. But Finn gave her a good-natured smile and helped her up. "It's too sandy here anyway." Oh, so gently he brushed grains of sand from her shoulders. She didn't want him to ever stop.

"I t-totally agree." How was it possible that he could turn her on like this? She couldn't catch her breath and shook like the leaves on the birch trees above them. "I don't want sand getting in, well, everywhere."

"You're cold, pretty girl. Let me warm you." When Finn enfolded her, she dropped her head to his chest and listened to his heart. Had she ever heard such a comforting sound? She'd never felt this safe and secure with Stephan.

He rocked her, as if they were dancing. Where had Finn developed all these moves? "Yep, you would have had sand, well, everywhere."

"Is that a promise or a threat," she whispered.

He chuckled deep in his throat and led her back to the stairs. The cool sand on the soles of her feet brought a return of reason. One arm tight around her waist, he snatched her shoes from the sand and pocketed them. "Come on. I'll walk you up to your car."

"Thanks." She felt relieved and disappointed.

"You let me know."

"Let you know about what?"

"When you're ready," he whispered.

Chapter 13

The smell of disinfectant stung Mercedes' eyes. She sat back on her heels and studied her work. So it had come to this. Her self-esteem depended on how well she scrubbed a floor.

The week had been a blur after Kate's wedding. How could she feel this much for Finn when they'd only known each other a few weeks? But they had a history. High school counted and she was just finding that out. She'd never felt this dizzying obsession for Stephan, and Mercedes questioned her judgment.

Now it was Friday, and she was back cleaning cottages. The scrubbing kept her focused in a weird way. She was tackling the gunk in the corners. No mop for her. Mom had taught Mercedes and Kate to "get in the corners with your fingers" when they cleaned Breezy Point on weekends. Today she had time. Only two cottages on Lindsay's list for her, and the guests wouldn't arrive until later in the day. The kids were back in school, so business was slowing down.

Outside the trees shook in a gust of September wind. The leaves were turning gold and orange from cooler nights. Glancing out the kitchen door she'd purposely left open, Mercedes felt as restless as those papery leaves dancing from the trees. She had to be honest with Finn. New York was where she belonged. She'd created a life there. No matter what she felt for Finn, she wasn't staying here. That much hadn't changed.

How could Kate face a future in Gull Harbor, where ice floes packed the shoreline during long winters of endless snow and raw winds? Mercedes' jaw ached, and she lifted a rubber-gloved hand to her cheek. No matter how much she read about TMJ, she still couldn't relax her jaw and stop this throbbing. Of course, the session on the beach with Finn didn't help.

In her restless dreams, she was out on the lake in Gator but had lost her kayak paddle. When it came to her personal life, she had no direction. Tossing her scrub brush into the bucket, Mercedes considered her future. She needed to raise some cash to get back in the game in New York. And she had a plan. Late at night, she sat in bed with a pad of paper on her knee, scratching out dates and figures. She hoped Lindsay would go along with this. The last thing she wanted was to alienate Finn's sister.

Hauling herself to her feet, Mercedes packed up her cleaning supplies before taking one final sweep through the three-bedroom cottage on Townline Road. Bathrooms sparkled; the towels were neatly folded. The kitchen counters had been cleared, the refrigerator emptied and the stove wiped out. The dryer buzzer made her jump, and she hurried back to gather the warm sheets so they wouldn't wrinkle.

As Mercedes made up the master bed, she wondered what Tiola, her cleaning lady, had done all day? Her condo had never needed the attention these homes required. She pictured her good-natured cleaning woman reading magazines on the wrap-around terrace, a cup of coffee in hand. Mercedes chuckled.

Moving from one side of the king-size bed to the other, she pulled the sheets tight. The fresh clean scent rewarded her. She was working on one of the twin beds in a guest room when she heard the front door open.

"Hello?" Her notes indicated the owners were not expecting guests for the coming week, and she trotted out to the front room.

"Just me." Her hair in pigtails accented by a mauve streak, Lindsay could have been sixteen.

"Looks like Phoebe worked some magic with your hair."

"Thought I'd live dangerously."

Right. This was "living dangerously" in Gull Harbor. "Looks cute." Lindsay was an attractive young woman but she sure didn't smile much. But after hearing her story, Mercedes couldn't blame her. How did she manage in a town like Gull Harbor? Of course, she had her family here and her girls.

"So you're just about finished up here?" Lindsay's eyes fell on the foam kneeler Mercedes had grabbed from her mother's garden shed. "You were scrubbing on your knees?"

"Ridiculous, right?" What had this job done to her? "My mother's influence, I guess."

"Up to you. Mostly I just use a mop." Leaning against the counter, Lindsay studied her tennis shoes.

"So what's up?" A sense of *deja vu* crept over Mercedes, only she'd been at the opposite end of the stick. Was Lindsay going to fire her?

Lindsay's gray eyes circled to meet hers. "Listen, I really

appreciate your helping me for a while at the end of the summer but the truth is…"

"You don't need me anymore," Mercedes supplied. "Got a minute?" It killed her that she had to share her plan. However, Lindsay had given Mercedes access to the summer people. This idea might never have occurred to her without this short summer gig as a cleaning lady.

Lindsay perched on the edge of the blue plaid sofa. "What's up?"

Mercedes sat next to her. "I'm pretty entrepreneurial. My agency billed well over seven figures annually."

Lindsay didn't look impressed.

Get off it, Mercedes. That was all in her past. "Anyway, I've been thinking of what I might create here in Gull Harbor."

"What does that have to do with me?" Lindsay grew guarded.

"I've been thinking… How do people find your services?"

"The Chamber website or southwestern Michigan. That kind of thing, including word of mouth."

Excellent. "I'm thinking of starting a service that would gather all these homes together and manage their rentals, from summer season through Notre Dame football games and cross country skiing season…" Her voice faltered. Lindsay's face had turned red and her eyes snapped. She looked furious.

"How like you, Mercedes."

"W-what are you talking about?" She hadn't finished explaining.

"Take my business and spin it off as your own. Are you kidding me?"

The words felt like a slap. "That's not what I'm talking about. Were you planning on starting a property management business?"

That was a low blow and Mercedes regretted it. Lindsay was busy with her kids, even though her parents and Finn helped her out. But she didn't understand why Lindsay was so mad. "If anything, this could help your cleaning business."

"Oh, sure. Right." Lindsay folded her arms tight across her chest.

Her lack of trust stung. "You don't have to be a part of this. I'm just being open and honest, trying to include you." Mercedes started to back pedal. Why had she even considered Lindsay in the first place? Well, there was the matter of her client list. Mercedes wanted to send a direct mail piece to a list of existing customers.

Ramrod stiff, Lindsay's hand shot out. "I'll take your keys to this cottage, Mercedes. Then get out."

Shock made Mercedes numb. She couldn't even feel her fingers.

"You heard me." Lindsay jerked a thumb toward the front door. "Take your fancy car and go home...or back to New York where you belong. I've had it with your condescending ways. You're not better than us, you know."

Somehow, Mercedes stumbled to her feet. She dropped the keys in Lindsay's palm and grabbed her purple cleaning caddy. When her odorless window spray thudded to the floor, she left it. Eyes filling, she stumbled down the steps. Clicking her trunk open, she tossed everything inside. Sand spun under the tires when she left the driveway and sped to Townline Road. Her head pounded with anger all the way home.

Her mother looked up from stirring something in a pan when Mercedes burst through the back door. "What are you cooking?" Whatever it was, it smelled burned. She drew closer.

"Applesauce."

"My favorite." Well, that was a lie but something was wrong here. When Mercedes peeked over her mother's shoulder, her interest turned to concern. What should have been a fragrant mixture of sweetened apples and cinnamon looked like a dark brown mess. "Maybe too much sugar?"

"You think? Oh, darn." With a sigh, Mom swung the pan into the sink. "Makes me so mad. How many times have I made applesauce? How could I goof this up?"

Her mother's frustration tugged at Mercedes' heart. "Come on, let's go into town for ice cream." The trip would distract both of them. Her mother would never notice that Mercedes wasn't eating the dairy whip.

Wiping her hands on a dish towel, her mom looked delighted. "That sounds wonderful. I'll just clean up first."

"I'm going to shower," Mercedes said over her shoulder as she dashed upstairs. "Turn off the stove, okay?"

She waited on the stairs until she heard the faint click of the knob. As she showered with her eucalyptus soap, the heated argument with Lindsay pricked at her conscience. Did Lindsay have a right to be angry? Toweling herself off and spritzing on some Spellbound, Mercedes slipped on her black jeans, forest green T-shirt and hoodie, and headed downstairs.

Thirty minutes later they were breezing down Red Arrow

Highway, top down on the black Mercedes. The sun had lost the blazing heat of August to become September soft. Next to her, Mom wore a huge smile. Although they'd each tied their hair down with a scarf, the wind played havoc. Soon the scarves loosened and blonde curls flew everywhere. Mercedes didn't care and neither did her mother. They were like Thelma and Louise going off on an adventure.

"Isn't this just the best?" her mother called to her, adjusting her rhinestone trimmed sunglasses. She'd been Internet shopping again.

"The very best," Mercedes agreed, letting her shoulders relax and tipping her face up to the sun. In Manhattan, she never put the top down. The car had been a luxury used for trips to the Hamptons with Stephan. For transportation, she took the subway or walked to her office. Here? She'd never enjoyed this black Mercedes more.

Once in town, she drove down Whittaker and pulled in next to the Swirly Top. The smell of grilled food wrinkled her nose but her mom perked up. "Hot dog then ice cream? How does that sound?"

Her stomach tumbled at her own suggestion but her mother beamed. "Sounds ducky, honey."

In a few minutes, Mercedes had Alice seated comfortably at one of the picnic tables outside the ice cream stand, while she went inside to order. During the summer, the picnic tables were jammed but today? Only two tables were taken when Mercedes returned with a full tray. Her mother concentrated on her hot dog, licking ketchup from her lips with appreciation. Mercedes threw out plenty of diversion that gave her time to break up the bun and toss it to the birds. Then she buried the hot dog under her napkin.

Her argument with Lindsay still bothered her. She was sorry that Finn's sister had gotten so upset. And then there was the practical side. Lindsay had the starter mailing list. Was Mercedes' plan circling the drain? Just as they were finishing up, Kate's friend Sarah wandered down the street. Smelling of the bakery, she gave Mom a warm hug.

"Kids with your mother?" Mom asked.

"Yep." Sarah nodded. "My mother's a saint. I promised the boys hot dogs today, and not the kind I boil in the pan. I'll be right back." She disappeared inside.

"Lucky Lila," Mom murmured, staring after Sarah as she went in to order. "Those two little boys are so cute. I hope Kate..." Then she stopped, pinching her lips together.

The bottom dropped out of Mercedes' stomach. "Gives you grandchildren, right?"

Reaching over, her mother squeezed Mercedes' hand. "You'll meet someone, sweetheart." Amazing how her mother still read her so well.

"Of course I will." Maybe she already had and that was a problem. "But not here, Mom. Not in Gull Harbor."

~.~

Finn came up behind her and overheard. His eyes met her mother's glance, and he held a finger to his lips. Mercedes didn't know her own mind. He wouldn't let it get to him. Not yet. Elvis yelped and

Mercedes turned. "All right if we join you?" he asked.

Curls wild around her face and freckles sprinkled across her nose, Mercedes looked like a different girl from the uptight woman he'd saved from the tar not long ago. Elvis and Wiggy started sniffing around the table.

"Aw, you brought your pets." Her mother dangled a hand, and Wiggy trotted over to give her a quick lick.

"Maybe I should buy them a hot dog."

Mercedes smiled up at Finn and his heart turned over. "I thought dogs weren't supposed to have people food?" She brushed a strand of hair from her lips, and he wanted to kiss her.

"Dogs? Maybe. Mutts? They've had a lot worse. I found Elvis and Wiggy at the no-kill shelter." No details necessary. "They were four years old and cautious, with good reason. Elvis wasn't easy."

"Lucky pair to be rescued by you." She scratched behind Elvis' ears, and he squinted his eyes closed.

"Sit down, Finn." Mrs. Kennedy patted the bench next to her.

"I wouldn't want to interrupt."

"We were just talking." Mercedes tossed a bit of bun to the dogs. "Come here, you two rascals."

He angled his long legs under the picnic table and Mrs. Kennedy turned to him. "Mercedes was just telling me that she didn't plan to—"

"Let this sun go to waste," Mercedes said quickly. "I was thinking we might go down to the beach this afternoon."

Her poor mother looked confused.

"Really? Interesting." He pinned Mercedes with a look, and she began to clear the table.

"Oh, let me." Scooping the plates from her hands, he was about to dump them in the trash when he spotted the bits of hot dog under the napkin. "Hey, Elvis. More lunch."

Elvis was on it but Wiggy yelped. Her bark distracted Elvis, and Wiggy grabbed the meat. Elvis was outraged and Finn laughed. "She does this all the time. Females are great with diversions." His attention swung back to Mercedes. "Not hungry?"

Mercedes squirmed. "My stomach's been upset." She lifted her heart-shaped chin, daring him to question her in front of her mother.

"Lindsay was just telling me that you have plans for a business here." He laid the words out casually. Mercedes didn't need to know his sister had gone ballistic about the plan.

Her mother's face brightened. "Is that so, Mercedes?"

A frown puckered Mercedes' forehead. "Nothing big, Mom. I'm working on something to tide me over so I can get back to New York."

"You grew up here, Mercedes," her mother said. "I don't know why you don't want to settle down here."

Crossing her legs, Mercedes looked down at the table, one foot bobbing.

"Yes, Mercedes." Leaning his head on one hand, he studied her. "Why don't you explain that."

Confusion clouded Mercedes' beautiful green eyes. Sweet Mrs. Kennedy sat waiting.

"I miss Barney's," she finally said.

"What's that?" Finn tossed another chunk of hot dog to Elvis. Wiggy had retreated and curled up in the shade of a small maple tree, just planted by the beautification committee.

"Barney's is a big, beautiful store."

At least she didn't say she missed Stephan.

"Do you mean you want to go back because you miss shopping in a big store?" Her mom was trying to understand. "Have you tried the Internet?"

Finn choked back a laugh. Mercedes glared at him. "It's not that simple."

"You can always drive down to the mall in Michigan City." Her mother's face brightened. "I'd go with you."

Over the years, messages had been carved into the picnic table. Her jaw clamped tight, Mercedes traced one heart with her finger.

"When will Cole and Kate be getting back?" Finn was rewarded for changing the subject when Mercedes smiled.

"This weekend. Can't wait to see her," Mom said, her eyes turning misty.

"So they went to the Grand Hotel on Mackinac Island. Is that what I heard?" Finn continued.

"Oh, yes." Her mother looked ecstatic, like he'd mentioned Paris. "Isn't that romantic?"

Jumping up, Mercedes pitched her empty cup in the trash. She wouldn't even look at Finn. What was this? After what he considered a pretty hot night on the beach, she ignored his texts and didn't pick up his calls. Mercedes sat back down. This had to stop. He didn't care if her mother was sitting there.

"Hey, give us a chance, Mercedes, okay?" Picking up a straw, Finn twisted it. Sometimes he could be creative.

"You're right, Finn." Her mother nodded and Finn wanted to hug her. "Give Gull Harbor a chance."

The straw he'd bent into a heart didn't look too bad. When he passed it to her, Mercedes closed her fingers around it but her mother saw it. "Oh, my," Mrs. Kennedy murmured. Mercedes threw him a pleading glance, as if to say, *No more. Please.*

Finn pushed on. "How would you ladies like to go for a drive tonight? Hear an outdoor concert up in St. Joe?"

"Oh, Finn..." Mrs. Kennedy clapped her hands, looking delighted. Then her glance swerved to Mercedes. "You go. My goodness, I'm way too tired."

"How about it, Mercedes?" He glanced down at the crumpled heart and smiled. "Around seven?"

"You should go, sweetie," her mother chimed in with an impish grin.

"I'm kind of worn out."

Worn down would be more like it. Panic made her wide-eyed, not exhaustion. He wasn't letting this go. "From what I hear you only cleaned one cottage today."

Her eyes flared. "All right. What time?"

He loved a woman with spirit. "Seven." *Game on.*

Chapter 14

"This is some car." Mercedes circled the forest green convertible parked behind Breezy Point. She wanted to run her fingers over the gleaming finish but didn't. Obviously this was Finn's baby. He opened the passenger side door and she got in, inhaling the cushy cordovan leather. "I'm serious, Finn. This is gorgeous."

"The Austin Healy is one of my toys." He closed her door with loving care. "Did you bring a scarf?"

"Sure did." *Who is this man?* Mercedes knotted a lime green headscarf around her hair while Finn slid into the driver's seat. "I didn't see you as a convertible kind of guy."

Grinning, he started the car and eased it down the bumpy driveway. "No? What kind of guy am I?"

"Unpredictable?"

"I've been told I'm a risk taker." They'd reached Lake Shore Road and he revved the engine.

She tightened her scarf. "What kind of risks do you take?"

"I like having the odds stacked against me." His gray eyes turned smoky. "How about you? Ready to take some chances?"

"Try me." He was getting under her skin tonight.

They'd reached Red Arrow and Finn picked up speed. The wind ruffled his dark curls in the most distracting way. She gripped the door handle with one hand and battled the wind tearing at her scarf with the other. The wind won and she rolled up the scarf, shaking her hair out into the night air.

They sped past shops and restaurants. "The trip will take forever if we stay on Red Arrow. What about Hwy 94?"

"A trip that took forever with you would be too short."

A shiver chased down her spine. "Really?"

His nod seemed serious. Then Finn waved a hand toward Paul's Wood Shop. "Besides, we'd miss all this charm."

"We've seen these places a million times."

"Mercedes, that's the point," he said, his voice even. "These shops and restaurants hold our history, right? A lot of them are owned by families we know."

"But I'm a New Yorker now. A Fifth Avenue girl...kind of." Who was she kidding? Her condo had been close to Fifth Avenue but not quite.

"You've come home. Enjoy it." He squeezed her knee. A rush of heat turned her leg to jelly. "Doesn't Gull Harbor run deep in your blood?"

"Maybe." She felt torn. His hand on her thigh didn't help. But she missed its comforting weight when he lifted it to shift gears.

"You're being so quiet."

"Guess I don't know where I belong right now." The unexpected truth brought an ache to her throat.

"You belong here." The warm hand was back on her knee. "With...well..."

She looked over. Finn's full lips tightened. Had he almost said "with me"?

His easy going smile returned. "I'll match you memory for memory as we drive up the road. How's that?"

"You're on." Anything to change the subject.

Finn went back to shifting, and she slid lower in her seat.

"Blue Plate Cafe," he called out, as they whipped past the restaurant. "Favorite thing on their menu?"

"Stuffed french toast." But the gooey apple stuffing was just a memory. "You?"

"The Chicago Hustle. It's got everything in it, remember? Eggs, bacon, onions."

"That's Kate's favorite. She ordered it every time our mom brought us there."

"Bet it's good to be home with your sister." He gave her a side glance. "You're lucky you have each other."

"We're not that close. Anymore."

"Why's that?"

"Hard to say. Things have shifted."

Silence fell. The wind whistled in her ears. "You've both grown up," Finn finally said. "Relationships change, right?"

"I guess so." Looking at the profile she wanted to trace with her fingers, she wondered about their own relationship. In high school, he'd been the nice guy who helped her with a class that was definitely over her head. Back then, nice didn't qualify as hot. Now when it came to Finn, nice felt very, very sexy.

"How about the Harbert Swedish bakery?" The man wasn't going to let up with this game. The brown frame structure came up on the left.

"Never went there. Too many calories. How about you?"

"Bring on the apple strudel. I never had to watch my weight and neither did you."

"Those were the days." Mercedes turned her attention to the dashboard. "Is that a CD player?"

"Right, a friend retrofitted my dashboard." He pressed a button. The smooth notes of a saxophone flowed over her, and she knew she was in trouble. Dressed in a navy V-neck sweater and khaki shorts, Finn looked wickedly handsome. And the best part? Unlike the New York men who knotted their Burberry scarves just so and used a ton of hair spray, Finn was totally unaware of himself.

"Look." He pointed to a sign. "Tabor Hill Winery. My folks always took me there."

"Prom night," she said without thinking. Had she even seen Finn at prom?

"And you went with Chuck."

"You sound disappointed."

He gave her a rueful smile. "You'll never know."

No, she wouldn't. Finn was fitting together pieces of her past, like stuff he'd carried in his pockets through the years. "It-it wasn't that much fun," she finally said. "The dinner was, I guess, but not the dance. The guys were sneaking back to the car to drink. So stupid."

"High school could be stupid. But we're adults now. Let's have dinner there some time. Watch the sun set over the vineyards.

Make new memories."

Making memories sounded like planning a future. An alarm sounded in her head. "Maybe."

Was he chuckling or was that the air rushing past? "Oh, Mercedes. I'm going to turn your *maybe* into a *yes*." With a devilish smile, he hit the accelerator. She held her breath when her back was pressed into the leather. To her relief, conversation became impossible.

When they reached St. Joe, Michigan, they found a parking spot on a side street and took off toward the bluff where the town had built a band shell. Perched above St. Joe's harbor, the small open stage gave a fabulous view of the lake. Her steps slowed as they approached. So much had changed since she'd last been here. A cool wind gusted over the water. Thank goodness she'd worn her green-striped sweater with her white jeans. Mercedes followed Finn into the seating area. "I remember coming up here to some art fair but this cute little stage? Is this new?"

Finn nodded. "Not exactly Broadway but the community supports the concert program. Very popular. St. Joe turned the old hotel into a senior living facility right behind us. They've done some great things to encourage tourism. The kind of efforts Cole and Gull Harbor are working on right now."

They settled onto the bench seats. "Kind of small but quaint...the band shell and everything."

"Quaint?" His forehead wrinkled.

"Lordy, you can be as sensitive as your sister." Did she have to watch every word?

Finn leaned forward, elbows on his knees. "Small doesn't always mean less, Mercedes. Sometimes small is good."

"I didn't say it wasn't." Time to bite her tongue.

Okay, the thought of Finn and her tongue made her crazy.

Their attention swerved to the front when a conductor took the stage and welcomed them. The band launched into a medley of oldies, from "The Very Thought of You" to "My Man, I love Him So."

The sun hovered on the edge of the horizon and they were here together. Didn't get more romantic than this. It could give a girl crazy ideas. She'd never had crazy ideas with Stephan. Together, they'd been very pragmatic, so this was all new territory. "I love these old songs," she said during a break when they wandered over to a refreshment stand.

"My parents play them all the time. Frank Sinatra, Nat King Cole. They love the classic oldies."

"Your folks must be near retirement. Are they going to stay in Michigan?"

He grinned. "As long as their grandchildren are in Gull Harbor, my parents will be here. How about some wine?"

She looked over the posted list. "Chardonnay would be great. I doubt that my mother will ever leave Gull Harbor either. She grew up here."

"A lot of folks like living where everyone knows them."

"Point taken."

Finn handed her the plastic cup, and she took a sip of wine from one of the local vineyards. "Is there a message there for me?"

"Not at all." The light in his eyes told her different.

"Sometimes I don't know how to take you. You confuse me."

"That's because you're trying to shove me into that box."

They were leaning against a railing that ran along a walkway. He stroked a strand of hair from her eyes and let his hand linger.

"Which box?" Her body wanted more of Finn's hand.

"The box marked *the past*. I'm not going to stay in your past, Mercedes. Deal with it."

Their eyes locked and her stomach plummeted. She had to look away from his determination and face some facts. "Break's over. We should probably take our seats." The musicians were filtering onto the stage and tuning their instruments. They followed the crowd back to their seats, glasses in hand.

Deal with it? His determination unnerved her. She was beginning to think Finn was serious. This wasn't another joke that they tossed back and forth while Mr. Daley scribbled formulas on the white board in class. During the music, they couldn't talk. One romantic tune after another filled the air. She could almost hear sighs among the couples who cuddled closer. Night fell, whispering across the lake while the street lamps came on. Boats rumbled slowly up the channel below, their running lights glowing in the darkness. It felt so natural when Finn draped an arm over her shoulders, and she leaned into his warmth. Maybe he was right. They might have different memories but they shared a lot of the past together.

"You've never seen my place," Finn said casually after the second encore.

"Your house? Guess I thought you might live with your folks."

She'd never given it a thought.

He barked out a laugh. "Give me a break. I built my own place. In fact, Cole designed it for me."

"Really?" All this time she'd pictured him in the home where he'd grown up, wherever that was. Maybe she *was* keeping him in that box. Finn Wheeler was frozen in time, a geeky guy who lived in a bedroom probably crammed with IT equipment in his parents' home.

Except he wasn't. Far from it.

Suddenly she was curious. "I'll bet it's beautiful."

"Come and see for yourself. I'd be interested in your opinion."

"Sounds good." Nerves skittered through her stomach. He took her hand, and they wandered along the bluff back to the car.

"Mercedes, have you been avoiding me since your sister's wedding? Feels like it. Are you unhappy about what happened?"

She studied her sandals, putting one foot in front of the other. "Hard question to answer."

"I thought we made progress."

She burst out laughing. "Is that what you call it?"

"What would *you* call it?"

"More like foreplay."

His thumb brushed the tops of her fingers. "Not if you don't want it to be. You hold all the cards, Mercedes."

His honesty amazed her. "Are you always so open about everything?"

"I just call things like I see them. You upset about the guy in New York?"

"Not really. Stephan and I, well, I don't know." Her uncertainty left her sad. But she tossed her head back. No sadness for her tonight.

"Was there a future with him?"

"I thought so." But the condo in New York and the house in the Hamptons would have just been buildings, not an enduring relationship. Seeing Kate and Cole together made Mercedes question what she'd had with Stephan.

They'd reached the car, and she was relieved to put this conversation behind her.

~.~

Like every little boy who grew up along Lake Michigan, Finn had learned to fish. His dad had taught him to be patient. With Mercedes, he was tossing out the line and letting it sit on the water, the red and white bobber rippling with the waves. He knew he had to give her space and time, which was why he hadn't suggested his place earlier. Finn wanted her full attention.

Maybe she was still mooning over the man who'd walked away. What kind of idiot would break up with Mercedes Kennedy? Not that Finn wasn't happy about it.

His Google search had turned up information about Stephan Forbes that infuriated him. Things he wasn't about to tell Mercedes. No matter what other people said, including his sister, she was sensitive, a girl who could be hurt. He wasn't that man.

The ride down the highway became quiet. He turned on his favorite music and soon Mercedes nodded off. Her head ended up on his shoulder. She looked exhausted. No one should have those lines around her eyes or lips. Even though he slowed down, the ride back to his place ended too soon.

"Hey, sleepyhead." Her skin felt so soft when he stroked her jawline. Probably the rest of her felt just like that. His mouth dried and he pulled his hand away.

She blinked and sat up, rubbing her eyes. "The music mellowed me out. Are we there?"

"Yep." He'd left the car out, and overhead a million stars studded the sky. Without city lights, so much more appeared across the inky canopy.

"Guess I needed that little nap." She stretched like a kitten, sending a wave of her perfume his way. She had no clue how sexy she was without even trying. Jumping out of the car, he came around.

She stared up at his house. "This is yours? It's huge."

Words any man would treasure. Taking her hand, he led her up the back steps. "Too big for you, huh?"

"Sorry, Finn. I wasn't expecting this." Distracted, she tripped. He had her in a second.

"Watch your step, pretty girl."

Her huge green eyes turned his way. "Oh, I sure will."

He wanted to kiss her. Hell, he wanted to do a lot more than that.

But he left that fishing line in the water.

With the outside lights on, the place looked pretty good. They kept climbing the stone steps until they reached the lawn.

"So Cole built this?"

"Yep, with a guy he knew from Chicago. I wanted the place to be open and modern with lots of windows. A lot of the cottages are older and boxed in with small windows. Let's go in the front door." He wanted her to get the full effect of the wall of glass that faced the lake.

Her eyes grew as they rounded the corner of the house. "This is no cottage."

Chuckling under his breath, he clicked a button on his key ring and the door unlocked. "I never said it was." Inside, he'd left a light on over the sink. The dark granite, stainless light fixtures and copper pans gleamed.

"No privacy right?" She looked from the sink to the wall of windows and frowned.

"Who's going to see me? People out on their boats?"

"Maybe." Her head swiveled. "Look at all the TVs."

"Football season and then basketball. I like to flip between games."

She studied him. "That was always the way your mind worked, wasn't it?"

"What do you mean?" He hated to be categorized.

"Multi-tasking. You always seemed to have a million things going on in your head."

"That's like the pot calling the kettle black, Mercedes."

She was so pretty when she blushed. "I guess so."

Wiggy and Elvis came barreling down the stairs. But when they realized food was not involved, they went right back up.

"Time for a tour. That area to the right with the three TV screens is the living room area. Dining room to the left."

"Modern furniture." She ran a hand over one of the black leather chairs pulled up to a glass table. At either end of the lower level, a stairway led upstairs. Swallowing hard, she turned her attention back to the kitchen. "Very nice."

"How about some wine?" He cracked open the huge wine cooler that was part of the kitchen island.

"Sounds lovely." She wandered into the living room area. "Are the coloring books on your coffee table for Lindsay's girls?"

"Yep, I babysit for Rebecca and Susan sometimes."

He uncorked the bottle, took two glasses from a cabinet and poured.

"Hmm, women must love to visit."

"I don't bring many women here," he admitted, handing her a glass of wine.

"Except Lindsay, I suppose. Does she clean your house?"

"No, she does not. I want her relaxing when she visits."

Mercedes was studying him like they'd just met. "I'm sorry that your sister and I haven't hit it off." That was putting it mildly.

Settling onto the sofa, Mercedes kicked off her sandals and folded her legs under her. "I think I make her mad."

He chuckled. "That's an understatement. You two are quite a pair."

"I guess she hates me now." She looked so sad.

"Not really." How could he explain this without hurting either one of them? "You've had a life Lindsay can only imagine. Starting your own business in an exciting city. Your life sounds glamorous to my sister. She's had heartbreak."

"Do you think I haven't known crushing disappointment?" Mercedes blinked those gorgeous green eyes. Maybe he'd said too much.

Putting down his wine, he opened his arms. "Come here."

Hesitating for only a second, she set her glass on a stone coaster and curled up in his arms. Her hair smelled like apples, wild and fresh. He kissed the top of her head. "In my experience, projects work better when you add other people to the mix. That's all I'm saying. Now can we forget it?"

Her long, creamy neck was so tempting. Dipping his head, he kissed it. Once. Twice.

Hands tightening in his hair, she trembled. "Do you..."

"What?" He flicked his tongue in the soft hollow at the base of her throat.

"Know..."

He groaned. "Please don't tell me no, Mercedes."

Her eyes were squeezed tight. "No. I mean do you *know* what you're doing?"

"Of course." Now where was he? That pulse point on her throat. "Yes, I do."

"Good." She cuddled up in his lap like a kitten.

"Let's not overthink it." Her lips begged to be kissed. Dipping his head, he started slow. Soft and sweet, her lips parted.

"Finn... I..."

"Your skin is so soft." He ran his hands up her arms. She was shaking. "Hey, pretty girl, what's this?"

The pleading in her eyes really got to him. "Finn, I just...want to be here with you."

"Well, okay. Don't look so surprised. You'll hurt my feelings."

"Oh, I'd never want to do that. I mean tonight." She patted the sofa. "I just want to be here. No overanalyzing what we're doing or how we feel."

"Works for me." He'd add those details later. She wound her arms around his neck, bringing everything closer. Even with his eyes closed, he knew just how she looked and felt. Her curves, her warmth, her soft breath on his face. The black leather didn't squeak when he stretched out, pulling her down on top of him, all long legs and fragrant hair. "You are so sweet."

"Oh, Finn." When he slipped his hands under her sweater, she groaned. Pushing herself, she smiled and dropped kisses from his forehead to his chin.

Her lips clung like warm wax. He liked it. "So I guess this means you had fun at the concert?"

"I had fun with you," she whispered before nipping his ear lobe.

"I'm glad." His hands found the tight muscles in her shoulders. "Let yourself go, babe."

With a whispered sigh, her body loosened. She became clay and he molded her body to his, taking care where it mattered most. Throwing back her head, she let him explore. Her skin felt like silk.

"You are so soft," he whispered, cupping her fullness in his hands and brushing his thumbs against the tips.

She was back to trembling.

He tugged at her sweater. "Too much stuff getting in the way."

Soon clothes littered the floor. Good thing Elvis and Wiggy had scampered off.

He'd turned off all the lights. With the glass walls and skylights, moonlight bathed her body. She was so beautiful. "Look at you. Don't lose a pound, okay?"

"I've been eating too much." She stiffened.

His hand followed the curve of her hip bone. "You're perfect."

"And you're deranged." But a smile tilted her lips.

"Come on. Let's get comfortable." Taking her hand, he led her to the stairway. She'd made up her mind. That was Mercedes. Nothing coy or stupid. Decide it and do it.

They started up. "But Finn...?"

"So there *is* a but?" Disappointment tightened his throat. "Out with it, Mercedes."

When she bit her bottom lip, his imagination felt the nip of those lips. But only if she were willing. "You know I'm, well, leaving, right? You know this isn't really anything."

Heat surged into his cheeks. This *was* something, dammit. Guess it was up to him to help her see that. "Yes, I hear you. Now, come."

"Race you up the stairs." Her backside gave him quite a view.

Chapter 15

The following afternoon Kate and Connor burst into the kitchen with Natalie and Priscilla trailing behind them. The newlyweds grinned at each other like kids. Still feeling the glow from her date with Finn, Mercedes waited to hear about the honeymoon.

"Welcome home, you two. How was Mackinac Island?" Mom gave them both a big hug as they all stood in the kitchen. Prissy sniffed the tarragon chicken baking in the oven.

"Mackinac was wonderful. Just fabulous." Kate curled into Cole's side and he kissed the tip of her nose. The gesture was something Finn would do, and Mercedes was flooded with memories of last night.

"Enough of this lovey dovey stuff. I'm going to watch TV. Come on, Prissy." Natalie marched into the next room with the Great Dane trailing behind her.

"Natalie's ticked that she didn't get to go on a honeymoon," Cole said in a stage whisper.

"Oh, for heaven's sake." Mom picked up her potato peeler. "She'll get over it."

While Cole went to join Natalie and Prissy in the front room, Kate talked endlessly about how good the fudge was up in Mackinac.

"Right, so you two spent the whole week in the fudge shops?" Mercedes asked. Mom shushed her and handed Kate a bunch of parsley.

"And we biked around the island." Grabbing a knife, Kate began to chop and Mercedes hoped she didn't hurt herself.

"Glad you fit that into your schedule," Mercedes teased. Seeing Kate so happy gave her hope. She'd been a mess when she came home to Gull Harbor in the spring. Mercedes could hear it in her sister's voice every time she called home. Then she ran into Cole and things happened fast. Mercedes began to snap the ends off a pile of beans and threw them into a pot.

"Your sister's starting a new business," their mother announced to Kate.

"No kidding. How cool is that? What are you going to do?" Kate popped the parsley potatoes into the oven.

Mercedes kept her head down and put the pan of beans on the stove. "Property management. Lindsay cleans a lot of cottages, but I think there's a real opportunity to list rental homes. From what I can see, there are a couple national companies offering beach rentals but no local company getting a piece of that pie."

Opening the oven door, Mom eyed the chicken. "You always were so smart, Mercedes."

The unexpected compliment took her by surprise. Lately, all she heard about was Kate. Kate and Cole. Kate and Natalie. "Thanks, Mom. But I'm a long way from launching."

"When do you think you'll have it up and running?" Kate took the chicken from the oven, and Mom began to make the gravy. "I'll send out some press releases. Get it on the Gull Harbor website."

"I'd like to have it up before the holidays. It's too late to list houses for the Notre Dame games. But maybe we'll be ready for cross country skiing season."

"We? So Lindsay will be involved."

"Hopefully. Lindsay and Finn."

"Ah, hah." Jubilation rang in Kate's voice. "So I guess this means you'll be around for a while?"

"For a while." Mercedes kept her tone breezy. She saw Mom exchange a look with Kate.

"Finn seems like such a nice young man," her mother said, sprinkling salt and pepper into the bubbling gravy.

"Yes. Yes, he is."

"If you're seeing him, he probably wants you here, right? Not a thousand miles away in the big city."

"I'm not really seeing him." Even to her own ear, that comment felt lame. Lame and disloyal, especially after last night.

"Nonsense, Mercedes." Mom shook a closed jam jar that held water and flour to thicken the gravy. "You were out awfully late last night."

While Kate roared, Mercedes felt her face flame. Was nothing a secret around here? "Where are you going to base your business?" her sister asked, grabbing the silverware from the drawer.

"Right here. The wonder of the Internet." Mercedes swept one hand toward the round kitchen table.

"You could camp out in the PR office." Kate took the dinner plates from the cupboard. "No one would mind."

"I hate to put you out." But Mercedes had already considered setting up shop in the empty store. She had mixed feelings about it. Did she want her younger sister looking over her shoulder? But Finn's words came back to her. She might need all the help she could get.

"Tons of room there." Kate waved a reassuring hand. "You'd be fine. Besides, I'd like the company."

Mom grabbed a gravy boat from the cupboard. "Girls, why don't you set the table."

"Girls," Mercedes mouthed to Kate.

"And why do I feel as if I'm still sixteen when I'm in this house," Mercedes mumbled as she passed Kate.

Later as they sat around the farm table, Cole and Kate told them all about Mackinac Island, as if they hadn't been there ten times. Stretched out under the table, Prissy nudged her knees for scraps. Mercedes was happy to sneak chicken to the dog.

"Next time you have to take me." Natalie pouted, pulling at one blonde braid. She looked so much like her mother Samantha, who had been a beauty in high school. Kate really had her hands full there and Mercedes didn't envy her. Did marriage ever come without complications, especially the second time around?

"Maybe next summer we'll schedule a Mackinac trip for all of us. The whole family," Kate offered. Her sister had a generous way about her. Did a man do that to a woman? Mercedes' mind definitely wasn't on dessert as she cleared the table. A warm flush heated her body when she thought of Finn last night. Where had he learned to do, well, the things he did so gently, so lovingly?

"Hey, what are you blushing about?" Kate asked, scraping the dishes clean before plunking them in the sudsy water. "How is Finn?"

"He's fine." She had no control over the silly smile spreading across her face. Ducking her head, Mercedes opened the refrigerator and took out chocolate silk pie her mother had made it the night before.

"From that smile on your face, I'd say he's a lot more than fine."

Picking up a knife, Mercedes began to slice the pie. "He's, ah, going to help me with the website for my business."

"Excellent. He's talented. But I guess you know that."

Mercedes gave a dazed nod. "Yeah, he knows that IT business all right."

Kate turned in the doorway, pie in hand. "He's lot more than that, Mercedes. Finn Wheeler is not one to brag, but he's developed at least two companies. Both involved security, and I hear he sold them for tons of money. Cole thinks he's a genius."

Why hadn't he told her? Maybe Finn hadn't been so honest with her after all. Or had she been so busy with her own problems that she'd never asked him? A cold hand closed around her heart.

~.~

The following week Mercedes met with Lindsay at Rosie's Breakfast Club. Convincing Finn's sister to come hadn't been easy. Lindsay had a big chip on her shoulder, maybe with reason, considering her loss. The sizzle and smell of hash browns and bacon made her stomach growl as she took a booth. Lindsay came in shortly, looking disheveled and out of breath.

"Good morning." Mercedes dug deep for her cheery tone. "Windy out there this morning, isn't it?"

Lindsay snatched a ballpoint from the spine of a notebook. "Why don't we just get down to business?"

So much for a friendly chat. "How about some coffee?" Mercedes motioned to a waitress.

"I've already had mine but sure. Hey, Susie." Lindsay smiled at the petite waitress with a bouncy ponytail.

"Decaf like always?"

"You bet." The girl left and Lindsay's lips returned to a thin line.

Mercedes was having second thoughts about this venture. Remembering Finn's advice, she handed Lindsay a copy of her project plan. "Here's the breakdown of what I see happening. We need to do a mailing, put up a website..." The list was long. Lindsay studied the chart while Mercedes walked her through the plan.

Susie came and went, but the steaming coffee mugs sat untouched.

Feeling unnerved by Lindsay's lack of response, Mercedes finally came to a halt. Time for some caffeine and she hooked her mug. The first sip seared her tongue and she grabbed her ice water. Lindsay lifted charcoal briquette eyes. "What makes you think you'll get all this done before Christmas?"

"F-Finn says he can get the site up and running by then," Mercedes said. Cripes. Even she heard her voice soften on Finn's name. "If we're functional by Thanksgiving, that would be great."

Lindsay's face reddened. "What's your hurry?"

Mercedes' burning tongue began to swell. "I'm a get-it-done person?" She wasn't about to tell Lindsay that she needed everything to be functional and successful by spring, so she could divest this little venture for a tidy profit. She'd leave Gull Harbor and temperamental girls like Lindsay behind.

The thought didn't bring its usual satisfaction.

With hands rough and red from all the cleaning, Lindsay lifted her coffee and took a gulp that made Mercedes' mouth throb in sympathy. The girl never flinched. Ripping open a creamer, Mercedes emptied it into her coffee.

"Don't hurt my brother. I'm warning you." The comment came out of nowhere. Mercedes stopped stirring, her coffee now a soft, diluted brown.

"Why would I ever do that?"

"I'm just warning you. You've got a hold on my brother. I don't know why."

"What, you think I'm not good enough for him?"

"I think you're not permanent enough for him. I do not want him hurt." The words snapped across the booth, and Lindsay's jaw jutted out. Mercedes thought she'd be sick.

"Let's get one thing straight." Leaning forward, she tapped the plan on the table between them. "What we're doing together? It has nothing to do with your brother. You gave me a job a couple weeks back. I appreciated it and I'm happy to include you, *if* we get along. To be honest, I can't work with an attitude."

Her own words almost cracked her up. All her life, people had accused her of having an attitude. Now it was her turn to blush. Settling back, she broke her stir stick neatly in two. "The business will belong to me. I'm happy to include the cleaning component. But technically, the company I intend to form will be in my name. We can work from the PR office in town. My sister is based there." Didn't that sound grand? Like that bare-bones office came with leather chairs, gleaming desks and lake vistas.

"Fine." Lindsay jumped up out of that booth so fast she tripped. Mercedes reached out a steadying hand but Lindsay twisted away. "When do we start?"

"Day after tomorrow?"

"See you then." Swinging her purse over her shoulder, Lindsay wheeled around and left. The door shuddered behind her, she closed it so hard. Mercedes slumped back into the booth. Every eye in the place turned her way as she fingered her mug and exhaled. What the heck had she gotten herself into?

Chapter 16

The chilly autumn air had turned Mercedes' cheeks the prettiest pink. Finn nearly fell off the ladder just looking at her. Reaching down, he dropped a Macintosh apple into her basket. His hand lingered, wanting to brush away the strand of hair caught on her peach lipstick. Just last night that hair had swept his chest. Finn's stomach clenched. Focusing, he twisted another apple from the tree and jumped down.

"When I was growing up, we would go apple picking. All four of us." Mercedes' voice was filled with childlike wonder. He imagined her as a little girl and hoped one day she'd show him some pictures.

"Sounds like fun." Finn took a bite of the apple, chewed a bit and then kissed her.

"It was." She nudged his nose with hers, the way Wiggy did with Elvis sometimes. "We would make pies. Every winter our freezer was packed. My father loved it."

"Sounds like you had some good times with your dad."

Mercedes shook her head. "Not nearly enough. Kate was the one who hung out in the back shed with our dad. She was our fixer. But he wouldn't be fixed."

If she gripped that shiny apple any tighter, it would be mush.

Finn carefully took it from her hand and placed in the basket. He hated to see competent Mercedes looking like a lost little girl and pulled her into his arms. "That's all in the past, okay?"

"Thought you didn't want me to forget the past."

"Some parts. Let go of the sad things, okay?"

With a soft sigh, Mercedes snugged her arms around his waist. Smoothing back her hair, he felt stupid for bringing up something so painful. He was still peeling back the layers of her life, the things he hadn't seen in high school. A reckless breeze rattled the branches above them. "Didn't mean to hurt you, Mercedes. Guess I was living my own life back then."

But she'd been a part of that life. The dream part, although she didn't know it. Were the problems at home the reason Mercedes would stare off into space in class? Her dazed expression had always irritated him. He'd thought she was daydreaming about Chuck Lindner and his red jeep. Finn imagined Mercedes and Chuck doing all kinds of stuff in the sporty vehicle his father had bought for his son's sixteenth birthday.

Mercedes ran her hands down his navy jacket. "How could you know? My father always had a smile on his face, right? But he never even went to a game when I was a cheerleader. My mother would sit in the bleachers with Kate, yelling until she had no voice."

"Trying to make up for him?"

"Always."

A chilly wind rustled the branches overhead. Looking up, Finn scanned the dark clouds moving across the sky. "Guess we should get back to the picking. We don't want to get caught in the rain."

He handed her the basket. "You going to make me a pie?"

Mercedes hooted. "I'm not a baker. My mother, on the other hand, will be happy to bake for you. She's come under your spell."

Good thing this was a weekday and they were the only pickers in the orchard. With her green turtleneck snugged up around her neck and her hair blown about on a gust of wind, Mercedes Kennedy was gorgeous. The basket of apples lay forgotten on the grass while he kissed her again.

"You taste like apples," she whispered.

"You smell like the breeze."

"What?" Laughing, she glanced up and her eyes felt like a caress.

"Hey, I don't know where those words came from. You do crazy things to me." But he did have a question. "What about you? Are you coming under my spell?"

The question seemed to surprise her. Maybe that was the only way to win. Catch her unaware. Right now she was thinking. He traced a finger down the frown between her eyes.

"Let's just say you ruin my concentration." She could be so serious. "I'm trying to get a business together."

"And I'm trying to get your website ready. We're in this together, right?"

"You don't have to spend so much time on this project, Finn."

Better come clean. "Listen, I farmed it out. Hate to admit it, but I'm working on a deal that should earn me big bucks, so I let someone else take it on. I call it encouraging the economy."

She pulled back and her frown deepened. "Then shouldn't I pay that person?"

Finn was sorry he'd brought this up. "No. Absolutely not." Mercedes had slipped into her business mode and he didn't want that. He knew her financial situation, although she'd given no details. "Let's just say your credit's good with me."

She shivered, pulling her head into her turtleneck. "All right. But I want to keep track of any expenses you have because of me."

Yep. Business mode and as long as they were there, he'd bring up a very delicate subject. "I wish you and Lindsay got along better. Together you could knock this ball out of the park."

"But it's my idea." She stiffened.

He cupped her soft cheek in one hand. "Lighten up, okay? This isn't New York. This is Gull Harbor and we're the folks you grew up with, not some Manhattan shark trying to cheat you."

Wrong words. He groaned when she twisted from his arms, grabbed the basket and began snapping apples from the nearest tree. Poor tree. Unable to reach them, she jumped up, yanking at the branches.

"I'll get those for you." He moved the ladder over.

"I can do it myself." She marched on to the next tree. He followed.

Sometimes it wasn't a good idea to push Mercedes. He'd seen that in school. She came around in her own time. Now he trailed behind her, helping where he could. Three apple trees later, she turned and sighed. "I'm sorry, Finn." Her eyes darkened like Lake Michigan on a rainy day.

"Oh, Mercedes. What am I going to do with you?"

She tipped up her beautiful nose. "You don't have to do anything with me. I'll do it myself."

"That's silly. What are we talking about here?"

"You asked me to include Lindsay, so I tried but she's not cooperating. I just wanted you to like me." The final words were whispered, and tears brimmed in her eyes.

"Sweetheart. Mercedes. I don't like you... I..." But something in her eyes made him stop. This was way too soon. His sophisticated Manhattan woman swiped at her nose with the sleeve of her sweater. Finn burst out laughing.

"What? What?" She jabbed his chest with one finger. Frustrated tears trembled in her eyes.

"Nothing. You just make me laugh. Sometimes I can't believe the things you say."

"Me neither. What is wrong with me, Finn? Sometimes I can't even believe the things I say myself."

He tried to brush the tears away with his fingers. "There's honesty in your words. I respect that. You're more softhearted than you think."

She made a raspberry with her lips, and suddenly they were back in high school. "Softhearted? Me? You don't know what you're talking about."

"I know you're kind and thoughtful."

"You're dreaming, mister." She blinked up at him.

"You don't remember, do you?" He pulled back a bit but his hands stayed snug at her waist.

Mercedes looked mystified. She really didn't remember? When

she ran one hand over his chin, his mind emptied and his body roared to life. "No, Finn. I have no idea what you're talking about."

"Remember that time under the bleachers? You were coming from cheerleading practice. Billy Kramer and some of the other guys were at it again."

Her lips pursed, like she was thinking back. Then she shook her head. "They could be creeps. I was tired of it."

"Billy was about to beat the crap out of me. I wouldn't tell him what had been on the calculus test. He had the class third period and I'd taken it first. The guy was dumb as a box of rocks and ditched class all the time."

"You mean our current mayor?" She laughed and he joined in.

"One and the same. Like most guys, he grew up. Actually apologized to me one day. Anyway, you were breezing by when you saw us. 'Billy,' you said, 'what do you think you're doing with my chemistry partner?' " He loved remembering that moment. It was so Mercedes Kennedy. Her green eyes lightened and she chuckled softly.

"Sudden change of attitude with Billy and his two friends. They were not about to gang up on me. I hightailed it out of there."

The whole thing was so ludicrous. That moment had stayed in his mind all this time. Finn started to play with her hair. "How did those guys know I'd become the town's major donor?"

Tucked in his arms, she became very still. His hand fell from her curls. Was he being an idiot? Had he just shot his mouth off like some of the other tech millionaires he didn't respect?

"I didn't know that myself, Finn." Suddenly Mercedes felt

distant. "Not that it would've made one bit of difference. Billy was a linebacker and he was trying hard to stay on the team. But that doesn't make what they did right."

"You saved me and after that, they left me alone." He almost hated to admit it.

"Aw, you could have taken care of it yourself." Eyes thoughtful, she twisted a curl around her finger. "They could be stupid. You were always so smart, Finn. Maybe back then they knew you were way out of their league."

What a revelation. "You think that mattered? I thought they were ticked because I didn't play football or even run track."

"Trust me. It mattered." A small grin danced across her lips. "You bopped down the halls with your earbuds, jiving to your own music. It was like the teachers couldn't even touch you. You were their AV guy, their ace in the hole. The guys must have hated that."

Really? "I never thought of it that way."

"I like the fact that you're different."

"And I like the fact that you don't know how kind you are."

She touched her forehead to his. "You say the sweetest things."

His mind filled with the words he wanted to tell her. Every day. Morning, noon and night. But this wasn't the time or the place. Suddenly he felt hungry for more than apples. "You know what an afternoon delight is?"

She gave a soft gasp and smiled. "I think so, but I've never done it." Her eyes turned to warm moss.

Taking her hand, he grabbed the basket with the other. "Glad I could be first for something. Come on."

Chapter 17

Mercedes stood in the kitchen getting her notes together before meeting Lindsay. Outside, the sun was shining on a crisp fall day when she heard a vehicle rumble down the driveway. Didn't sound like Finn's car and she peeked through the white eyelet curtains. Kate hopped out of Cole's green truck, Natalie and Prissy right behind her. My word, Kate looked so beautiful with her cheeks flushed. Was it that cold outside? Mercedes opened the door. "Hi, stranger."

"Got news for you!" Natalie burst out.

"Where's Mom?" Kate asked, eyes sparkling.

"Yeah, where's Alice?" Natalie echoed and then glanced up at Kate. "Sorry, Kate. I know my dad says I'm not supposed to call her Alice."

"Did I hear my name?" Mom came dancing through the door in a new teal blue outfit. Plastic peacocks dangled from her ears. "Why, Katie. What is it?"

Kate threw out her arms. "I'm pregnant."

"That's wonderful!" Mercedes felt dizzy with delight. Mom looked like she might faint. All hell broke loose. Natalie chattered about having a baby sister to play dressups.

"But we don't know about that, honey," Kate gently reminded

her stepdaughter.

"My goodness, you know already?" Mom was counting on her fingers.

"Yep. Those pregnancy tests are accurate in a matter of days." Leaning against the sink, Kate looked pleased with herself. "I took a pregnancy test and bingo."

Mom hugged Kate tight, and Mercedes felt tears in her own eyes. "Oh, my. Isn't this wonderful? We'll have to have a baby shower."

How amazing to hug her sister and know she really had her arms around two people.

"When do you think you're due?" Mom glanced at the calendar hanging next to the refrigerator.

Kate just shook her head. "Next summer I guess. I mean it just happened."

"It just happened." Natalie beamed.

Not wanting to be late for her meeting, Mercedes crammed her notebook into her tote. "Hate to leave but I have an appointment. See you later and congratulations, Kate."

As she dashed out to her car, she could hear her mother and Kate talking about a baby shower. Good grief, gifts from the last bridal shower were still stacked on Kate's old bed. This all seemed to be happening too quickly, although her sister was twenty-eight. Or was it her own life moving to a slower beat? Slinging her tote into the front seat, Mercedes got in her car and took off. The black Mercedes lurched over gnarled roots in the driveway, reminding her of the bumps in her own life.

A baby. Kate would have her own family. Her life had come together.

Oh, she was happy for her sister. But never had Mercedes felt so alone. In New York, the pace had kept her so busy, she never had time to think. Here in Gull Harbor, the soft summer nights gave her too much time to think about her life. Questions started to surface. Where was she going? What would make her happy?

Lately, she'd started to wonder where Finn fit in all this. She couldn't imagine life without him. The night before they'd gone to Weko Beach. Every evening two veterans played taps on the dunes as the sun set. Dressed in jeans and sweatshirts, Mercedes and Finn had stretched out on a blanket, his arm around her.

Mercedes always felt so safe with Finn. His easy-going confidence buffered her from the world. How would she feel back in some apartment in Manhattan? She pictured a stark empty room, a messy desk and a computer that would occupy a lot of her time. Would the excitement of some new business fill her life? Or would she think back to these special times with Finn?

She didn't have an answer.

As she drove toward The Blue Plate Cafe to meet Lindsay, uncertainty fluttered in Mercedes' stomach. She couldn't face another tense showdown. Mercedes had purposely chosen the cozy eatery along Red Arrow so there would be no reminders of Rosie's. Was Finn right? Could she accomplish more with Lindsay than if she took on the project alone? Mercedes wasn't so sure. She wasn't good at relying on other people. It felt like she was venturing out onto the ice floes that banked the frigid shore every winter. As kids, they'd played a dangerous game, taunting each other and listening for the faint crack of ice under their boots before scurrying back to shore. She felt the same now with Lindsay.

Just a few cars were parked in front of the Blue Plate when she pulled up alongside Lindsay's old family sedan. Mercedes sat there for a minute, hands in her lap. They were so different. How could they possibly be a team? Squaring her shoulders, she grabbed her tote. No matter how uncomfortable this situation was, she wasn't going to disappoint Finn.

The smell of fresh bread and pastries greeted her when Mercedes pushed through the door. Her stomach growled. Lately, Finn was always waving food in front of her. With his huge appetite, the man could be persuasive. She'd rediscovered the wonder of fresh salads, grainy breads and even a thick steak, although Finn preferred chicken or blackened salmon. Some days her poor stomach yowled like a hungry beast, awakened from a long sleep. The cookies on display at the reception counter looked mighty good.

"I'm meeting a friend," she told the girl at the front desk. *Friend?* Well, that was a stretch but she sure hoped they could work out any differences.

Lindsay was studying the menu at a back table when Mercedes pulled out a chair across from her. "Good morning."

"Hi, Mercedes." Looking up, Finn's sister smiled. Mercedes' stomach settled a bit and she reached for a menu.

The waitress came over. "Coffee," Mercedes told her, skimming the breakfast offerings. "Two eggs over easy, grapefruit and a blueberry muffin."

"Not me," Lindsay said with a dry chuckle. "Orange juice, of course. Then I'll have the French toast with one egg on the side, over easy. Got have your protein. Right, Sheila?"

"That's what you always say, Lindsay." Scrawling on a small pad, the girl bobbed her head.

"Do you know every waitress in Gull Harbor?" Mercedes asked as the girl walked away, her dark ponytail swinging.

"Everybody knows each other in Gull Harbor," Lindsay said pointedly.

Biting back a sharp retort, Mercedes opened her notebook. "Look, I'm sorry our last meeting didn't go so well. I'm hoping we can work on this together. The project could benefit both of us."

Lindsay's lips twisted. "Spoken like my brother."

Mercedes knit her fingers together so tight they hurt. "Finn has good business sense, I guess."

"You *guess* he has business sense?" Lindsay's eyes widened. "Mercedes, don't sell my brother short."

Flipping her notebook to a fresh page, Mercedes frowned. "I'm not. After all, we've known each other since high school."

"I mean today, Mercedes." Lindsay thumped her fingers on the table. She could use a manicure but then so could Mercedes. "For the past eight years, Finn has been developing and then selling tech companies. The last one went for way over seven figures, not that you need to know that."

Lindsay had Mercedes' full attention. The floor seemed to shift beneath her chair. Why hadn't she heard all this from Finn? "At first I thought he was the local IT guy but Kate clued me in. And of course he owns that restaurant."

"How do you think he renovated that building? Design like that doesn't grow on trees, not in Gull Harbor." Sheila had brought the orange juice and coffee. Mercedes had a minute to gather her composure. Her thoughts spun. Had she been so wound up in her need to get back to New York that she hadn't really appreciated Finn? The possibility nauseated her.

Across from her, Lindsay sat, waiting to pounce. "Now you'll probably hunt him down like every other woman. Shouldn't be too hard. He's really into you."

The words turned in her chest like a knife. "Look, Lindsay, we're here to talk about business, not your brother."

Lindsay sucked in her cheeks. Grabbing two packets of sugar, she dumped them into her coffee.

Mercedes took a sip of coffee The acidity didn't do her stomach any good. Had she underestimated Finn? That thought didn't sit well and she tried to focus on her notes. "I thought we'd begin with a Facebook page, establish a Twitter presence and develop a website with booking capabilities. Then a mailing and some targeted ads. Although it might be too late to book for the Notre Dame games, we might be up and running for the holidays, right?" She sure hoped so.

"Maybe. We can try."

Hardly the words of an enthusiastic partner.

"We can start with my mailing lists." Digging around in a quilted handbag that looked handmade, Lindsay pulled out some papers stapled together and smoothed them onto the table.

Mercedes eyed the messy pile. Maybe Lindsay would be a help after all. Her list was a critical starting point.

For the next hour, they brainstormed. Some of Finn's Internet smarts must've rubbed off on Lindsay. She knew a lot about search terms and online advertising. Things were looking up.

"I'll ask the shop owners if they have any email lists," Lindsay said as they tossed ideas back and forth. "A lot of them ask people for contact information. The bed and breakfasts too, along with the restaurants."

"Sounds great."

Lindsay's French toast had arrived, along with the eggs. "That smells heavenly." Mercedes sniffed the air.

"It's the cinnamon," Sheila told them both, sliding the heavy plates onto the table. "I put on at least five pounds since I started working here at the beginning of the summer."

"Sure you don't want one? Just a taste?" Lindsay cut off a corner of the French toast, speared it and then handed Mercedes the fork.

"Why not. Thanks." Taking the fork, Mercedes dipped the small piece in the powdered sugar and syrup before popping it in her mouth. The sweetness sprang to life. Her own order sat in front of her but she couldn't pass this up. "Oh, this is delicious. Sheila, could I have an order? Just one piece, please."

She could hardly believe she'd said that. In her mind, she pushed those size two clothes to the corner of her closet.

"And Sheila," Lindsay said as the girl turned to walk away.

"You think you can give us your email list of customers? We're starting a new business and we could use some customer contacts."

"Sure. I'll ask Ned, the owner. I don't think he'll have a problem with it. Be right back with the french toast," she said to Mercedes.

"Great move, Lindsay." Mercedes viewed her business partner with new respect.

"It's what people do for each other here." Lindsay doused the golden-edged french toast with a generous serving of syrup. "We help each other out."

"What was it like for you growing up in Gull Harbor?" Mercedes asked as she nibbled her blueberry muffin. "I'm sorry but I don't remember…"

Lindsay snorted. "Why would you remember me? I was a lowly freshman, and you were a senior. The girl who had everything, including my brother's undying devotion."

"How did you know that?" Mercedes pretended to work on her eggs and grapefruit but her ears were tuned to Lindsay.

"Finn swore me to secrecy when I saw your senior graduation photo on his bulletin board, hanging right next to his favorite picture of Steve Jobs."

She set her fork down. "You're kidding, right?"

"Wish I were." The words made Mercedes wonder. Was Lindsay protecting her brother, the way she'd often protected Kate?

"I didn't know. High school was so long ago." How had she missed all that?

"For some people." Lindsay stabbed her fork at Mercedes. "Most guys get over their high school crush, especially when she moves away. Finn didn't. That's why I'm saying, take my brother seriously."

"Well, I-I am." *Wasn't she?*

"For years after he graduated from MIT, my parents asked Finn when he was going to find a nice girl and settle down."

"Wasn't he dating?" Mercedes had to fill in the blanks.

"Sure but no one lasted." Lindsay's forehead puckered. "It was weird. Made me wonder if you were still on his mind."

It made Mercedes wonder, too. The anonymous Facebook friend she never confirmed because there was no picture. The daytime phone calls that left no messages. "I did get calls, not enough to make me nervous but some calls. Guys get over crushes, right?"

"Not my brother." Lindsay Wheeler was dead serious, and that put a different spin on things. Was Mercedes being careless with Finn? She didn't want to ever hurt him, but with every day her confusion deepened. Finn didn't press her but the message was clear. He wanted her to stay here, in Gull Harbor. That had never been Mercedes' plan.

The silence seemed to swell with her own embarrassment. She cleared her throat. "How about you, Lindsay? Did you meet your husband in high school?"

Lindsay's eyes softened. "Oh, Rich and I went way back. He sent me this really fancy valentine in third grade. Too much glue on doilies dotted with those candy hearts. Corny but cute, know what

I'm saying? We got married right out of high school. He joined the Marines as soon as he could." She lifted those big gray eyes—eyes that reminded Mercedes so much of her brother. "The truth? I hardly remember what it was like to be married. Sure, we had a family but Rich wasn't really there for the important things. I don't know what I would have done without Finn. He was even my Lamaze coach when I had Susan."

"I'm so sorry." She felt like hugging Lindsay instead of strangling her.

Pushing her plate to the edge of the table, Lindsay reached for her notes. "So what are you going to call the company?"

"Do you have any ideas?"

Lindsay's lips tweaked up. "Something about the lake, maybe? Beach Rentals."

"Lake Rentals. Flip-Flop Time. Beach Vacations." Mercedes joined in, and they tossed names back and forth like beach balls until the mood lifted with their laughter. Maybe this could work. When the bill came, Mercedes snapped it up. "I have it."

Lindsay tossed a credit card onto the tray. "Let's split it this time."

Chapter 18

She'd always done well under pressure. Now Mercedes threw herself into mapping out a website and writing the mailer. Anything to keep her busy. Deep inside, she knew she had to come to a decision about Finn. She didn't want to blindside him the way Stephan had treated her. But she couldn't find the words. "You see, Finn. This just won't work, not long term…" or "The city is my life. I have to go back." But her feeble attempts in front of a mirror felt like a lie.

So she threw herself into organizing her office space. Mercedes was going to take Kate up on her offer but unlike her sister, she needed a fundamental order. Everything in its place. "Okay if I come down to the office?" she asked Kate the following Sunday after they finished with dinner. "I want to set up shop."

"Excellent. It'll be nice having company." Kate had picked at her roast beef all through dinner and was looking queasy. "I'm there most days."

"Can I come too?" Natalie asked, plucking at Kate's sweater. Since the baby announcement, Natalie clung to Kate, asking every day if the baby was "done" yet.

"She thinks I have a cake inside, instead of a baby," Kate told Mercedes. They laughed, but it was sweet. Must be nice to have a stepdaughter who adored you and wanted to spend time together.

Now Kate reached over and smoothed Natalie's long blonde curls. "Sorry, you can't come. You're in school. Besides, Mercedes and I have work to do."

Natalie pulled a frown until their mother piped up. "Chocolate chip cake in the kitchen when everyone's ready."

That got Natalie's attention fast. "Oh, man. I love that cake."

While Kate and Mercedes cleared the table, Cole talked to Mom about his latest construction project. They were stacking dishes next to the sink when Kate turned to her. "Why haven't you ever asked Finn to Sunday dinner? Mom adores him."

Panic seized her. "It's not that serious."

Kate didn't look convinced. "But you're seeing a lot of him, right?"

"Too much." When she wasn't with Finn, she was thinking about the next time she'd see him. Like he was a force field, drawing her in. This was crazy.

Scraping the leftovers into the trash, Kate shook her head. "When you find a guy who's right for you, the man you love, time together can never be too much, right?"

A fork slipped from Mercedes' hand and clattered onto the linoleum floor. *Love?* Did she love Finn? She bent down to pick up the fork and shoved it into the drawer.

"Hey, lady. Isn't that fork dirty?" Kate cast her a curious glance.

"Oh, right." Blushing, Mercedes retrieved the fork and laid it in the sink. Then she began to cut Mom's cake. "It's not like that, Kate. With Finn, I mean."

"Uh, huh. Right." Kate didn't look convinced as she put the coffee on to perk.

"Do you mind if Lindsay uses the office too?"

"I thought you two didn't get along."

"We're making progress." Mercedes arranged slices of cake on the plates. "Look, if it's a problem having her there, that's fine. She just asked."

"Nope, the more the merrier, right?" But Kate cast a curious glance over her shoulder as she sailed from the kitchen, two plates in her hands.

Seated back at the table, Mercedes felt safe from further questions when her mother regaled Cole with stories of what Kate was like as a baby. She gave her full attention to the cake and considered a second tiny piece. She was just that hungry. Ravenous. And she licked her fork after the second helping.

The next morning, Mercedes traveled into town to Kate's office, cartons of supplies in her back seat. Finn had agreed to meet her there. Together they could maneuver a desk from a back room. No way did she want to be closeted in a small area that had served as a stock room. That would have been cruel punishment after her spacious New York corner office. How she'd loved the sweeping view of New York City, even though the suite still had radiators. When she'd worked late, the city looked magical, all lit up.

Setting her box of office supplies on Kate's desk, she squeezed her eyes tight, trying to call up the image of the skyline. How frustrating. Nothing. Blinking her eyes open, she glanced around at Kate's messy desk, stacks of boxes, empty shelves and bare racks that still had to be taken out.

A knock came at the door and Finn stood there, beaming. She felt as if her own private sun stood shining in that doorway. "Morning, pretty girl." When he kissed her, she drank in the smell of a crisp fall day. Finn was like that. Refreshing. And so darn sexy. His tongue nudged her lips open, and she melted back into summer heat. "Missed you," he murmured.

"Yeah, me too." With a sigh, she surrendered, twining her arms around his neck until she was dizzy from his kisses. She broke away.

"Well, let's get to work or we'll be using that desk for something else." Finn gave her a look that sent her scurrying to the back.

"The two of us should be able to move it up here." She led him through the abandoned showroom. The door of the storeroom area squeaked when she shoved it open.

One hand squeezing her shoulder, Finn sized it up. "I'll get it. You just keep out of the way, okay?"

"Sure you can handle it?" One look from Finn and she stepped back. When had Stephan ever taken on a project for her? When it came to remodeling her condo, he found contractors to do the work. The man who remodeled her kitchen said something about a "finder's fee" that made her wonder if Stephan benefited from the referral.

She hadn't heard a thing from her former boyfriend. Watching Finn wrestle with the desk, she wondered what she'd ever seen in Stephan.

When they were all finished, the old metal desk sat back a few feet back from Kate's. Both faced the window overlooking the street, where Oscar Werner was setting out fall banners in front of his shop, Sun and Sail. Visitors still trickled into town from the harbor, but nowhere near as many as during the summer. Mercedes wondered if Oscar had a mailing list and made a mental note to ask him.

Finn surveyed the layout. "I'll put a privacy screen between your desks if you like."

"Don't bother. I'm sure Kate won't care." Mercedes laughed. "My sister's mellowing out now that she's going to have a baby."

Turning, Finn cupped her chin in both hands. "You're happy for her, right?"

She twisted away. Sometimes Finn saw too much. "Of course I am. Yeah, sure." She couldn't put a name on the uncomfortable feeling in her chest when she thought about her younger sister becoming a mother. Having a family was another expectation she'd held without thinking about it too much. An expectation that hadn't come to pass. And now she didn't know how she felt about it.

Perched on the edge of the desk, Finn pulled her in between his knees. "Want to come over tonight to watch Monday night football? I'll make pizza."

Maybe the moment had come. "I don't think that's a good idea."

"No?" Finn studied her. "What's up, Mercedes?"

Her heart pounded as she stepped away and shifted the box of office supplies from Kate's desk to her own. While he watched, she yanked the center drawer open and inserted a plastic drawer divider. Then she began to arrange her paperclips, pens and clips. Her hands were shaking.

"No, Mercedes. You are not going to do this." He was around the desk in a second. "What is the problem? Have I done something wrong?"

"No, it's not you. You've done everything right." Eyes furiously blinking back tears, she studied the pulse at the base of his neck. "Oh, Finn, I've been honest with you from the beginning. I'm going back to New York. Maybe we should take a break. Be practical." Lindsay's warning came back to her. She did not want to hurt him.

He looked at her as if she'd just grown another head. "What are you saying?"

"Maybe it will be next spring or next summer. But I'm not staying in Gull Harbor, and that's not fair to you."

"I think I'll be the judge of that." The tendons in his neck became rigid wires.

"I don't want to hurt you."

"Too late for that, Mercedes."

"Oh, God, Finn." She could hardly breathe.

Then his gray eyes softened. He gave her one of those looks that turned her bones to putty. "You need to think about this, Mercedes. I'm what you want. I'm what you need. You just don't know it. Yet."

But she wasn't finished. "Maybe we can deal with each other on

the business level. But I think we should, you know, cool it a little."
There. She'd said it. Finn backed away. Her heart told her to reach
out. But her head said that this was the right thing to do, the
considerate thing. She kept her hands clenched at her sides.

His eyes hardened to steel, his glance threatening to drill right
through her heart. "This is how it's going to be, Mercedes
Kennedy. I'm sticking around. Got that? I'll help you get this
business up and running. You can really see what success feels like
in Gull Harbor. You can know what love and loyalty are. Then you
can judge if that's what you want for the rest of your life."

Feeling miserable, she watched Finn walk away. He closed the
door behind him. The sun went behind a cloud, and the office fell
into darkness. Where was the damn light switch?

For the past ten years, her work had always been enough. When
Stephan came along, he'd felt like an addition to her business.
Truth was, she missed her agency more than she missed Stephan.
This was different. This felt like she'd been ripped open and left
bleeding on the dusty floor.

Dust motes floated in the air. The silence felt oppressive. She
glanced around and finally clicked on the lamp on Kate's desk.
She'd organize her files. Opening a side drawer, Mercedes started
to cram her old folders into the space. The files held marketing
promotions and social media and all the other strategies that would
make her a success so that she could return to Manhattan.

But the files didn't fit. Corners bent and several folders slid to
the floor. The drawer wouldn't even close when she slammed it
shut and collapsed into the hard wooden chair.

She didn't hear Kate until her sister burst through the door, skidding to a stop next to Mercedes' desk. "Hey, what's going on here? I just passed Finn, and he wouldn't even talk to me. Just got in his car, slammed the door and peeled out of the parking space."

"He's mad." She sniffled.

"What about?" Kate sat on the desk, facing her.

Mercedes swept her hair behind her shoulders. She had to get in to see Phoebe soon. "I'm going back to New York, Kate. It's just a matter of time. And Finn doesn't want to accept that."

Kate puffed out a breath. "Mercedes, that sounds crazy. Besides, it's a long way off, right? You might change your mind, especially with Finn in the picture."

"But I don't want to stay here all my life."

Her sister tilted her head. "You sure about that? Cause you act like one happy woman around Finn Wheeler. Happier than I've seen you in years."

The tears came and Mercedes didn't stop them. When she brushed her hands under each eye, she stared at the dark mascara on her fingers.

Lips pinched shut, Kate grabbed a handful of tissues and handed them to her. When Mercedes blew her nose, she ended up with a headache. "I guess we can find another desk somewhere for Lindsay. Think I saw one in the back."

Kate's eyes had narrowed. "Lindsay doesn't have anything to do with this, does she?"

Just then Sarah swirled through the door, bringing her usual white box. "Time for a snack for the new mother." Mercedes' stomach betrayed her with a growl. Right, she was ready to eat the entire box.

"Oh, Sarah. You are too good to me. To us." Kate patted her stomach.

Sliding the box onto Kate's desk, Sarah gave them both a sharp look. "Am I interrupting something?"

Mercedes grabbed another tissue. "Not at all. Just having a sob fest."

Sarah shook her head. "Finn Wheeler just gunned it down Whittaker Street. He wouldn't be involved in this, would he? If so, I'll kill him."

"It's not his fault, Sarah, really." Getting up, Mercedes walked over to the pastry box on Kate's desk and nudged it open. Chocolate brownies. But she hesitated. After all, these were for her sister.

"Dig in." Sara must be a mind reader. "One for each of you."

Kate had turned green, and Sarah rubbed her shoulders. "The nausea really getting you down? I hated that when I was pregnant. It passes. And so does the exhaustion."

Coming closer, Mercedes noted her sister's obvious discomfort. "Maybe you should go home and go to bed."

But her sister shook her head. When she didn't reach for a brownie, Mercedes did. The first bite made her forget her problems. The second mouthful tasted like mud. Nothing could replace Finn. She pushed the box toward her sister. "Go home, Kate, and take these with you."

"There's no way I'm going to curl up in bed. At least not

alone."

Sarah's smile widened, and then her sparkling eyes dimmed. "Have you heard about Diana?"

Kate pushed the box farther away. "What are you talking about?"

"She had an accident."

"Is she all right?" Mercedes managed around another mouthful.

"What kind of accident?" Kate asked.

"A burn. Something at the care center. She was helping Tim at the October Fest, working with the deep fryer and dumped in too much frozen food. The grease splashed."

"Oh, no. That sounds terrible." The short time Mercedes had spent at Hippy Chick, she'd really liked the pretty blonde.

"Her hands and arm will be fine. Painful but they'll heal. But her cheek?" Sarah ran a hand over her own face. "That's something else."

Kate groaned and Mercedes cringed. The brownies had been forgotten. Her own hand went to her cheek.

"Yeah. She doesn't want visitors but Chili has a plan, and we're going to the hospital tonight."

"How does Will feel about it?" Kate asked.

"Devastated. Blames himself of course." Sarah's phone pinged and she checked the message. "Gotta run. Mom's having trouble with Nathan. Kindergarten can't come soon enough."

"See you later." Kate dashed toward the back. The nausea must be something fierce. Picking up the last brownie, Mercedes figured her sister wouldn't care.

Hours later, Mercedes sat in the chair facing the mirror, Phoebe standing behind her. "Trim?" the hairdresser asked.

"Yes, I guess." Cripes, nothing felt good today. "I have to do something with this hair." *This hair. My life.*

"Yeah, you look like you've seen a ghost. Getting enough sleep?"

"That's not it." She couldn't talk about it. The caffeine in the chocolate brownies had made her jittery. Mercedes bounced her right knee.

Phoebes looked so kickass, standing behind her with mauve hair gelled into soft peaks like the meringue on a pie. She ran her fingers through Mercedes' hair. "How about that green streak we talked about?"

"Let's do it."

~.~

"So how did your meeting go with Mercedes this week?" Finn asked when Lindsay came over with the kids a day later. He hadn't seen his sister's eyes sparkle like this in a long time. This gig with Mercedes might give Lindsay a new interest. But having the two most important women in his life working together? Might not be the best thing. He couldn't account for Mercedes' abrupt change and wondered if his sister had unknowingly sabotaged him. The image of Mercedes standing at her desk while she shut him out was burned into Finn's mind. She'd looked miserable. "Everything working out okay?"

"Great. She's not such bitch after all." Grabbing an apple from the basket Mom kept on the kitchen counter, Lindsay bit down.

"And?" He stared at his sister, wanting to hear more.

"What?" She wiped the corner of her mouth. "Finn, you've got that look on your face. You know, like when I was playing with your computer in sixth grade and accidentally deleted your files?"

"Exactly. Thank God for Carbonite and backup." But how can you back up your love life and keep it safe from meddling? "Lindsay, Mercedes is very special to me."

His sister's chewing slowed, but he could tell her mind was busy. She swallowed. "I know that, Finn."

"Look, I know you love me, but no messing around with my personal life, okay?"

She paled. Bingo. Yep, she was definitely involved. "No girl to girl sharing. No well intentioned efforts, understand?"

"Okay, I get it. Enough." Her face blazed red as the apples.

Lindsay opened her mouth and shut it again. He held up a hand. "Business, just business. Working together, you two can be very successful. But it stops there, got it? No sharing confidences about me, okay?" He eased off at the end. After all, Lindsay had been through so much.

"I know, big brother. I know." She went to give Finn a high five, but he pushed her hand aside and hugged her.

Chapter 19

Did avoiding Finn hurt more than being with him? After their conversation, Mercedes held him off through emails about the website. Didn't matter. She scrolled through his messages line by line, analyzing each word and searching for any cleverly disguised subtext. She tried to imagine his expression when he wrote the words. Was he wearing that sexy half smile? Running a hand through his thick dark hair? Pulling the lobe of one of the ears she found adorable?

The Full Cup became her morning stop. This just wasn't her, but every brownie or cheese crown temporarily filled a void, followed by the sharp aftertaste of disgust when she got on the scale. When she switched to pecan sticky rolls, she didn't feel any better.

"My, oh, my," Sarah said as she tucked Mercedes' latest choice into a white bag. "You're becoming one of my best customers."

"I know. Thank you, Sarah." Mercedes carried the bag to her car as if it were stolen jewels. Her hands shook when she slid into her front seat. The dry rustle of the tissue when she reached inside pumped up her heart rate. How she loved the sugary coating that stuck to her front teeth. She worked it with her tongue and licked her fingers one by one when she was finished. Truly disgusting and oh, so good.

But not Finn.

Some days she practiced self-control with tiny bites. Other times, she wolfed down the pastries in record time. At least once, she considered a quick dash back for more. All self-control had vanished. Her hunger raged, unchecked. What was happening?

Lindsay joined Mercedes and Kate in the PR office two days a week. Turned out Finn's sister was pretty good at graphics to use in their email blasts. She also designed the direct mail card that would go out in the mail. Finn would foot the bill for the mailing, or so Lindsay said. Mercedes kept track. No way would she become his charity case.

Dividing the list of merchants and restaurants in the area, they made cold calls and asked for mailing lists. Altogether they ended up with a database of 25,000 names. The mailing should be ready mid-November.

Today Finn was coming to the office to test the new website. When Lindsay showed up with a wide fuchsia streak in her hair, Mercedes smiled. "Maybe we've both gone crazy, right?" Her own thatch of green had sent her mother into giggles.

Lindsay blushed. "Maybe." Taking a seat at the card table she'd brought from home, Lindsay immediately got to work and hardly broke for coffee. Did Mercedes imagine that tension hung in the air between them? Wistfully, she thought back to The Blue Plate, when they seemed to stand a chance of being friends. That had never developed. Instead, Lindsay withdrew, leaving Mercedes to wonder what she'd said or done.

The day Finn stopped in to demo the new website, Kate was at a doctor's appointment. Only Lindsay and Mercedes were there when the back door opened, the same door Finn had carried her through that day in late summer. The air shifted. Her body tensed, prickles chasing down her neck. The sudden burst of air smelled like Finn, fresh and invigorating. Lifting her hands from the keyboard, she turned.

"Lindsay, Mercedes?"

"Hey, bro. What's up?" Lindsay looked up from her keyboard.

Mercedes stumbled to her feet. "Hi, Finn." Seeing him took her breath away. He looked way more handsome than she remembered, dark hair disheveled and cheeks ruddy from the November wind.

"Got the goods?" When Lindsay jumped up, Finn enfolded her in a hug. Hungry for those arms, Mercedes studied the stripped trees outside, branches quivering in the cold lake gusts.

"Ready for a demo?" Finn asked, sliding a burlap case onto the card table.

Unnerved, Mercedes turned back. "Sure."

"You bet." Lindsay shoved her own laptop aside.

While Finn connected his computer to the Wi-Fi, Mercedes tried not to stare. Glancing up, she found Lindsay's eyes on her. But Finn's sister quickly looked away.

"Okay, let's get to it." Finn jumped up and patted the chair right in front of him. "Why don't you sit here, Mercedes, and Lindsay next to you." He was talking to her as if she were a client while he pulled another chair over for his sister. The distance between them felt like a concrete restraining wall.

Finn smiled. "With those colored stripes in your hair, you two look like sisters."

Mercedes sucked in a quick breath while Lindsay gave her brother a look that said *don't be an idiot*. After a few awkward moments, they turned their attention to the staged website. "Oh it's beautiful, Finn." The words Beach Vacations scrolled over an eye-popping beach scene. "Where did you get this shot?"

"I have my sources."

"It's breathtaking. Releases have been signed for usage?"

"Of course." Finn was blushing, and it was hard to turn away. On the screen, a couple lounged in beach chairs close to the water. Children played in the shallows. The sun beamed across the blue water while a few clouds hung on the horizon.

For the next twenty minutes, Finn took them through the site. Mercedes was impressed by the functional menu. He'd thought of everything. "People can search by the number of bedrooms. They can choose a beach site or a cottage one or two blocks away." A long checklist appeared. Lindsay had gotten permission from one of her clients to use his property in Finn's demo. Viewers could click on the calendar to see what was available and at what price range.

Looking at the trial site for Beach Vacations, Mercedes felt the company come to life. Her dream was within reach. "Finn, you thought of everything." Glancing up, she fell into those gray eyes.

"Right," Lindsay chimed in. "You sure did."

One look from Finn, and Lindsay grabbed her purse. "Think

I'm going over to check in with Sarah. She's got something for me."

"Just don't bring back any more of those cheese crowns," Mercedes called after her, running one hand along her tight waistband.

The door closed. They were alone together. Panic struck. Grabbing the mouse, Mercedes began clicking randomly through the new site. "Is it set up so that it can process payments?"

Taking the seat vacated by his sister, Finn launched into an explanation of the website and what it could do. As long as he kept talking, Mercedes felt better. Why hadn't she come up with some excuse to keep Lindsay here? Hands moving deftly, Finn eased the cursor from one point to another.

Suddenly he stopped. The silence stretched. "Mercedes, are you sure?" Finn's question took her by surprise. She looked up.

Wrapped in his wounded eyes, she fumbled for the words. How she longed to say, "Oh, Finn. What am I doing? I love you."

Instead she mumbled, "Sure about what?"

"You know." He leaned closer. The door opened. Lindsay stepped inside. "You'll never guess what I found."

Finn and Mercedes both exhaled and fell back in their chairs.

"Bad timing?" Poor Lindsay. Her eyes darted from Finn to Mercedes. "I bought chocolate chip cookies, not brownies. Is that okay?"

Catching her breath, Mercedes whispered. "I'll take three."

Finn took the box from his sister.

Insomnia had started to plague Mercedes. What other reason

could she have for her strange behavior? At night, she watched TV with her mother until Mom went to bed. Then Mercedes trudged up the stairs with her electronic reader. She liked romances because they were so relaxing. Now she found the love scenes downright disturbing.

She slipped so easily into the scene. Stretching out in her bed, she imagined herself in Finn's cool gray sheets, his hand skimming her skin. Longing twisted through her. Heck with the dialogue in the book. Instead, she heard his voice coaxing her with words she wanted to hear. Finn Wheeler had become the source of her happiness and that was frightening. No wonder she couldn't sleep.

"Mercedes?"

The office chair creaked when she jerked upright. Had she nodded off? Lips twitching, Finn studied her. "Where were you just now? What are you thinking about?"

"The business," she lied, running shaky hands up her thighs. "The numbers. We have to get everything up and running."

Finn gave her one of his secret smiles.

"Did you know that Sarah sells little cartons of milk, too?" Slipping the purse from her shoulder, Lindsay grinned at them, totally unaware.

"How convenient." Grabbing a letter opener, Finn slit the tape on the bakery box.

Mercedes peeked inside, where huge chocolate chip cookies were stacked in thick layers. "I should be on a diet."

Nudging the box closer, Finn whispered, "You should indulge."

"Sarah said they were on sale. I've got napkins." Lindsay tossed them onto the table and took a cookie. "Man, I am so tired. The girls kept me up so late last night. That Charlie Brown show for Thanksgiving was on. Can you believe we're almost to the holidays?"

Finn glanced over. "Ladies first."

Still babbling, Lindsay drifted to the front window, chattering about Oscar Werner arranging Thanksgiving decorations in front of his shop to lure customers. Huge cardboard turkeys sat next to grape vine pumpkins. Lawn flags of orange and yellow autumn leaves billowed in the breeze.

"Mercedes, you decide," Finn said in a hoarse whisper.

"Oh, I couldn't," Mercedes whispered, her gaze shifting between the box and Finn. "I shouldn't."

"Why do you deny yourself things that you know you want?" His lips barely moved.

"My mother taught us self-discipline."

"Alice would want you to be happy, wouldn't she?" Lines radiated from his eyes. Were those from lack of sleep or the sun?

"She asks where you are all the time," Mercedes murmured.

"And what do you tell her?" He was so close she could see the dark stubble on his chin. Her palms tingled.

"That you're working." This was beginning to feel like an interrogation.

His smile poured over her like July sunshine. "I'm working at getting you back in my life, Mercedes. Back in my bed."

Her legs buckled and she gripped the edge of the desk. "R-right. But it would just be temporary." Was she bargaining with him?

This was so wrong but she couldn't help herself. She ran one hand up the front his navy jacket and leaned into him.

Catching her, Finn cocked his head. "Temporary? No way."

She'd offered herself and he'd refused. The disappointment tugged her down.

"Make no mistake, I'm in this for the long term, Mercedes. And so are you. You just don't know it."

Her body screamed yes, so she had to change her focus. Picking a point of concentration, she studied the scar at the right corner of his lips. "Always meant to ask you about that scar." She touched the same spot on her lip with her tongue.

"Metal truck. Lindsay hit me with it."

"Your sister should be careful." Her hand crept up to brush his lip as if she could fix that white nick, heal the past hurt. When his tongue leapt out, electricity sizzled through her body.

Lindsay turned from the window. "I wonder if those outdoor displays work. Maybe we should put a sandwich board sign on the sidewalk about Beach Vacations. Would the town let us do that?" She glanced down at the box and then up at them. "Hey, Mercedes, I thought you said you wanted three?"

"I shouldn't."

Hands on hips, Lindsay stared down. "If you're not, I will."

Scooping up a cookie out, Finn handed it to Mercedes. "You need some meat on your bones."

"Right. Like that'll do it." The plump cookie broke between her teeth and melted in her mouth. Finn and Lindsay talked about the website while Mercedes nibbled, eyes drifting from his crazy hair to the broad shoulders, and finally resting on those persuasive hands. The man's body might be imprinted on hers, but his words were also imprinted on her heart. *Mercedes, are you sure?*

No, she wasn't. Two cookies later, Finn was gone and she was on a sugar high that in no way had filled that empty place inside.

That night Mercedes dreamed she was seated alone on a runaway train that screeched through the night, the empty car rocking like crazy. Station signs whipped past: Cleveland, Pittsburg and Philadelphia, New York. Panicked, she made her way through the empty car, grabbing handrails and finally flinging herself into the next car, only to find it empty. "I have to get off. I've missed my stop."

But no one was there to hear her.

No one cared. The train hurtled through the darkness.

When she woke up, her pajama shirt was drenched. A great loneliness overtook her.

That's when she decided.

Chapter 20

Mercedes studied the black Oscar de la Renta sheath hanging in her closet. Too dressy for a family Thanksgiving and it was sleeveless. Outside, the temperature had dropped below freezing, and her mother's frugality always kept Breezy Point cool. Down below the house, angry waves battered the shore. Definitely not a day to go sleeveless, and she pushed the dress to the left.

The tiny closet was crammed full with her New York wardrobe. Hangers squealed as she plowed through them. Maybe the Nina Ricci pleated blouse would work? The creamy fabric felt deliciously slippery. But Mercedes could picture her favorite splashed with gravy or, even worse, cranberry sauce. The blouse went to the left. Maybe the black Stella McCarthy Portia top would work with skinny polka dot jeans. Turkey dinner and skinny jeans? She squirmed just thinking about that.

Her mattress squeaked when she fell back onto her elbows and regarded the fortune in designer clothes sandwiched into her closet like a bargain basement sale rack. If only she could have sold some of them when her company was failing. But New York consignment shops would have paid a fraction of what she'd spent. Back in those days, her clothing had to strike a certain tone, especially with her clients.

Closing the closet door, she rooted around in her dresser for her old standards. Finally, she pulled out a pair of black jeans that seemed sophisticated in high school. She wiggled into them. Mother of all surprises, they still fit her burgeoning hips. She studied herself in the full-length mirror before digging out a pale aqua fleece from high school. Delicate beaded snowflakes winked on the sleeves. Too cutesy for New York but comfortable here in Gull Harbor. Today she wanted to be comfortable. Pulling her hair into a high ponytail, she smiled at the green streak in her blonde hair. Crazy but it was growing on her.

The smell of the turkey in the oven seeped up the stairs. Time to help her mother, who was banging pans around downstairs. The back door slammed open and she heard her mother say, "Well hello, Prissy." Cole brought the poor dog everywhere. Something about separation anxiety. Mercedes knew the feeling. Tucking her feet into her black ballet flats, she hurried down the steps.

The warmth of a busy holiday kitchen greeted her. "Happy Thanksgiving!" she called out with a gaiety that didn't reach her heart. Cole's mother-in-law had come with them. "Hi, Marie."

"Hello, dear." Marie McGraw looked cute in a purple pantsuit. Like Mom, her hair was dyed blonde. If Phoebe had anything to say about it, the two older women would probably sport streaks of color in their hair before long. Her mother looked up from basting the turkey, face flushed from the oven.

"Let me help you, Mom." Mercedes pushed the rack back in and closed the oven door.

"Oh, sweetheart." Her mother handed her a peeler. "Potatoes, please?"

"Sure." Her least favorite job in the world but it was Thanksgiving. She reached inside the refrigerator for the plastic bag of Idaho spuds.

Kate was busy hanging up coats and getting Natalie and Marie settled in front of the TV, the dog panting beside them on the blue sofa. Slipping into a Wonder Woman apron, another relic from her past, Mercedes began to peel the potatoes.

Cole disappeared into the front room, and some good-natured kidding ensued over whether they would watch a football game or reruns of the Macy's parade. Kate drifted back into the kitchen, looking dreamy and probably cocooned in a prenatal fog.

While Mercedes hacked at the potatoes, Mom plied Kate with questions about her pregnancy. The discussion felt like it was in a foreign language. Morning sickness, fatigue, due dates and names. Natalie wanted to call the baby Crystal and Cole voted for Kaitlyn. Their mother had suggested Nora for a great-grandmother. Marie wanted Maria.

"What about you, Aunt Mercedes?" Kate looped an arm around her shoulders.

"What you mean, what about me?"

"Any suggestions about the baby's name?"

The potato peeler slipped and sliced her thumb. Mercedes yelped and dropped everything. Peeling had never been her strong point. And neither were babies, apparently.

"Good heavens, Mercedes." Her mother glanced over with concern. "You're bleeding all over the potatoes."

Kate lifted Mercedes' hand and inspected the finger. "You need a bandage. Come on."

Feeling like a fool, Mercedes followed Kate into the powder room. "I picked up some Tinkerbell Band-Aids for Natalie last month. She thinks they're too childish." Kate rolled her eyes. "So I stashed them here."

"Childish for Natalie but okay for me? Love it."

Rummaging around in a drawer, Kate didn't meet her eyes. "Like your outfit, by the way." She'd found the box and ripped a packet open.

"High school. This was all I could find that still fit."

Peeling the backing off the colored design, Kate applied the Band-Aid tight as a tourniquet around Mercedes' finger. "You always looked beautiful in high school and you still do. Love the hair." She motioned to the broad streak that zipped down Mercedes' long ponytail like colored lightning.

"Phoebe's work. By the way, she mentioned you were going to visit Diana. How is she?"

Kate's smile disappeared. "She's having a hard time."

Mercedes cringed at the thought of having burns. "Diana is so beautiful. The oil hit her face too?"

"Right, her cheek. Will feels guilty." Clamping the metal box of Band-Aids closed, Kate tucked them back in the drawer. "How did the trial run of the website go the other day?"

Mercedes' stomach swirled. "Awesome. Great searching functionality. The direct mail went out last week. We've had over one hundred hits a day on the website with a ten percent close rate." The marketing terms kept her emotions in check. Her body turned to warm taffy when she remembered her conversation with Finn.

"Are you shivering?" Kate looked at her carefully. "Maybe Mom should turn the heat up."

"Are you kidding?" Mercedes turned back to the kitchen, banishing thoughts hotter than any furnace. "It's suffocating in here."

Kate caught her arm. "Hold on a sec, okay?"

Mercedes stepped back into the powder room.

"About Mom. What do you think? You've been here for three months or so." Kate looked so concerned, and this conversation needed to happen.

"She's different," Mercedes said slowly. "Sometimes, she comes through like gangbusters. Look at her today. She knows this meal like the back of her hand."

"It's written on her heart."

"She can use the remote. Remembers her friends' birthdays. Driving?" Mercedes shook her head. "Probably not a good idea. We can check that out with Dr. Kumar."

Kate nodded. "Right. That scares me."

Helpless and in new territory, the sisters looked at each other. "Do you want me to have that conversation with Mom?" Kate finally asked.

Her finger was throbbing. Peeling off the Band-Aid, Mercedes reapplied it but not so tight. "I will, Kate. I'm the oldest and, well, I'm here."

Clearly relieved, Kate gave her a quick hug. "Love you, Merc."

"Love you too." She squeezed her sister with great care.

"Girls." Their mother clapped her hands, as if they were still in grade school. "Could one of you lift out the turkey? Got to get going on that gravy."

The potatoes were boiling, and the green bean casserole and yams were baking. Grabbing two hot pads, Mercedes opened the oven. Heat singed her cheeks as she lifted out the pan that strained her arms. At least she wasn't poor Diana. For the next half an hour, the three of them worked around each other. After draining the potatoes, Mercedes grabbed the mixer and got to work. Kate helped lift the succulent turkey onto a platter, and Mom began on the gravy.

"Any snacks out here? I'm starving." Natalie appeared in the doorway, looking so cute in her grey tights and purple hoodie.

"Well of course, sweetheart." Reaching into a cabinet, Mom brought down a couple cans of nuts. "Forgot all about these. Think you can open them? I've got some pretty bowls here somewhere."

"Of course I can." After pouring the nuts into the small glass bowls used for special occasions, Natalie turned to Kate. Edging closer, she laid a hand on Kate's stomach, which was still flat as far as Mercedes could see. Natalie leaned closer. "Can you hear me, Crystal? When are you going to come out and play paper dolls with me?"

With a laugh, Kate shooed her stepdaughter away, handing her the two bowls of nuts. "Hate to disappointment you, Natalie. This baby will not be Crystal."

"Whatever." With a shrug, Natalie disappeared and a howl went up in the living room. "Grandma, did you let Dad turn off the parade? Who wants to watch stupid football?"

"I was outvoted." They heard Marie's laugh.

Kate smiled as Natalie began to scold her father. "Now you switch that back on, Dad."

"Poor Cole," Kate said. "This goes on all the time. And it's just going to get worse,"

Turning away, Mercedes gathered the silverware, the young family's happy chatter echoing in her heart. Her sister had everything.

About an hour later, they all bowed their heads over the Thanksgiving meal. The table should be groaning under the platters of turkey, mashed potatoes, candied yams and side dishes. Sitting next to Natalie, with Cole on her other side, Marie McGraw looked in her element. Mom beamed from the head of the table. With great care, Cole carved the turkey and moist slices fell away from the nicely browned bird. Stretched out at their feet under the table, Prissy remained alert for any falling morsel. Hunger gnawed at Mercedes. She was finding it increasingly hard to tame the beast.

"Let's go round the table and say what we're thankful for," Mom said. "Today means a lot more than food, doesn't it? I'll start. I'm thankful for my friends and family." Her eyes circled the table. "Especially the new additions."

Cole was next. " And I'm thankful for my beautiful wife. A year ago, I never would've believed this." Reaching across the sweet potato casserole, he squeezed Kate's hands.

Marie jumped right in. "I'm just glad to be here. Thank you for including me in your family." It must be hard having a daughter in California who never called.

Natalie wiggled in her chair. "And I'm thankful we have pecan pie *and* pumpkin pie for dessert."

"With whipped cream or ice cream," their mother threw in. Natalie grinned.

Mercedes fidgeted. Did they really have to do this? The year had brought so many endings for her.

But everyone sat waiting. These dear people had supported her when she came back to Gull Harbor, and she did owe them a debt of gratitude. "I'm just glad to be h-here with you." She almost said *home*. Was this home for her?

"And now, let's eat." Mom motioned to the platters. "Let's pass the fowl and the filling, as my grandfather used to say. Gravy last."

The delicious food proved to be a distraction. After her second helping of mashed potatoes and gravy, Mercedes opened the button on her jeans. She battled the guilt, but today felt justified. Clearing the table and putting the coffee on gave them all time to breathe a little. Natalie slipped pieces of turkey to Prissy. Then they dove right into dessert. The pumpkin pie was perfectly spiced. Mercedes even took some of the pecan pie with chocolate chips, although that second serving seemed flavored with guilt. She didn't care.

Surrounded by family, she pictured Finn and his loved ones gathered around the table together. Later, he'd no doubt settle down to watch football. The fact that she'd created this distance between them twisted a knife in her stomach. Was Finn right? Did she know what she really wanted?

"You feeling okay?" Kate asked as they did the dishes later. The TV blared in the next room. Cole had one eye on the game while he played Monopoly with Natalie, Marie and her mother.

"Preoccupied that's all. Getting the business together and everything."

"What's it like working with Lindsay?"

Kate was washing and it was hard to keep up with her. "Not too bad. She has a lot of connections, and I'm glad she shared them with me. Besides that, if I do succeed in developing and selling this business, she would be here to help the new owner."

Setting the sponge on the lip of the sink, Kate turned. "How can you talk about going to all that work to start a company and then just leave it? Is your life really just about business?"

Mercedes blushed. "Kate, I've always wanted to get ahead with my life."

"Oh, sweetie, what does that really mean?" Her sister looked so sad, like Mercedes had just told her she had a terrible disease. "Isn't life about people? When we were growing up, you were so happy. You smiled a lot more often."

The words felt like a slap. Looking away, Mercedes wiped the plate in her hands carefully, front and back. Had she been happy with her work in New York? Or had the excitement turned to drudgery? Picking up the sponge, Kate went back to work. "Any word from Stephan?"

The name sounded foreign now. "No and I'm glad. Stephan's

someone I want to forget."

"Who do you want to remember?" Kate asked quietly.

"Are you turning into my therapist now?"

Her sister sighed. "Okay, change of subject. We really should get Mom that dishwasher for Christmas."

"Where would she put it? This is a pretty small kitchen."

"We can let Cole figure that out." Kate's eyes got all dreamy again.

After that, they worked in silence. In the end, they decided to soak the pans until the next day. Mercedes had to get out of there. When she poked her head into the other room, all eyes were glued to some holiday special on TV. "I'll be right back." No one moved. Everyone was in a food coma.

"Where are you going?" Kate whispered as Mercedes pulled her black, quilted jacket from the coat closet at the back door.

"For a walk. "

Mercedes couldn't spend another second with Kate, not right now. Jerking open the back door, Mercedes drank in the frigid air.

"Give him a call." Those were Kate's last words before Mercedes slammed the door shut behind her. As if it were that easy.

Outside the wind howled high in the trees. Winter and Christmas lurked just around the corner. She was not in a holiday mood. Hollyhock stalks were shriveled against the siding of the house, and frozen geraniums stood tall and stark in the blue window boxes. She'd have to help her mother pull up last summer's plantings before the snow came. Zipping her jacket tighter, she pulled the hood over her head. Thank goodness leather gloves were still stuffed in the pockets from last winter.

Her breath formed a white cloud as she stood there in the dark. In weather like this, the beach was out of the question. An angry lake thundered against the shore. Before too long, the ice floes would form along the shoreline.

She started down the driveway, her flats slipping on the gravel. Too late, she realized she should've worn a pair of boots. No time to go back. Stumbling along, Mercedes wondered if a girl could have PMS all month long. Sure felt like it. The winding road felt eternal, darker with each step as she moved farther from the house.

When she finally reached Lake Shore Road, she edged onto the center of the road. No need to meet some raccoon or possum scrambling from a tree to forage. Lights glowed in some of the houses, although many were shut up tight for the winter. The owners were probably back in Chicago, toasting Thanksgiving with the people they loved.

The emptiness inside grew, as if she'd swallowed a huge bubble of loneliness.

Kate was right. But how could Mercedes bridge the chasm she'd caused between herself and Finn?

The rumble of a car startled her, coming up behind. Turning, she held a hand up to block the headlights. Her heart revved up as she retreated to the edge of the road. How creepy being out here alone, even though this was Gull Harbor. Then she recognized the silhouette of the Bentley. Her chest eased. Finn frowned at her over the wheel, and she laughed with relief. Mercedes was that glad to see him. Pulling up beside her, he rolled down his window. She came closer.

"What the hell are you doing out here alone?" A lock of hair fell in his eyes when he leaned across the passenger seat.

She sniffed, wiping a hand under each eye. "Working off dinner."

Her body burned for this man. The car jerked when he shoved it into park. Suddenly he was there beside her, smelling of his leather bomber jacket and wearing a fierce frown. "Happy Thanksgiving," she whispered. "Good holiday?"

"Fair to middling until now." His forehead smoothed. Hands reaching to cup her head, Finn kissed her. Shameless, she pressed her body against his like she wanted to climb inside.

"Oh, Finn." Mercedes trembled while his lips roamed her face. Breathless, she met him kiss for kiss.

Finally, he broke away with a ragged sigh. "Guess you miss me, right?"

Swallowing hard, she nodded. "Could be."

"What should we do about that?" His thumb brushed her cheek, flicking away a tear.

"My house is full of people."

"Mine isn't." He opened the passenger door.

Chapter 21

The only sound in his car was their heavy breathing. Had Mercedes been crying? That rattled Finn. Made him feel pretty good, too. He kept his eyes straight ahead. If she sniffed one more time, he'd lose it. When he took her hand, a sigh swept through the car. "You're killing me, pretty girl." She tugged off her gloves. "Do you have a boo-boo?"

"I cut myself peeling potatoes."

"Want me to make it better?"

"Yes." The husky voice just about sent him through the roof.

Lifting her hand, he kissed the bandage and then her palm. From now on, dish soap would always smell sexy. Thank God they were almost home. The November winds howled outside, but he felt warmed now that Mercedes was with him. When she squeezed his hand, other parts of his body responded.

Home. He wanted to bring Mercedes home.

When Finn pulled up behind his house, he didn't bother with the garage. Just turned off the car and hopped out. Thank goodness he'd left the outside lights on when he went over to his folks for dinner. He opened her door, and Mercedes reached for his hand. Together they ran up the steps. Inside the heavy paneled door, Finn kicked off his shoes and Mercedes followed.

Elvis and Wiggy came leaping down the steps from their favorite perch in front of the upstairs windows. Snatching a box of dog biscuits, he tossed one to each yipping dog. "Now beat it, okay?" They knew that tone of voice and Elvis headed back upstairs, Wiggy behind him.

Mercedes stood in front of him, swaying with heavy eyes.

"Come here." He extended his arms and she stepped into them. It felt so right.

"Love the smell of your leather jacket." She kissed him, lips soft and sweet.

"Love the smell of your dish soap."

"No way." She got real quiet then pulled away.

Suddenly he was Goofy again, back in high school and feeling clueless.

But her lips tilted up. "Hey, I just might do the dishes for you. I have a great Wonder Woman apron."

"Now that's a picture. Nothing more." He ripped off his leather jacket and dropped it to the floor, crazy to feel her warmth. Nestling in his arms, she murmured appreciation when he kissed her. Felt like forever since he'd tasted her. She parted her lips and fed his hunger.

"More," she whispered, hands clutching his biceps. "I want more."

"Glad to hear it. Upstairs?"

She nodded. "Now." Her quilted jacket landed on the railing as they scrambled to the landing overlooking the first floor. He undressed her like the precious gift she was, draping her pretty blouse over the railing. "I feel like such a lecher, dragging you upstairs like this."

Mercedes threw her head back and laughed, her old, bold self again. "I've always liked older men."

"Really? You don't seem like the kind of girl." Teasing her was fun.

"Oh, you don't know everything about me."

But he thought he did. Knew her like the back of his hand.

Taking out her clip, she shook out her hair.

"Have I told you how much I like that green streak?"

"Have I told you how happy that makes me?"

"Sort of reckless. I never would have believed it."

"Oh, Finn, tonight I feel reckless."

"Bring it on." Finn tugged her to him, ran his hands down her back while she moaned. They were both breathing like they were in the last leg of a marathon. He had to slow this down, wanted to savor every second. The past weeks had been miserable. Moonlight poured through the skylights and accented her delicate features. And those damp tracks on her cheeks? Yes, she'd been crying.

Love just about knocked him senseless. "I missed you so damn much."

"You did?" A cloud passed over the skylights, and they were plunged into darkness. He couldn't see her face.

"Let me show you." Scooping her up, he made tracks for his room. Her head fell onto his shoulder, the soft hair tickling his face. It reminded him of that first day when he'd seen her struggling on Whittaker. Wanted her then. Needed her now.

Once in his room, he gently laid her on the bed and stretched out beside her. She reached for his Henley shirt and tugged it over his head.

"Oh, Finn." Her fingers brushed his chest, and he almost lost it.

She seemed as desperate as he felt. He'd spent the last few weeks crazy for her touch, missing her zany comments and hungry for her Mercedes sass. Because that's what she was. She was a first-class girl who knew her own mind. He might not deserve her but he would have her.

Elvis and Wiggy pattered into the room and leapt onto the bed. Damn dogs. "Don't even think about it, you two." He scooted the wriggly Jack Russells to the floor.

"Maybe later." Mercedes turned back to him and the dogs settled at the foot of the bed.

"For them? Later. For us, now." Finn turned back to the matter at hand. "We're still wearing too many clothes." Slowly he peeled off her jeans. The clouds apparently had cleared overhead, and the blue moonlight threw her body into stark shadows. "You put on a little weight."

"Have I?" Where was his head? Her hands immediately flew to cover the most interesting parts.

"Oh, babe. It's all good. If anything you look even better." After a few kisses and some serious coaxing, she dropped her hands. Gradually, she teased the pants right off him.

"Finn, I was afraid we'd never be like this again." Such sadness in her voice.

"Don't be silly, Mercedes. You're *always* on my mind. I was willing to wait." He skimmed one hand along her curves and with a sigh of surrender, she fell back. When he spanned her flat stomach with one hand, he just about stopped breathing. She was so perfect.

A mischievous smile tilted her lips. Turning, she propped her head on one hand. "You mean even when you were talking me through the website, you weren't thinking about business?"

His laugh felt ripped from his gut. "*Especially* then. With every click, I was taking a totally different tour in my head."

Mercedes giggled like they were still in high school. "Sounds naughty."

"You don't know the half of it." He tilted her chin so she had to look at him. "I'll always love you, Mercedes, so get used to it."

Her features contracted, and so did his heart. Maybe he was an idiot to put himself out there like this.

"You know the way things are, right? That hasn't changed." She frowned.

"Yeah, I know." It hurt to say it.

Twisting a length of hair around her fingers, she fell back against the pillows. He pressed his lips tight.

She shivered and looked uncertain. "So cold in here."

"I'll turn up the heat." He was about to jump out of bed when her hand caught his wrist. So delicate, yet so strong. The mood shifted.

"No. Let me."

~.~

Morning sunlight poured through the skylights. Mercedes hadn't felt this relaxed in a long time. She gave a long stretch as she sat on one of Finn's leather stools at the breakfast bar. He smiled over at her, pouring their coffee. Elvis and Wiggy curled up in a patch of sunlight in front of the glass windows. Outside, the world had become a winter wonderland.

"Tired?" he asked, handing her a mug.

"Nope. Not that kind of tired anyway." Looking out at the gray lake, Mercedes shivered in his fisherman knit sweater. Tightening her grip on the coffee mug, she took a sip. "Last night was really nice."

Finn looked cozy in grey heather sweats that matched his eyes. "More than nice."

What girl would argue with that? "Got bread for toast?"

"English muffins." Jumping up, he opened his bottom freezer drawer and tossed the package to her. She was struggling with the cold plastic when it hit her. This all felt so natural. The box slipped from her hands. Finn scooped it up. "Let me do it."

As they worked together in his chrome and black kitchen, the morning breakfast thing continued to feel like some other girl's life. But it was a nice life. Finn made eggs, hash browns and turkey bacon while she toasted the muffins, poured the juice and found his silverware.

"So what's this thing you have about eating?" Finn asked her later as she dipped her English muffin into the egg yolk. The man knew how to cook an over easy egg just right.

"That's all behind me. I am fat as a Christmas goose." Grinning, she dragged her muffin through the egg yolk as if to prove her point. No more senseless diets for her.

Finn closed one hand over hers. "Glad to hear it. It's just not healthy, Mercedes. You had me worried. Your body needs fuel, like gas for a car."

Definitely a guy's comparison but it made sense. Brow furrowed, he looked so concerned. Mercedes was touched that he cared that much.

Three months ago, this tasty mess of eggs and hash browns would have nauseated her. Now she just felt hungry. The guilt she once felt after eating had faded. She picked up her fork.

He leaned closer, ticked a finger at the corner of her lips and came away with a toasted crumb. "Take it from one who knows. Your body is perfect."

"Oh, is it now?"

They let the eggs cool. Later, they laughed when Finn fixed a second batch. Even that felt natural and right.

The contentment stayed with her all day. Like she was in a familiar dream but not that haunting train nightmare. Of course, her mom had a thousand questions when she got home, even though Mercedes had texted Kate, who was still at Breezy Point, to tell her where she was. Somehow that Friday, Mercedes avoided her family's questions.

Over the next days, Finn was a frequent visitor to the office. Mercedes didn't know what was more distracting, the business that had taken off like a rocket or the romance that followed that same track.

At first Lindsay was very quiet at work. And then she changed. Mercedes never knew if Finn had a conversation with his sister, or if Lindsay just reached her own conclusions. To Mercedes' relief, their relationship began to feel comfortable. Trying to present Finn as just a friend to her mother or Kate was useless.

"My, you certainly are seeing a lot of that young man," her mother commented one night the following week. Dressed in her leather miniskirt with knee boots and a leather jacket, Mercedes waited for Finn to pick her up. They were going up to St. Joe for dinner. The week had been hectic. They now had forty-seven houses signed up, and most of those were booked for at least one weekend in the coming two months.

In the comment section of their website, homeowners were saying that they never realized that they could rent out their cottages during the cold weather. Sure, some of the Chicago people had friends that they would let use their property. But that kind of generosity could lead to strained friendships and hard feelings. "Now I can just direct my friends to your website and you take it from there," one of their new clients wrote.

"I have never had so much business in the winter. One year I almost took a job at Clancy's deli, the way Carolyn Knight, the high school teacher, does every summer." Lindsay was clearly impressed by their success. She'd hired two women to help her with the cleaning. Both ladies appreciated the winter work, especially as Christmas approached.

"Excited?" Finn asked her that night in St. Joe as they faced each other over a glass of wine.

"Very. I like working on something I can build, create on my own."

"So you can go back to New York?" His handsome features darkened.

Reaching out, she took his hand. "Hey don't, okay? Sure I want to build the business. The rest? I honestly just don't know."

The knot in her chest released when the tension eased in his face. She would never do anything to intentionally hurt Finn. And she thought she'd made everything clear.

But as the days passed and their relationship deepened, she had to push her initial plan to the back of her mind. The emptiness she felt at Thanksgiving came back to haunt her. She found herself back where she'd been in November, not wanting to hurt Finn.

When the early Christmas card arrived from Stephan, she took it to her room. Heavy vellum in her hand, the large card felt crisp and corporate. The envelope was lined in gold when she opened it. A sparkling, stylized tree greeted her and she groaned. The glitz was so Stephan. At the bottom, he'd scratched out his printed name and had scrawled *Love, Stephan.*

Really? Love, from Stephan?

She sat down on her bed to read his short note. *I see that you have a new business going. Good for you! Always knew you could do it. I hope you'll fit a trip to New York into your schedule during the coming year.*

Why hadn't she ever noticed Stephan's patronizing tone? Instead of giddy excitement, she felt disgust. The authoritative script even made her mad. Studying the bare branches that rattled against the gutters outside, she made a mental note to trim them.

Then she tucked the card into her purse and went down to help her mother make dinner. They planned to watch *White Christmas* together that night. When she mentioned it to Finn, he asked if he could come. She surprised herself by saying yes. Her mother was in seventh heaven. "About time Finn comes over to our house." In her heart, Mercedes knew this was only the beginning.

One sunny December day, Kate and Mercedes took Mom on an outing to St. Joe. They checked out the Christmas decorations and then had lunch at Clementine's. Over burgers oozing with bacon, cheese and caramelized onions, they talked over the car issue. Their mother listened. "My word, I don't want to worry you," she finally said, fingering one red Christmas bell earring. "But there aren't any cabs in Gull Harbor, girls."

"Just let us know where you need to be and when," Mercedes said. "We'll work it out." But in the spring Kate would have the baby. Mercedes wasn't really sure how they'd meet that obligation, but she had time to come up with some options.

The PR office continued to hum with activity. Kate brought a tiny, pre-lit Christmas tree into the office. "Remember this?" she asked Mercedes, arranging it in the front window so passersby could see it.

"Sure do. But I haven't seen it in decades." Their mother used to set the small tree out on the porch "to dress it up." This year Mercedes would help Mom put up a larger tree inside next to their fireplace. In New York, she never had time for Christmas decorations. This year she was looking forward to all the traditions she'd left behind.

When Gull Harbor residents saw the tiny tree in the window of the PR office, they began to drop off wrapped gifts. Sarah brought the first one. "Just a pair of booties my mother crocheted," she said. The tag was made out to Baby Campbell. Beaming, Kate placed the present under the tree.

Baby Campbell. The whole world knew Kate was pregnant even though she hadn't started to show yet. Soon she'd reach the end of her first trimester. Mercedes couldn't wait until Kate felt the first flutter. She was looking forward to becoming Aunt Mercedes.

Things were almost perfect. Unlike Thanksgiving, Mercedes approached the coming holiday with hope. She was taking her relationship with Finn one day at a time.

All that changed one morning in mid December. Mercedes was sitting in the office with Lindsay and Kate enjoying cinnamon coffee. The three were arguing over who was going over to Sarah's to buy cheese crowns. Kate dashed back to use the restroom, and Lindsay left for the Full Cup. When Kate returned, her face was drained of color and her hands cupped her tummy. Mercedes leapt from her desk. "What is it, Kate?"

"I'm spotting."

Chapter 22

What did this mean? In her book, blood was never good. Mercedes guided Kate to a chair. "Sit down. Let's call your doctor."

Face drained of color, Kate fumbled for her phone. Outside it was snowing and the white stuff curled along Whittaker Street like waves rippling over a cold shore. Mercedes shivered.

While Kate talked to the doctor, Mercedes straightened the piles of paper on her desk. She had to do something. Lindsay sat forward on her chair, not even bothering to pretend this was normal. She'd had two babies. If Lindsay was worried, this wasn't good.

The call was brief. Kate jammed the phone back into her purse. "The nurse said I should come in."

Mercedes rocketed from her chair. "I'll drive you."

"Can I do anything?" Lindsay asked as the two sisters headed for the door.

"We'll let you know what's up, okay?" The ride would be tense enough. Grabbing her sister's elbow, Mercedes steered her out the door.

"Right. Call me." Lindsay's voice followed them down the stairs.

How amazing that Lindsay had become one of them, but she

had. Mercedes led Kate out to the car and helped her inside as if she were made of fine china. When Mercedes started the car, Christmas carols blasted over the radio. She clicked it off. Kate called Cole. "No, I don't know what this means." More conversation. "No, I don't know if this is normal. Look, just meet me there, okay?" Her voice was shaking.

"Should we call Mom?" Kate asked as they pulled onto Highway 12.

"Absolutely not. This could just be nothing, right?" Kate glanced over, her face pale as the snow drifted over the highway.

"I don't know anything about pregnancies." In New York, her friends had been mostly professionals who delayed having children.

"Well. Right." Biting her lip, Kate stared out the window. Train tracks ran along the road. Mercedes wished they could jump on a train that would speed them to the doctor's office. They needed answers and they needed them now. She hit the accelerator and the car skidded.

"Easy, Mercedes." Lifting a hand from her tummy, Kate squeezed her arm.

Pumping the brakes, she eased up. The last thing they needed was an accident.

"Maybe this happens all the time."

"I don't know. I've been reading a book but I'm almost into my second trimester. I didn't think...I didn't know." Kate's voice choked.

Reaching over, Mercedes squeezed her sister's arm. "Let's wait 'til you talk to the doctor."

"Right. Of course. Silly to worry until then, right?" Kate's chin came up. For a few minutes they rode along in silence. Mercedes tried to talk sense to herself. Maybe this happened to women all the time when they were expecting.

Then Kate's sigh pierced the air. "Oh, my God. Cole just painted the baby's room. If anything happens, we'll have to look at that every day. He'll feel terrible."

"You are going to use that nursery." Strong words but inside Mercedes' resolve melted like the snow hitting the warm windshield.

The rhythm of the windshield wipers seemed to match the beating of Mercedes' heart. Except for that sliding sound, the drive to Dr. Jensen's office was quiet and felt way too long. Cole's green truck was the first thing Kate saw when they pulled into the parking lot. Jumping from the pickup, he was at their car in two strides, his open navy parka flapped in the wind. He reached for the passenger door before Mercedes turned off the car.

Kate spilled into his arms. "Oh, Cole."

"Katydid, it'll be fine." Cole wrapped his arms around her as if that would heal everything. "Let's just see what Dr. Jensen says, okay?"

Inside, the waiting room was crowded with women. Most of them looked uncomfortable but happy, hands folded complacently over rounded stomachs. Cole led Kate to a chair and walked to the receptionist's counter. One glance over at Kate and the receptionist pasted a reassuring smile on her face. A few terse words and Cole came back to sit next to Kate. Seconds later, a nurse appeared in the doorway leading to the exam rooms. "Kate Campbell?"

Kate and Cole disappeared and Mercedes was left alone. A couple women sent curious, sympathetic glances her way. Picking up one of the magazines, Mercedes paged through it. She barely saw the words.

Guilt tore at her. Since she returned home, Mercedes had envied her sister. Oh, yes, she had been jealous of the husband, the security. Life wasn't secure, though. She could see that now.

Maybe life was littered with debris. Accidents, illness or business failures created hurdles you never saw coming until you hit them, smack on. Mercedes rolled a magazine into a tight cylinder in her hand. Suddenly there was just one person she wanted with her. Digging her phone from her jacket pocket, she stepped into the hall. Seemed like the phone didn't even ring before Finn's voice came on. "Lindsay told me. How is Kate?"

"I don't know. She's with the doctor now."

"Where are you? Do you want me to come?"

Her composure cracked like one of the icicles that had just fallen from the gutter outside. "Yes."

The trip from Gull Harbor to Michigan City usually took twenty minutes. Somehow Finn made it in ten. Bursting into the waiting room, he stopped, eyes searching until they found her huddled in the corner. Taking the chair next to her, Finn took her hand. "Everything will be all right."

"How do we know that?" She nipped her lip against the break in her voice. Unzipping her purse, she dug around for a tissue. Stuff flew everywhere and she watched the card from Stephan fall to the floor. Finn snatched it up, his concern turning to curiosity. Oh, why had she put that in her purse? The huge card wasn't in an envelope and the heavy vellum opened in his hands. One eye sweep and he jabbed it back at her.

"Finn, I –"

"Later."

The word lacerated any calm she'd woven together so carefully as she sat waiting. Time dragged. The nurse appeared periodically, carrying a file and calling out a name. A woman would stand and follow the staff back into the exam area. The larger their stomach, the slower they walked.

Finally, Kate appeared with Cole. He had an arm around her like he was holding her up. Mercedes had never seen Kate look so helpless. A few words at the desk and the four of them headed for the door and walked out. Moments before Mercedes had felt like part of a couple. Now Finn seemed distant and pensive.

Outside, Cole turned but his eyes veered off. "The doctor said she should go home and rest. Call if anything changes."

Kate swayed, clutching her coat around her.

"That's it?" Mercedes asked.

Cole and Kate shared a glance. Had Mercedes ever seen such heartbreak in her sister's eyes? "There's no heartbeat," Cole finally said. "It's just a matter of time before..." He gulped hard.

Silent tears squeezed from Kate's eyes. Opening the door of the pickup, Cole helped her inside. "Katydid, we have each other, all right?" Mercedes heard him whisper to her sister.

Feeling like an outsider, Mercedes backed away. "Call me if you need anything," she called out as Cole shut the door.

Devastated and confused, Mercedes shuffled to her car. Finn walked quietly behind her. When she got up that morning, she'd been happy to see the snow. The wintry weather put her in a Christmas mood. Now the snow felt icy and so did her heart. Finn took her elbow when she missed a step getting to the car. But he looked preoccupied.

"Thank you for coming."

"Of course I'd come." The words were an exasperated growl.

But that had been before. Before he saw that stupid card with a scrawling name so large you'd have to be blind to miss it. Mercedes wanted him to hold her. Needed to feel his warmth. Instead, she stood shivering in the cold. "I wish we had come in the same car."

"Do you?" He stared at her as if she were a stranger.

"Finn, what is it?"

"Let's start with that card in your purse, Mercedes. Carrying it around so you can read it, what, five or ten times a day?"

Her heart stuttered. "No, it's not like that. I was in a hurry. It just ended up in my purse."

His laugh was short and sharp. "The stuff in a woman's purse is pretty important—at least that's what I hear." He opened the door. No way was she getting inside.

"That's not true. You don't understand."

A blast of cold air swirled through the parking lot. With his crazy dark hair and red cheeks, Finn looked wild and wonderful and mad as all get out. He was scaring her. And this was all her fault.

"You have to choose."

"Finn, no. You don't understand."

Eyes steely, he was on a rampage. "I'll loan you the money to start a new agency in New York."

"That's not necessary." What was he doing?

"You build your company in New York. See if it's what you want. But you have to choose. Stephan or me. Even if you choose Stephan, I'll loan you the money. I believe in you, Mercedes. I do. And I want to see you happy."

Shock ran cold in her veins.

"And if you choose me, well, I can weather a long distance relationship, as long as it's with you. Fact is, I can work anywhere. I can hire someone to manage Mangy Mutt or sell it."

He'd do that for her? "But you hate New York. You told me so yourself. And you love Gull Harbor." The snow had turned to sleet, coating her cheeks. Or was that tears?

He nodded. "Yes, I do. But I love you more. And I choose you. I'll be happy where ever you are, Mercedes."

Finn was backing away. The rigid set of his shoulders scared her. Her throat expanded around a lump the size of a beach ball. "Do you want me to call you when I have news?" She could hardly get the words out.

"Sure." He stared off down the street. "Call me when you figure all this out."

Mercedes didn't know what to say. The idea he'd thrown at her was so outlandish and crazy.

His eyes swung back, a cauldron of anger and distrust. "Look, I know you have other things on your mind right now, with Kate and everything. But what we have is important too. At least to me."

"Finn, you *are* important."

His lips thinned. "Right. Today. But where do I fit in your future?"

Not having an answer, she climbed into her car and watched him walk away. This was about much more than a card. The Bentley started and he roared off down the road. A light coating of snow obscured her vision. Resting her forehead on the cold steering wheel, she'd never felt more alone.

Finn and the future? She thought about that all the way home. Watching Cole comfort Kate today, Mercedes knew Finn held that same devotion. Shame heated her face. Could tall skyscrapers, business acquaintances and grinding deadlines substitute for personal relationships? When she came home to a Manhattan apartment every night, what comfort was offered by a glittering skyline seen through a plate-glass window?

Stopping at the red light on Whittaker, she could see the Christmas decorations arching over the street. The leaping reindeer had held such magic when she was little. Back then Mercedes thought Santa's reindeer really could fly. Smiling at the red, white and green blinking lights, she loved them more than the brilliant splendor of Rockefeller Square. The reindeer were part of her history, and a warmth glowed in her heart. A horn honked and she jerked forward.

Later, at Breezy Point, she sat her mother down on the blue sofa and explained what had happened. "There was no hope for the baby, Mom."

"Oh, my poor girl. My poor girl." Mom's eyes emptied. "You know, I had a miscarriage about a year after I had you."

That snapped her attention back. "You did?"

Her mother stared out at the bare trees visible from the front porch. "Saddest thing ever. Course when that happens, you think you're never going to have another baby. But I did. You and Kate are three years apart, and that was a little bit more spacing than I wanted."

"You have to tell Kate. That might help her." Mercedes left the room to put some coffee on. Outside the wind howled. Absolutely no use going back to the office. Besides, her mother seemed upset, pacing from the kitchen to the front porch and back again.

"How about a fire?" Mercedes was already slipping on her quilted jacket.

"That would be nice. I'll crunch up some paper." They always kept the Sunday newspaper in a bin next to the fireplace.

Outside, the cold wind burned Mercedes' ears. Thank goodness she'd grabbed the gardening gloves. They kept the firewood in a metal rack a few feet from the house, safe from termite infestation. After heaping as many split logs her arms could carry, she trudged back into snow that kept mounting. Tomorrow she'd have to dig her car out.

When she got inside, her mother was waiting, paper bunched in the metal cradle. Mercedes stacked the logs crosswise on top of the newspapers that she lit it with a long match. Minutes later, they settled on the sofa with their coffee while the storm built outside.

The afternoon went slowly. Mercedes threw one log after another onto the crackling fire. Her mother turned on the TV but if she had to watch one more talk show, she would lose her mind. No wonder she had worried about losing weight. That was about all the shows talked about, and it was sickening. Going into the kitchen, she made peanut butter and orange marmalade sandwiches for herself and her mother.

Around ten o'clock they went up to bed. The day had been so exhausting that she had no trouble getting to sleep. The clanging bells on her phone woke her up in the middle of the night. She grabbed the cell. It was four o'clock. "We're on our way to the hospital," Cole said when she picked up. The resignation in his voice told her everything.

"I'll be there." She hung up and threw on some clothes.

Her mother was waiting in the doorway of her own bedroom, blue nightcap on her head. "Should I come?"

The winter wind shook the house, and snow pelted the window on the landing. "It's snowing pretty hard, Mom. Besides, the fire might not be completely out."

They'd been taught never to leave the house with a fire live in the grate. "I'll just wait for your call." Her mother trailed downstairs after her, wringing her veined hands while Mercedes grabbed her jacket and slipped into her boots. Then she bounded out the door.

The snow was so high in their driveway that she'd have to park on Lake Shore Road when she came back. All the way down the road, she said the prayer she hadn't said in a long time. Kate had been so excited about this baby. How would it feel to be pregnant and then have that pregnancy end?

Salt trucks had come through on Highway 12. The layer of sharp crystals could chip her finish if she didn't slow down. Even with the salt, the car fishtailed twice. When Mercedes reached the hospital, the receptionist at the front desk directed her to the second floor surgical waiting area. Lights were dim in the hospital, and her boots squeaked on the tile floors. In the waiting room Cole sat alone, head on his hands. "Cole?"

When he lifted his head, he looked defeated.

"Oh, God. I'm so sorry." She rushed to sit beside him.

"It's over."

Her heart wrenched.

He swept one hand over his red eyes. "Dr. Jensen told us not to blame ourselves. There's no telling when the baby d-d-stopped developing. Mercedes, I never should have let her carry in groceries or take out the trash."

"Don't do this to yourself."

"I'm waiting for some word. Your sister's so strong but she was over the moon about this baby."

"She needs you, Cole. More now than ever. And she'll need you to be hopeful."

The poor man blinked and nodded. He looked like he'd been run over by a truck.

Eventually the doctor appeared. Kate had done well. She would be fine.

Mercedes seriously doubted her sister would be fine. At least, not for a while.

Of course Cole questioned him. The doctor was patient but there were no real answers. "Your wife is healthy," Dr. Jensen said when he turned to leave. "That's the good news."

When they could finally see Kate in her room, huge circles rimmed her reddened eyes. And this was the girl Mercedes thought had it all? How she regretted every envious thought she'd had in the past months. Maybe the more you had the more you had to lose. Life was not a card game where everyone was dealt the same hand.

And what could Mercedes say to ease this loss? After a tight hug and a promise to tell Mom, Sarah and the book club the sad news, Mercedes left Cole sitting on the edge of the bed, his arm around Kate. Mercedes knew where she wanted to be. That is, if she were welcome.

It took her forty-five minutes to reach Finn's house. Plows were on the highway but the side roads were drifted over. As she maneuvered the car down his snowy drive, she wondered if she'd get stuck. The garage doors were closed, snow mounded against them. She left her car where it stalled and got out. Grasping the cold railing, she pulled herself through the deep snow to his door.

Finn answered. He looked terrible.

"I need to talk to you."

"Come in out of the snow." The comment was more a command than an invitation. She unwound her wet scarf and snow fell to his grey stone entry floor.

"How's your sister?" he asked, taking her coat.

"In the hospital. She'll be fine, but…"

Her face must have told the story. Finn cocked his head toward the sofa. "Let's sit down."

But Mercedes stood her ground, not knowing if he'd want her to stay. Maybe she had totally messed this up, like she'd messed up so many things in her life. Turning to look at her, he stood waiting, arms loose at his sides. Like he didn't know what was coming and doubted that he'd like it.

"I don't know if you want to hear this. I don't know if it's too late. But I love you, Finn."

"Right. Okay." Giving her a cautious side glance, he braced his legs. "If there's a 'but' coming, I want to hear it now. I know you, Mercedes Kennedy."

He was still pushing her away, and she didn't blame him a bit. "I want to be with you, always. Here in Gull Harbor."

A crooked smile lifted his sad features. "Really?"

"Forget New York. Forget the career that's not worth creating again. I just want you."

Two steps and Finn had her in his arms. "Oh, pretty girl," he whispered into her hair. "Thought I'd never hear you say that."

"Why am I such a slow learner, Finn?" She laced her arms around his neck and held on.

"You tell me. No handwritten Cliff notes for this one."

"I might need you to help me figure this out." She pushed him back into the room and onto the sofa. "You know, the finer points."

Outside the storm raged. Finn gave her a sultry smile. "Might take some time. You could get snowed in."

"Sounds good to me." She buried herself in his arms.

Epilogue

A harpist played Pachelbel's Canon next to a crackling fire as Mercedes stepped carefully down the staircase of the Inn at Gull Harbor. Kate and Lindsay had decorated the lodge with pine boughs and hearts, since it was Valentine's Day. Standing next to the minister, Finn stood tall in a black suit with a red shirt and black bowtie. He looked unbearably handsome and so proud.

After his Christmas Eve proposal, they decided not to wait. Mercedes knew no other man would ever have a place in her heart. "Pretty girl, we're burning daylight here," Finn had told her. Her mother had been so excited and now stood beaming next to Finn's parents.

Behind her, Kate fussed with the long veil they'd found at Second Hand Rose. No train on the gown for Mercedes but the veil had been right from the first glance, just like Finn. Her Alecon lace wedding dress had been dropped off at Second Hand Rose in September, the girl told them. The elegant gown with a flared skirt and fingertip bell sleeves was more gorgeous than anything Mercedes could have found in New York. Besides, she was through with big city glamour that came with price tags that matched. The glow in Finn's eyes told her she'd made a good choice.

Organizing the wedding hadn't been easy since this was their busy season for booking rental cottages at Beach Vacations. With Lindsay and Kate to help her, Mercedes welcomed the chaos. Their teamwork energized the budding company with amazing potential. Today her future sister-in-law stood next to Kate in a blue velvet bridesmaid dress. Kate wore green that matched her eyes. Mercedes' heart warmed to see her sister smile again.

Clutching her bouquet of red amaryllis and baby's breath, Mercedes swept the small group of friends and family with a grateful smile. They'd given her so much love and support. Then, taking a deep breath, she moved toward the man who would always have her heart.

"Looking beautiful, pretty girl." Finn whispered as Mercedes took his arm.

"Looking handsome," she whispered back, smiling up into those smoking gray eyes.

Later there would be a dinner celebration at the Whittaker Woods Golf Club. The minister cleared his throat, the music faded into silence and the group settled. Just as Finn dug his vows from one pocket, Kate made a break for the bathroom. She'd been doing a lot of that lately. The smile on Cole's face as he followed her out told a happy story.

"Friends of Finn and Mercedes, welcome to this wedding celebration..."

As she vowed to love this man forever, Mercedes saw her future unfolding in Finn's gray eyes. Sometimes bad times can bring a woman down. Sometimes they help her give life a second look. Her heart brimmed with love and gratitude that she'd found her way home to Finn...forever.

THE END

Finding Southern Comfort

For a heart-tugging romance set in the beautiful city of Savannah, Georgia, turn the pages of *Finding Southern Comfort*, usually FREE in ebook format on Amazon, Barnes and Noble, iBooks and Kobo.

Chapter 1

Harper Kirkpatrick shoved her Catwoman mask into place and rang the doorbell. Hard to look casual with a whip under her arm. A late evening breeze ruffled the Spanish moss overhead. Didn't matter. She was sweating big time under the black spandex costume. Savannah in February was a lot warmer than Chicago.

An older woman answered the door. "Yes?"

"I'm the entertainment for the party."

She stood aside. "Right this way, please. I'm Connie."

The heels of Harper's black boots clicked on the white marble floor as she followed Connie inside. Pink tulips drooped in a crystal vase on a long hall table. Harper sure hoped they were fake. Holding her breath, she scurried past.

Bypassing a parlor stuffed with antiques, Connie led her around the wide staircase where etchings of the Savannah squares hung above the wainscoting. She'd studied those squares as a design student and knew them well. A wide archway opened into a library and beyond that she glimpsed a dimly lit dining room with a long shiny table.

Pretty snazzy, as her mom would say. These sprawling southern mansions felt so elegant compared to the solid brick houses in Oak Park, the Chicago suburb where Harper grew up. Still, why was this house so quiet? Where were the birthday party decorations, the cake and the kids? The back of her neck prickled. In the three months she'd worked for Party Perfect, this was a first. Something wasn't right.

The note from Rizzo was tucked under the spandex so she couldn't check.

Good grief, had she goofed up again?

"Here you go, miss." Connie yanked open a door under the staircase. Raucous male laughter shot up a narrow stairway.

"Thanks, Connie." Harper reached for the handrail. These suckers looked steep. The door closed behind her, and she was left in the darkness. Maybe the children had brought their parents? She started down. Her wired tail flailed the steps, almost keeping time to the music.

"Keep 'em in line," Rizzo had told her with one of his sleazy grins.

Sure. Right. She'd thought he was talking about rambunctious first graders, not the howling group below.

A man waited at the foot of the stairs. The low lighting glinted off blond hair when he glanced at his Rolex. "You're late."

"Sorry, I had trouble finding the—"

"I'm Cameron Bennett and you're thirty minutes late."

Her cheeks stung. "I'm Harper Kirkpatrick and I said I was sorry." She'd had trouble with the zippers. Probably not the time to share. His blue eyes iced her. Stumbling on the last step, Harper pitched forward.

"Good God." He broke her fall with both hands.

"Sorry. So sorry." *Cripes.* She pushed away from a chest that had seen a gym or two.

"You okay?" Cameron Bennett looked more annoyed than worried.

"I'm fine. It's dark in here, in case you hadn't noticed." Squaring her shoulders, she peered into the room. "Where are the kids?"

"What kids?"

A chill shot down her spine. Guys with flushed faces lounged in leather chairs. The low-ceilinged room held a hint of Cuban cigars smoked long ago. Her lungs squeezed tight. She had rules and Rizzo had broken them.

But her rent was way past overdue.

"Nothing. Forget it." Her arrival time of ten o'clock didn't seem too crazy when Rizzo gave her the details. She'd worked a sleepover birthday party two weeks earlier for a bunch of cute second graders. She handed Baby Blues the CD Rizzo had given her. "My music."

"Good, because you're late."

"You said that already."

His lips pressed into a thin line. Anxiety chattered in her stomach.

"Cameron, ole buddy! Now, don't keep that sweet thang all to yourself," called out a guy who looked like a former lineman. He made a feeble attempt to stand before collapsing back in the club chair. They all roared. Felt like she'd stumbled into a locker room.

"Doesn't look like a sweet thing to me," said a guy with a pencil moustache. Her stomach flopped over.

"Gentleman—and we are gentlemen, in case some of you may have forgotten—y'all be on your best behavior now." Baby Blues pushed her forward.

Show time. Harper stretched a smile across dry teeth.

They began to clap in a steady rhythm —like this was a rock concert and the main act was late. Holding the black whip tight against her chest, Harper shimmied through the closely packed tables. A hip here, a hip there. Open bottles sporting expensive gold labels gleamed on the tables. Definitely not a beer crowd and they weren't on their first drink. A banner hung over the long bar. "Congratulations, Beau! Another Man Down!"

A blasted bachelor party. Her steps faltered. Grabby lap dances and straying hands. She needed chain mail, not spandex. Harper tightened her hold on the whip. She'd like to wind it around Rizzo's neck. Beau must be the one grinning at the end of the bar, a ball and chain cuffing one ankle and a mourning band on his arm. Head down, he looked close to passed out. Still, he shot her a sweet, wobbly smile.

She threw back her head. No going back now. Not unless she wanted to be out on the street. Swinging her hips, she smiled her way to the bar. When one heel caught in the berber carpet, she caught herself and glanced back. Leaning against the wall, Baby Blues raised his eyebrows.

Fine. She'd show him.

How? This wasn't exactly a hokey pokey group. That much she knew.

Breathe. Breathe. Just one foot in front of the other.

When she reached the bar, two men hoisted her up. Planting her feet wide, she nodded to Baby Blues. Sweat tickled along her hairline under the spandex hood. He pressed a button on the sound system.

"What's New Pussycat" blasted, and she shrank. *Really, Rizzo?*

The guys loved it.

"Come on, Sugga!"

"Dance for us, you pretty thang."

Her chin came up. What would McKenna do? Time to channel her older sister back in Chicago. This was just a group of southern boys goofy with booze. Drunk, but harmless. Harper began to strut. Keeping her balance was tricky. Wings, pretzels, and pork ribs sat in bowls along the bar.

"Dance for us, darlin'."

"Yeah, give us a show!"

Her stomach plummeted into her boots. Maybe a few kicks. Bright smile. Hands on hips. Toes to the ceiling, as Mrs. VanderPool, their cheerleading coach used to say.

The bouncing sure didn't help her breathing. So hard to keep her eye on everything. She froze when her right foot connected with a bowl of pretzels that sailed through the air like a missile. Baby Blues jerked when the snacks took out some shiny statues on a shelf. Pretzels flew and awards crashed to the floor.

A roar went up. Baby Blues closed his eyes. Harper kept kicking.

"That's okay, sugga." Propping his head up, Beau threw her a goofy grin.

She smiled back. Piece of cake.

But boy, it was hot in here. With every bump and grind, the spandex tugged on her skin. Were the black whiskers melting off her face?

When Baby Blues turned down the lights, it threw her off. Then he hit her with a spotlight. This was getting serious.

A pleased rumble rolled through the room.

"Whatcha got on under there?" A meaty hand slapped onto her calf.

"Play nice, now." She tapped his head with the fluffy end of her tail. The guy looked like he could play for the Chicago Black Hawks but he pulled back with an embarrassed smile. Harper's confidence grew. Mother of mercy, maybe this would be better than waitressing. At least she wouldn't get carpal tunnel. Maybe she'd be able to keep a roof over her head after all.

With renewed confidence, she threw herself into the rhythm. The guys clapped. Yeah, this was more like it. She kicked. She strutted. She smiled.

Then they started to chant, "Take it off! Take it off!"

Holy moly. Really?

Just… bump … *shoot* … bump … *me* … bump … *now.* She pictured the horrified look on Sister Gabrielle's face. Her sweet fifth grade teacher often sent her to the office with messages for the principal.

"You're so dependable, Harper," Sister Gabrielle had told her. "Such potential."

If Sister Gabrielle could see her now.

The room closed in around her.

But she wasn't going down. Not like this.

Her airway felt like two thumbs were jammed against it. Harper just couldn't do the fainting thing again. She could hurt herself falling from up here but these boys wanted something. With a quick jerk, she yanked back the hood. Her hair fell to her shoulders. Chin up, she threw her head up and sucked in a deep breath. What a relief.

Applause ruptured the close, warm air. Baby Blues was fooling around with the thermostat. Wheeling around, he saw her and settled back against the dark paneling. Cool air blasted her from a vent right above. She drank it in.

"More! Give us more!"

"We want more, Pussycat!"

Pussycat? *Didn't* ... bump ... *they* ... bump ... *recognize* ... bump ... *Catwoman?*

Now, if this were a children's birthday party, they'd know. Kids loved all the super heroes—Catwoman, Batman, the Hulk, and Iron Man. She'd worn those costumes for recent gigs, and the children loved it. The parties had been fun and she'd made good money.

Six year olds never expected her to take off anything.

The chubby guy with bleary eyes staggered to his feet and began to jiggle his hips. Not a pretty sight but he was having fun. She smiled at him and his friends wrestled him back into the chair. "Bubba, no. You're going to break something again."

Bubba sank back into the chair. The men cheered. Bubba smiled. And Tom Jones wouldn't quit. Up on the bar, breathing became a marathon event.

She never had to dance for the kids, just sing and clap. This group had definitely come for a show. Prancing along the bar, she tossed the whip lightly from one side to the other. Hands reached for the leather strips.

"More! We want more, Pussycat!"

What was she wearing under this suit?

Underwear hadn't been a consideration when she got dressed.

Slowly she unzipped her left sleeve. Angry pink tracks throbbed from when she'd snagged herself getting dressed. With every click of the zipper, the applause grew louder. Chest heaving, she stopped under an air vent. Cool air rushing over her, she closed her eyes. Big mistake.

"Gotcha." Fingers tightened around one booted ankle and she glanced down at Pencil Moustache Man.

"Stop that!" Harper jerked and the whip hit his cheek. Her heart stopped when an angry red line zipped across his skin.

"Bitch." He reared back.

"Oh, I'm so sorry, sir. I didn't mean…" When she bent over, she got dizzy.

His buddies found the whole thing hilarious.

"Randy, way to go!"

"Got what you deserve, buddy!" They thumped on the tabletops.

"Hands off, Randy. Let her dance." The host's voice sliced the darkness.

Randy fell back.

Baby Blues caught her eyes and tilted his head, like he was just waiting for the next mistake.

Fine, she'd show him. Forget the sleeve teasing. Her hands moved to the front of her costume. Wrestling with the zipper, she didn't see the wet patch on the bar. Before she could even think "white cotton," she was sprawled on her behind. Hurt like heck.

Baby Blues was there in a heartbeat. His nostrils flared and she could hear him breathing.

"I'm all right." She struggled to stand.

"Well, I'm not."

"You okay, darlin'?" Beau lifted his head from the bar. "Cameron, ya tryin' to kill my party?"

A muscle twitched in Cameron's jaw. "Sorry, Beau, but it appears our entertainment for the evening is a little under the weather."

"I am not," she hissed, heaving herself upright.

"You damn well are."

Beau's eyes flagged. "You did great, Pussy…cat."

"Catwoman," she squeaked.

"No! She can't go." Bubba tried to stand again.

"We haven't seen anything yet!" The others joined the rowdy protest.

Ignoring them, Cameron helped Harper down and steered her through the disappointed men. His grip would probably leave a bruise on her arm. She fought back tears.

My rent. She wrenched her arm away. "I can…finish."

"The hell you can. You can barely breathe." He marched her along.

"I'm okay." Twisting, she saw Bubba trying to climb onto the bar while Beau gave him a shove. She couldn't help her giggle.

But when she turned, Cameron's steely blue eyes lanced her. "If you're an exotic dancer, then I'm a…."

They'd reached the stairs. He pushed a button, grabbed the ejected CD and jabbed it in her direction. Anger flamed in her cheeks. The night was not going to end like this. Not one more man rejecting her. Harper grabbed his belt and pulled. "You have to give me another chance."

His eyebrows rose and he glanced down. "No second chances."

"Geez." She shoved him away and snatched the CD.

How long would it take for Charlie Roden, her landlord, to evict her?

Wails followed her up the stairs, Baby Blues right behind her, eyes about butt level. She was furious and heartsick. Rizzo had been asking if she wanted to earn better money. Maybe she misunderstood him. She thought he meant more gigs. Didn't matter. She was finished.

Upstairs, Cameron led Harper to the front door and yanked it open. "Thank you for your time but I asked Rizzo for a professional."

"I *am* a professional." She got a glimpse of herself in a huge gilded hall mirror. Melting makeup, crooked mask and tangled curls. Harper swallowed hard.

Cameron nudged her outside. The night air clung like cotton candy.

"You could've let me finish."

"Trust me. You were finished."

Her lips quivered. "Well, aren't you so… lah dee dah."

That was all she could manage? Harper clamped her lips shut. On the street, gaslights glowed. Leaves whispered overhead and she breathed deep. Felt so good when her chest loosened.

Baby Blues' lips tweaked up. "Lah dee dah, huh? Good thing the guys were too tanked to complain. Much."

"They weren't complaining." Leering but not complaining. "I wasn't that bad."

"Yes, you were." The ghost of a smile softened his frown. Baby Blues was really handsome when he smiled. Handsome and hot. Jamming one hand into a pocket, he sighed and dug out a roll of cash she wished she could refuse. "Here, take this."

"Thank you."

"You're welcome."

A wail came from deep inside the house. "Good night," he said, nodding politely—the perfect southern gentleman.

"Okay, fine. Good night." Turning on her heel, she limped down the stone steps. A cool shower waited for her at home unless Charlie had turned off the water.

Her footsteps echoed on the pavement as Harper walked toward the car at the end of the side street. She hoped to heck it started. When her ex-boyfriend Billy had taken off for California, he'd left her with this heap of junk. Two years out of college and all her friends were pairing up like fruit flies.

All except Harper.

The beige sedan with the bumper held on with duct tape looked ridiculous on the elegant street. She slid inside. Even though the sun had set hours ago, the front seat heated her back and thighs. Thank God she'd never see any of those men again. Savannah was small, but she sure didn't travel in their circles.

The smell of money hit her when she fanned out the bills Baby Blues had given her. Generous but not generous enough. Reaching under the seat, she pulled out her beat up Coach bag and dug around for her inhaler. The first breaths were almost painfully blissful. Lungs expanding, she slumped back and tucked the money into her purse. What was she going to do? She'd think about that later. Right now she needed a shower and some sleep.

But first one quick call. She whipped out her phone.

"How'd it go?" Rizzo answered right away, like he'd been waiting.

"You're a rat, you know that?"

She could hear him take a drag on his cigarette. "You were lucky to get a shot at this group. Elite customer and I hope you didn't screw up with Mr. Bennett. Stop by on your way home with the cash."

"Oh, I don't think so, Rizzo."

"Hey, Chicago girl, don't get all uppity on me. Didn't you say you were interested in career development?"

He really was a trip. "What happened to the kids' birthday parties? This was a bachelor party, for Pete's sake. I am not a stripper."

His laugh was more of a bark. "They all say that. You dames are all alike."

The words hit her like darts. Harper blinked back tears, glad he couldn't see her. "I quit."

"No, you're fired. And you better get that money to me or you're toast, little lady."

She ended the call. What a creep. Jamming the key into the ignition, she turned it. The click was like taking another dart. Resting her forehead on the steering wheel, she squeezed her eyes shut. If she started to cry, her chest would tighten up. She forced herself to take deep breaths. When the swelling in her throat subsided, she grabbed her phone again. Maybe Adam, her neighbor, would be home.

But it was Saturday and Adam usually partied on Saturday nights. The phone rang and rang until his voicemail picked up. She didn't leave a message.

~~

Cameron watched the taillights of the limousine pull away. Limo service was the only safe way home after a bachelor party, an unwritten rule in their group. But he'd never offer to host one of these parties again. Just not his thing. Unbuttoning his shirt, he welcomed the cool breeze. He didn't know whether to laugh or put his fist through a wall.

Stripper, my ass. Not that she didn't look hot in the Catwoman costume. And the hair? Definitely a turn-on. But something felt off. Any minute he'd expected to have to give her mouth-to-mouth resuscitation.

Cameron fought the mental picture that brought a warm rush.

Turning back to the house, he yanked his shirt tails out of his slacks. Was she one of the local college girls? Something admirable about that. He'd put himself through school washing dishes, valeting cars, bartending, and just about everything in between.

Gutsy girl who drew the line at stripping. At least she had principles.

The beat up car parked at the corner caught his eye. Really? Irritation made his head throb. People were always leaving their junkers on the street. Looked like this one had a license plate.

"Daddy?"

He swiveled. Inside, Bella gripped the banister at the foot of the stairs, a small pale figure in her yellow Tinkerbell nightgown.

Smiling at his four-year-old daughter, he stepped back inside. "Why aren't you asleep, sugar?"

"Too much noise, Daddy." She rubbed a small fist into her eyes.

"Yeah, I'm sorry about that." When he scooped her up, Bella felt so frail. His heart turned over. "You should stay in the air conditioning. Too much pollen out here."

Batteries of tests and the doctors still didn't know what made his daughter wheeze and turn pale. Scared the hell out of him.

At the end of the hall, Connie appeared in the doorway of the kitchen.

"Connie, can you take her back to bed? I have a situation

outside.”

“You bet. Come here, you little munchkin.” Connie opened her arms and he handed Bella off. The dark rings beneath his daughter's eyes wrapped around his heart and squeezed.

“Night, Daddy.” Bella leaned over for a kiss, her wiry dark hair smelling of baby shampoo.

“See you tomorrow, darlin'.” He watched them mount the stairs before stepping back outside and pulling the door closed behind him. The car was still there. His loafers scuffed the warm pavement as he walked down the middle of the road. When he got closer, a head of thick sherry-colored hair eased its way up. Mardi Gras beads dangled from the mirror.

Perfect. Just perfect.

“Why are you still here?” he asked when he reached the open window. “You can't park on this street overnight.”

Her back was toward him. Was she slipping the damn mask back on? When she turned, those green eyes sparked. “My car wouldn't start.”

What a surprise. “Have you called a service station? AAA?”

“I've left messages for a friend. Somebody will call back.” Her hands white-knuckled the steering wheel. “Any minute now.”

Jamming one hand through his hair, Cameron stared down the dark, empty street. Thank God his neighbors were well asleep by this time. A clunker was a red light for everyone, and he didn't want them calling the police about his stripper.

Well, the girl who wasn't a stripper.

Maybe he should just let the police handle it. Wasn't she

loitering or doing something illegal?

Then he saw the inhaler on the seat.

Damn. But not a total surprise.

"Give me a minute." He headed back to the house.

"Look, you don't have to do anything."

Like hell he didn't. He broke into a jog.

Two minutes later, he pulled his Porsche up next to her beat-up piece of crap. Leaning over, he pushed open the passenger side door. "Get in."

Mumbling something under her breath, she got out of the car and slammed the door behind her. As she slid into the Porsche, she gave him the name of her street. Then she folded her hands into her lap like a school girl, a Coach bag plopped at her feet. Must be a knockoff.

He pulled away. For a while, all he could hear was the sweet, low rumble of the car. Time for some music and he punched buttons until Billy Holiday filled the small car with "The Very Thought of You."

"Oh, I love this song." When she leaned forward a little, her reddish brown hair fell over one shoulder. The curls looked soft, like Bella's. She started to hum along.

"So, do you do this often?" he finally asked.

"Have a broken down car? Not if I can help it."

"No, I mean do you work for Party Perfect often?"

What he could see of her face turned sad. "Just worked some children's parties for him."

"Worked? As in the past?"

The soft hollow at the base of her throat pulsed. "Right. I just quit."

"Sorry. You didn't really do anything wrong. I mean, your kicks were good."

He caught her eye. They both burst out laughing, probably thinking of that bowl of pretzels.

"I am so sorry about your trophies." Her luscious chuckle hit him right in the gut.

"Not the first time they'd been knocked off that shelf." Damn, he needed to laugh. His latest restoration deal had fallen through that afternoon. He hated the thought of the wrecking ball taking that house down. For him every old structure in Savannah carried a precious piece of history. The stripper who didn't strip was just a bad end to a bad week. "Trophies only matter the day you win them. Besides, the football only broke off one of them. It's been glued before."

"Well, I won't be dancing on bars anytime soon." The sadness in her voice tugged at him.

She must have unzipped her costume to get some air. When she leaned forward and peered out the front windshield, he tried not to stare at the dusky valley between her breasts.

"Stop. Right there."

He jerked his eyes away. "Look, I didn't mean anything." What was wrong with him, ogling her like that?

But she wasn't looking at him. She was stabbing one blue-tipped finger at an older home with a serious lean. The building was like so many in this district of Savannah. Rundown. Probably cut into four different apartments. He pulled to the curb. She cracked open the car door. "Thanks so much for the ride. I hope I didn't ruin your party, Mr. Bennett," she added softly.

"You did fine."

"Yeah. Right."

What was he saying? She was terrible. But damn, that pinched look around her nose, the trembling of her soft lips—she was killing him.

She reached for her handbag and make-up spilled out. They both grabbed for it and their heads bumped. Her hair brushed his cheek, unleashing a crazy warmth that took him by surprise. Totally inappropriate for so many reasons.

"Sorry. I am so clumsy tonight. Thank you."

When he handed her a lipstick and a comb, their fingers touched and sparked. Damn. She sucked in a quick breath. He sat back. She stepped out until all he could see were those long legs.

"Well, thanks." One hand on the top of the car, she leaned forward.

"No problem." He trained his eyes on the empty bucket seat. It was hard.

"Good night, then." She pushed off and began to walk away.

Something purple on the floor caught his eyes. "Wait. You forgot your inhaler." Scooping it up, he handed the device through the open window.

"Thank you." She curled it tightly into her fist, backing onto the curb. "Aren't you going to take off?"

"Just waiting to see you in." This wasn't the safest

neighborhood.

"Right. That's nice." As she turned, her boots crunched on the gravel. She looked absurd and hot as she took the stairs with that tail swinging behind her, whip tucked under one arm. Took her a little time to work her key. The front door stuck but finally gave way to a hip. After she banged it shut behind her and the porch light was turned off, he eased away from the curb. The feeling that dogged him all the way home was ridiculous. Why did he care if the girl needed help? He had enough on his plate.

But Cameron knew what it felt like to have no place to turn.

Other Books by Barbara Lohr

Windy City Romance series
Finding Southern Comfort
Her Favorite Mistake
Her Favorite Honeymoon
Her Favorite Hot Doc
The Christmas Baby Bundle
Rescuing the Reluctant Groom

Man from Yesterday series
Coming Home to You
Always on His Mind

About the Author

Barbara Lohr writes contemporary romance with a flair for fun and subtly sexy love scenes. In her *Windy City Romance series*, feisty women take on hunky heroes and life's issues. Her *Man from Yesterday* series, launched in 2015, provides a provocative glance back at "what if." When she's not writing, she loves to bike, kayak, golf or cook. She makes a mean popover. Barbara lives in the South of the USA with her husband and a cat that insists he was Heathcliff in a former life.

For more information on the author and her work, or to sign up for her newsletter, please see:

www.BarbaraLohrAuthor.com

www.facebook.com/Barbaralohrauthor

www.twitter.com/BarbaraJLohr

Acknowledgements

Many thanks to Romance Writers of America and Central Ohio Fiction Writers. The loops and forums of writers who address writing and publishing issues are also invaluable to me. On a more personal level, I'm grateful for Sandy Loyd and Marcia James, who started this journey with me. And an extra load shout out to my Street Team, the readers who support me in so many way!

For my daughters, Kelly and Shannon, when we shared Judy Blume and Madeleine L'Engle together, we never saw what lay ahead. Keep those reading lamps on over your beds. My grandchildren, Bo and Gianna, bring me such joy and will probably appear in quite a few of Mama B's novels. To my husband Ted, words aren't adequate to thank you for your love and support, especially when my computer crashes and you have to provide tech support. May we have many more wonderful years together that include trips to Leopold's for ice cream.